THE
PARIS
LIBRARIAN

ALSO BY MARK PRYOR

A Hugo Marston Novel

THE
PARIS
LIBRARIAN

MARK PRYOR

SEVENTH STREET BOOKS®
AN IMPRINT OF PROMETHEUS BOOKS
59 JOHN GLENN DRIVE • AMHERST, NY 14228
www.seventhstreetbooks.com

Published 2016 by Seventh Street Books®, an imprint of Prometheus Books

Cover image © Media Bakery
Cover design by Nicole Sommer-Lecht
Cover design © Prometheus Books

This is a work of fiction. Characters, organizations, products, locales, and events portrayed in this novel either are products of the author's imagination or are used fictitiously.

Trademarked names appear throughout this book. Prometheus Books recognizes all registered trademarks, trademarks, and service marks mentioned in the text.

Inquiries should be addressed to
Seventh Street Books
59 John Glenn Drive
Amherst, New York 14228
VOICE: 716–691–0133
FAX: 716–691–0137
WWW.SEVENTHSTREETBOOKS.COM

20 19 18 17 16   5 4 3 2 1

Library of Congress Cataloging-in-Publication Data

Names: Pryor, Mark, 1967- author.
Title: The Paris librarian : a Hugo Marston novel / Mark Pryor.
Description: Amherst, NY : Seventh Street Books, 2016. |
    Series: Hugo Marston ; 6
Identifiers: LCCN 2016009757 (print) | LCCN 2016016012 (ebook) |
    ISBN 9781633881778 (softcover) | ISBN 9781633881785 (ebook)
Subjects: LCSH: Americans—France—Paris—Fiction. | Motion picture actors and
    actresses—Fiction. | Cold cases (Criminal investigation)—Fiction. | Murder—
    Investigation—Fiction. | BISAC: FICTION / Mystery & Detective / General. |
    GSAFD: Mystery fiction.
Classification: LCC PS3616.R976 P37 2016 (print) | LCC PS3616.R976 (ebook) |
    DDC 813/.6—dc23
LC record available at https://lccn.loc.gov/2016009757

Printed in the United States of America

This book is dedicated to my beautiful sister,
Catherine Eleanor, aka "Caci/Cat."
I know we're too far away from each other, but remember
we share so much more than just a birthday.
Your unwavering support for and delight in my writing career
mean more than you can know. I love you, super sis.

AUTHOR'S NOTE

As ever, I have tried to be faithful to the geography, traditions, and cuisine of the beautiful city of Paris, and any distortions or failings are my own, as are any exaggerations. However, to those who fear I've been too fanciful with my fictional American Library in Paris I feel compelled to point out that the real one does, indeed, have a secret door as well as a small, basement room that staff call the *atelier*. More than that, I cannot say . . .

CHAPTER ONE

The note sat beside his coffeemaker, the elegant handwriting unmistakable.

Café Laruns at 8:30 this morning.
Come alone and unarmed. Tell no one.

Hugo Marston read the note twice and sighed. Despite Tom Green's rough demeanor, hard-drinking ways, and sailor's vocabulary, his friend and current roommate had an artistic side that very occasionally revealed itself in his appreciation of classical music, several styles of painting, and, less occasionally, in his own handwriting.

The clock on the kitchen wall read eight, and Hugo considered the possibilities. Either Tom was back working for the CIA and needed his help with an undercover operation, or his friend was screwing with him. Given the tone of the note, Hugo was prepared to put his money on the latter. Even so, a trip to Café Laruns was welcome enough on a lazy Sunday morning, especially since the coffeemaker propping up Tom's note turned out either sludge or drain water depending on its mood. The decision was made easier when a quick check of the fridge showed that *someone* had eaten the last of the eggs and bread.

The only thing that gave Hugo pause was the time of the requested rendezvous. Rare enough for Tom to be out of bed by nine, let alone eight, on a weekend—or any day come to that—and also be in decent-enough shape to leave the apartment for a meeting.

Hugo opened the window to check on the temperature, the cool of the early morning already giving way to a mugginess that had clogged Paris for most of August. Half a dozen times that month the city had been battered by afternoon thunderstorms, rain pounding the pavements and the streets, turning them into little rivers as the sky crackled and snapped with lightning, thunder rolling angrily above. August was vacation month in France, and traditionally Hugo, along with many other employees at the US Embassy, was given the chance to work from home when he was able. Several afternoons he'd watched from his fifth-floor apartment as the tourists on Rue Jacob scurried for cover, filling the nearby cafés and bistros. The stores selling cheap umbrellas and plastic ponchos filled their coffers, too, opening their doors wide every time the sky darkened or a few heavy raindrops hit the sidewalk.

Hugo showered and dressed quickly. He ran a comb through his hair and frowned when he spotted a few more grays. *Time to stop looking too closely*, he thought.

He trotted down the stairs and waved at Dimitrios, the concierge for the apartment building. The Greek wasn't supposed to work weekends, but he lived three streets away in a tiny apartment with his wife and four children, and his comfy chair and sturdy desk were the perfect place to find peace and quiet, and to read a good book. He looked up and spoke as Hugo passed.

"*Bonjour*, Monsieur Marston, did the young lady find you?"

Hugo stopped. "'Young lady'?"

"She was here yesterday. You were at work. Don't worry, I didn't tell her anything about you, not where you work or your schedule or anything."

"I appreciate the discretion, Dimitrios, but I don't know who you're talking about. Not Claudia?"

"*Non, non*, of course not. She was younger, this one." His eyes brightened at the memory and he gave Hugo a mischievous wink. "Very pretty, though. I won't mention her to Mademoiselle Claudia, I promise."

Hugo shrugged. "I still don't know who you're talking about, I'm afraid. Claudia's the only woman I've dated in a long time. Perhaps one of Monsieur Green's friends?"

"*Non, certainement pas.*" Dimitrios shook his head. *Definitely not.* "This one was . . . she was dressed a little strangely, all in black but she seemed sweet, a nice girl. Not his type."

Hugo laughed. "You are an observant man. If she comes back, ask for her name and phone number. I'm curious now."

"*Oui, monsieur*, I will." The conspiratorial wink again. "And not a word to Mademoiselle Claudia."

Hugo chuckled and stepped out onto Rue Jacob, turning right and starting a slow stroll toward Café Laruns. He had no plans for the day other than a desire to peruse the stalls along the River Seine that offered mostly tourist items but also the occasional collectible book, which is where Hugo's interest lay. Since the disappearance of his *bouquiniste* friend Max, Hugo had subconsciously put a hold on his slow but regular book buying, stalling the gradual trickle of first and rare editions that he'd gathered for years. He owned almost a hundred, some in his bedroom but most in a locked glass cabinet in the main room of his apartment. Their colorful spines were a special display to Hugo, a touchable and re-arrangeable work of art more permanent than flowers but just as beautiful. And they were more than just trophies to admire. Hugo had read every single one, convinced that even rare and delicate books deserved the fulfilment of their purpose before being transformed into collectors' items, treasures that were no longer cherished for the words between the covers but for the covers themselves and the name printed on the front.

As he neared the end of Rue Jacob, his phone rang and the name Paul Rogers showed up on the screen. Rogers was the director of the American Library in Paris, on Rue du Général Camou, in the Seventh Arrondissment. Hugo had worked several functions there for the ambassador, and Rogers was his point of contact. He was in his late fifties, balding, and quiet but always ready with a smile—and ruthlessly efficient.

Hugo also knew that there was a little more to the man than his gentle demeanor suggested. As a matter of course Hugo was required to look into Rogers's background, and in doing so had unearthed a past that, in days gone by, would have been labeled "colorful." The librarian's interest in books was preceded by a career in film, making short movies that catered to a small but enthusiastic group of adults whose nocturnal activities were harmless, other than being potential fodder for the tabloids should a politician or movie star be found in their midst. Hugo and Ambassador Taylor had enjoyed a chuckle over some of the imaginative titles, but they quickly decided that his lack of criminal record, his bachelor's in English literature and master's degree in library science, and the trust of his young but highly cultured fiancée, Sarah Gregory, were better ways to judge the man.

Without hesitation they'd agreed that Paul Rogers was no security concern, and over their dozen or so interactions he'd proved himself devoted to his books, his girlfriend, and helping the diplomats and other guests of the American embassy enjoy the delights of the largest English-language lending library on the European continent. The library sold books, too, twice a month, and Hugo had asked Rogers to call him when he noticed something special up for grabs.

"Paul, how are you?" Hugo said, slowing his walk.

"Great. Just wanted to let you know about a little sale we're having."

"Oh yes?"

"Not just the usual fundraising thing. We have some older books we don't really have space for any more, and some others we don't want to spend the money restoring. Two or three hundred books—I'm sure you could find something."

"Any particular theme?"

"No, we have a little of everything. The big moneymaker will likely be a six-volume set of Gibbon's *History of the Decline and Fall of the Roman Empire*."

"Surely not a first-edition set?" asked Hugo.

"It most certainly is." A note of humor entered Rogers's voice. "Care to guess how much we're selling it for?"

Hugo stopped and leaned against the stone wall of a boutique clothing store. He could picture the books in his mind but couldn't even imagine owning a set like that. Or reading it. "Well out of my league, I'm sure. Twenty grand?"

"Thirty-five, in US dollars."

"That'll pay your salary for a couple of years."

"I wish you were joking," Rogers said lightly.

"You're worth every penny. Any stocking stuffers I might be able to afford?"

"You like the literature side of things, if I recall. As opposed to photography, religion, and philosophy, I mean. Couple of good travel books, too, if that's your thing."

"It is in theory, but I have to focus my collection. Until you mistakenly sell me a first-edition Jack London or H. G. Wells for a couple hundred bucks."

"Lord, I'd lose my job for that." Rogers laughed. "Let me think. We have a first-edition of Cormac McCarthy's *The Road* for a few hundred dollars."

"I prefer something a little older. Signed, too, if possible," Hugo added. "Almost all the ones in my tiny collection are signed."

"Nothing springs to mind, I'd have to look and see which ones are," Rogers said. "Oh, wait. How about a Truman Capote? *In Cold Blood*. I know it's a first edition and I think it has his autograph in it, too."

"How much?"

"Three thousand, I think. Let me pull it up on my computer."

"For that price, it better be signed."

"Here we go. Yep, three-and-a-half thousand, and it's signed. Want me to put it aside?"

"Let me think about it. That's still pretty expensive—I'm just a lowly government employee, you know."

Rogers laughed. "I know, Hugo, I know. The sale starts tomorrow, so I'll hold it for you until you get here, does that work?"

"Perfect. I'll take the morning off and be there by ten."

"Do me a favor. Bring your buddy Tom, he's a blast. And I like the way he spends your money."

"I'll think about it."

As soon as Hugo hung up, his phone rang again.

"You coming or not?" Tom asked.

"I'm on my way, five minutes at the most. What's going on?"

"It's a secret."

"Yes, one that I'll find out in five minutes. Why can't you just tell me now?" Hugo waited for a response. "Tom. Hello?" The screen on his phone was dark. "Typical," Hugo muttered to himself, and resumed his walk.

It took him ten minutes, and he breathed in deeply as he pushed open the door to Café Laruns, the aromas of coffee and freshly baked bread welcoming him into the large, cool room. He saw Tom at the back of the café, sitting with two people, a young lady he didn't recognize and another slight figure who was sitting with her back to him. He started toward them and waved when Tom looked up.

He was ten yards from their table when the young lady with her back to him turned around. Hugo stopped in his tracks, a smile of surprise and delight spreading across his face. She smiled, too, then sprang up and ran over, wrapping her arms around him and squeezing tight.

"Well, now, what are you doing here?" he asked, hugging her back.

She looked up and grinned. "I'm pretty sure you said I could visit anytime I liked."

"I'm sure I did," Hugo said. "But we have phones here; you're allowed to call in advance."

"Ha!" She released him, tucking her arm through his and leading him to the table. "Don't you remember our trip to the cemetery? The party we went to?"

"How could I forget?" Hugo grimaced playfully. "Ah yes, that's right. You're one for surprises, no doubt about that."

She squeezed his arm. "Especially where you're concerned."

They stopped beside her empty chair and Hugo looked into those clear, almond-shaped eyes. "It's good to see you again, Merlyn, it really is."

CHAPTER TWO

They sat around the table and Merlyn introduced Hugo to "my partner," Mikaela Harrison. She was, like Merlyn, a beautiful young woman. Her dark hair fell either side of an oval face, but where Merlyn's skin was *café au lait*, Mikaela's was just the *lait*, classic English pale, the perfect canvas for her striking blue eyes and cherry-red lips. She was slender, but not in the same way as the waiflike Merlyn, more athletic.

"Call me Miki," she said, shaking Hugo's hand. She smiled and held his eye for a shade longer than he expected. *Confident girl*, Hugo thought.

A waitress appeared and Hugo ordered coffee for himself and croissants for everyone. When the waitress left, Hugo turned to Merlyn.

"How did you get hooked up with this guy?" He thumbed toward Tom, who was looking smug. "And are you in Paris for fun or work?" He paused. "Or one of your . . . parties?"

Merlyn laughed. "Same old Hugo, full of questions. Someone I did some genealogy work for gave me access to his apartment as partial payment. We can even use his Smart car, though I can't imagine driving around Paris is a lot of fun. Anyway, we got in yesterday and we went to your apartment and then the embassy to find you. Tom was talking to the security people and heard me asking. He said we should surprise you here this morning."

"He's like you in that way," Hugo said. "Always a bundle of fun."

"Hey, be grateful I've included you at all." Tom winked but didn't elaborate. He didn't need to—sitting at a café with two pretty girls was about the only thing in the world likely to get him out of bed in the morning.

Miki rummaged in her bag and then stood. "I don't smoke much, but something about being here . . ." She gave an embarrassed smile, and Tom stood to let her out.

"Maybe I'll join you," he said, ignoring Hugo's *So you smoke now, too?* look.

When they'd gone, Merlyn reached over and squeezed Hugo's hand. "It's really good to see you again, you look good."

"So do you." Hugo smiled.

It had been several years but she looked the same, that hint of Asia around her eyes, the smooth olive skin. Her black bob was now streaked with a line of blue, but otherwise she looked the same as when she'd stumbled into the first investigation he'd conducted as an RSO, when he was heading up security at the US Embassy in London. Merlyn had been friends with a movie star Hugo was supposed to babysit, one who disappeared moments after they'd met. Without Merlyn he'd have had no idea where to look for the man. With her, he found himself chasing through the English countryside and, to his chagrin, wearing leather pants and a matching vest at a secret party at an English mansion. She'd opened his eyes to a different way of living, and loving, testing the unjudgmental part of himself that he so valued. In her world, anyone could be anything, and sexual exploration was to be encouraged, no matter how out-there it seemed. Hugo had gone along, mostly out of necessity, and had gained a valued friend in the process. They'd swapped a few e-mails after that case but, as often happens with hurriedly formed friendships, the lines of communication had thinned out and they'd not corresponded in almost a year.

"So tell me why you're here, and for how long," he said.

She released his hand and sat back. "I'm really just tagging along with Miki. She's a journalist and wants to write about the movie star Isabelle Severin. She lives here, and apparently her papers are now available at some local library. She's a little obsessed, seems to think Severin was a spy during the war."

"A spy for whom?" Hugo knew that the 1940s actress, now in her late nineties, lived somewhere in Paris, after having moved here in the 1970s when she upped and left Hollywood, ending her career on a high note and on her own terms. She'd never attended any embassy events despite numerous invitations, but Hugo's boss, Ambassador J. Bradford Taylor, claimed to know her, a little anyway. *She's still beautiful, Hugo, I promise you. The sweetest, kindest, and most elegant woman I've ever met*, he'd said. And something of a recluse, Taylor acknowledged, attended to by one or two close friends and a carefully vetted and fiercely loyal personal assistant.

"For the Allies," Merlyn said. "Her theory is that she used her stardom to buddy up with top people in the Vichy government, then passed on secrets to the Americans, British, and even the Resistance."

"You know, I may have read about that somewhere, many years ago."

"There's even a dagger involved."

"How so?" Hugo asked.

"The story goes that she was delivering secrets to a Resistance cell in 1944 and two Gestapo officers showed up. She pretended to seduce one and used his own dagger to kill him."

"That so?"

"Yeah, well." Merlyn rolled her eyes. "It's on the Internet, so I assume it's true."

"So what happened to the other officer?"

"No idea. I suppose the Resistance fighters killed him but you'd have to ask Miki, she knows all the gory details."

"I will. So where is this dagger and stash of papers?" Hugo had a pretty good idea, and he made a mental note to call Paul Rogers.

"No clue." She grinned. "Like I said, I'm just tagging along so I can see you."

"I'm glad you did." Hugo hesitated. "You said Miki was your partner. I wasn't sure if you meant in business or . . ."

Merlyn waved a hand. "It's complicated. We're good friends but . . . It's complicated, but mostly in a good way."

"Yeah, well, watch out for Tom. He likes complicated, and he especially likes innocent-seeming pretty girls from England."

"You know I can look out for myself," she said with a wink. "And don't call me innocent."

"I said innocent-*seeming*. And I know you can look out for yourself, just look out for Miki, too."

Merlyn chuckled. "That girl can handle herself, don't worry. Last night Tom came on a little strong and she shut him down lickety-split."

"That's good to know. So who is she writing this article for?"

"Freelance. She thinks it might even be a book. As well as the mysterious dagger, she's convinced there is a bunch of Severin's stuff that's never been seen before and that puts some people in a bad light. Politicians who are now dead, and a few old movie stars, but still. Those people have families and estates to worry about, which means it'll be controversial."

". . . And therefore will sell."

"Precisely," Merlyn said. "Assuming all that stuff exists and she can get her hands on it."

"Some grand conspiracy to hide the truth, eh?" Hugo said.

"Yeah, well, don't be sarcastic with her," Merlyn chided. "She'll stab you with her pen."

"Maybe I can help. I'm headed to the American Library tomorrow to look at some books they're selling. I'll ask my contact there; he'd know the whereabouts and extent of the collection."

"But will he tell you if there's secret stuff? Miki's made several calls, had important people pull all kind of strings, and the best she's got is, basically, 'Come have a look, we'll let you see what we'll let you see.'"

Hugo spread his hands. "I can ask. Isabelle Severin is still alive, and living here in Paris. You guys should try to talk to her."

Merlyn raised a delicate eyebrow. "Bloody hell, Hugo, what a great idea, she'd *never* have thought of that. You don't have a high opinion of journalists, do you?"

"Ah, you tried already. Sorry."

"Miki can't even get close to her. Apparently she doesn't like a lot of attention and her former personal assistant was a little, shall we say, tight-lipped. You know anyone close to her?"

"She and I don't move in the same circles," Hugo said. "Although my boss claims to know her a little. I can ask him, but no promises."

They sat quietly for a minute, watching the morning activity of the café, then Merlyn said, "We may be going to a party tonight, you wanna chaperone us?"

Hugo's mind flashed to the last party he went to with Merlyn, an underground, highly secretive BDSM event where he'd found an important clue in the case he was working on.

"What kind of party?" he asked suspiciously.

"Same as last time," she said lightly. "But French. Strict dress code, of course, but I can help you with that."

Hugo smiled and shook his head in mock disgust. At the party in England, she'd told him that he would be allowed in only if he was wearing leather, the party's dress code. She forgot to mention that a tuxedo was also permitted—a rule he would have followed quite happily, and one he discovered once he was already inside the party dungeon. *One of those things*, he thought, *that's a lot funnier in hindsight than at the time.*

"I'll pass," he said. "Feel free to take Tom, he may actually enjoy it."

"Scaredy cat."

They looked up as Miki and Tom rejoined them. Miki poked at her coffee and frowned. "That went cold fast," she said. She looked up at Hugo. "Merlyn said you're head of security at the US Embassy here."

"That's right," Hugo said.

"What does that mean, exactly? What do you *actually* do?"

"That depends on the day, the week. It varies a lot. Sometimes I'll escort guests, sometimes I'll arrange security for dignitaries, sometimes I'll work with local police when there's been a crime involving an American citizen."

"Do you carry a gun?"

"Whether or not RSOs carry weapons is decided by the two countries involved, so that also varies from embassy to embassy."

"I was asking about you," Miki pressed.

"I know you were." Hugo smiled. "Tell me about your writing project. Merlyn said you're writing an article about Isabelle Severin."

"I'm actually hoping it'll be a book. Amazing person. She wasn't just the most beautiful woman who ever lived, she was a good person, too."

"And brave, if she was a spy."

Miki watched him, as if wondering whether he was making fun of her. "Merlyn told you about that."

"I think I already knew about the rumors but yes, she said you were looking into whether or not that was true."

"I'm pretty sure it is, but she doesn't want anyone to know."

"So shouldn't it stay a secret?"

Miki smiled. "Merlyn said you were kind of a Boy Scout."

"Meaning?"

"Meaning, if one of the most famous actresses of the last century went up against, and defeated, the Gestapo, that should be public knowledge, especially seventy years later. What's the harm?"

"Maybe that's for her to decide."

Miki's voice hardened. "I've never known a historian or journalist to ask permission from their subject, so I'd say no, it's not."

"I'm with you on that," Tom interjected. "But aren't there books about her already?"

"One or two, but nothing published recently." Miki nodded. "But they barely touch on her travels, and whatever else she got up to in France. Since her papers have just been donated to the American Library here, I'm hoping there's something new and different I can share with the world about her role in the war."

"You're sure she had a role?" Hugo asked.

"Yes. At least, I think so." She flashed a smile. "If I get to see all her papers, I'll find out."

"Seems like a tough story to dig up."

"I like a challenge," she said. "And once I get my teeth into something like this I don't give up until I get the truth, all of the truth. If there's a story there, I'll get it one way or another."

"Very admirable. You know what, let me call my friend at the library right now." Hugo stood. "A little noisy in here, I'll be right back." He walked out of the café and found a shaded spot on the sidewalk. He dialed Paul Rogers, who answered quickly. "Paul, Hugo Marston again. Hope this is a good time."

"Change your mind about the book?"

"Not at all. It's about a new collection you guys have. Isabelle Severin's papers."

"Ah, yes, I'm in charge of those, as it happens. What do you want to know?"

"I have a friend here, she's planning to write a book about Severin. She seems to think the actress was involved in the war, some kind of spy or something."

Rogers didn't reply immediately. "Well, I've not gone through everything yet, a lot of it still needs to be catalogued. But I haven't seen anything along those lines."

"You don't sound terribly sure."

"She was definitely an interesting woman, so it's not impossible. But like I said, I've not been through everything yet. There's a ton of stuff on the Internet which might interest you, and we have one or two books in the library about her life, too."

"I may check those out."

"Not anymore, if you meant that literally. We've moved them into the collection, keeping everything related to her together in one place. You're welcome to come by and look at it, just not check anything out."

"Including the secret stuff?"

"Again, nice try. I'm just sorry I can't tell you more."

"I understand. I wouldn't ask you to compromise yourself, don't worry. Although maybe we can talk more tomorrow morning, I'm quite curious now."

Rogers chuckled. "Of course you are—that's your nature. I don't think I'll be able to tell you much more, but sure, we can talk. Oh, do me a favor and come around eleven will you?"

"Sure thing."

"Another secret, but this one I can tell you. I'm writing a book."

"You are? That's great, and seems appropriate for a librarian."

"I've always wanted to, and I'm not getting any younger. I decided

I just need to go for it, make myself do it. So every morning I shut myself in a spot in the basement that I've converted into a writing room, lock the door, and don't let myself out until I've written two thousand words."

"How long does that take you?"

"Well, I do my research at home the evening before—the Wi-Fi reception in the little room where I write is worse than useless. But that way I'm primed and ready to go the next morning, so anywhere from one to three hours, depending on my mood, inspiration, and work distractions. I try to start around eight or nine, finish by eleven."

"What are you writing?"

"It's kind of a science fiction crime thriller. Takes place in the future, and also the past. Time-travel stuff. Sounds silly, I know, but . . . there you have it."

"I think it's fantastic, actually," Hugo said. "I couldn't ever write a novel, so I admire anyone who can, regardless of subject matter."

"It remains to be seen whether I can finish it." Rogers laughed. "But so far so good."

"Well, best of luck with it; I'm impressed." Hugo turned as Tom, Merlyn, and Miki stepped out of the café. "I better get going. I'll see you tomorrow around eleven?"

"You bet."

Tom and Hugo walked slowly behind Merlyn and Miki, who linked arms and took in everything around them.

"That your buddy at the library?" Tom asked. "Bald guy in his forties, with the super-hot American wife in her twenties?"

"Fiancée, I think, or just girlfriend. But yes, that'd be him. Paul Rogers."

Tom wagged a finger. "He's one of those guys who's way more interesting than he appears. Like your buddy Max, the *bouquiniste*."

"Oh, I know, I vetted him for embassy-related reasons." Hugo thought of Max often, the gruff, grumpy, but painfully honest bookseller who'd been kidnapped from his stall beside the Seine. For a while, Hugo was the only one looking for Max, and in the process he had discovered the man's fascinating history as a Nazi hunter, something Hugo had no idea about. It was another lesson that you never really knew about people, only what they wanted you to see. Unless, like Hugo or Tom, you were very good at discovering people's pasts, digging up their secrets.

"Yeah, adopted by a rich but kooky French lady. She shipped him off to America to live with relatives, go to boarding schools on the East Coast. He grew up an American, only came here for the occasional vacation until about twenty years ago."

"How do *you* know all this?"

Tom nudged him playfully. "Guess."

Hugo thought for a moment. The two men had been best friends ever since they met at the FBI Academy in Quantico, living and working together over the years. Their paths had split when they left the FBI and Tom got recruited to work for the CIA, a move that suited his reckless side. But that last year at the bureau and the rigors and expectations of his new job had changed his friend. He drank too much and was prone to fighting in bars several times a year, a trait that was manageable except that Tom usually picked on people much larger than him. And, occasionally, cops. An interest in librarians like Paul Rogers was definitely not going to be recreational, even if the man had a beautiful girlfriend.

"I would say," Hugo began, "that since he's a dual citizen and gets to live in either country . . . and has a wealthy, presumably high-society mother, he came across your radar at the CIA as either a potential asset or a possible target."

Tom slapped Hugo on the back. "Smart man. Both, as it happens."

"Both?"

"He was zipping back and forth a lot as a kid. Some people at the Company have this phobia about sleepers, children raised in the US and groomed to be spies. There have been a few, but there were also a few dinosaurs in the past, if you know what I mean. As with dinosaurs, TV and movies keep the threat alive, so when baldy Rogers attracted attention he, well, attracted attention. Although he wasn't bald back then."

"How very interesting," Hugo said. "You guys have your beaks everywhere, don't you?"

"Some places you wouldn't much like, my friend. Anyway, that's not all of it."

"Keep going."

"He had a brother, a few years older. He wouldn't even remember him, because Rogers was not even two when he was adopted, this other kid was seventeen. Real kid, the old woman's flesh and blood, not adopted."

"This'll surprise you, Tom, but adopted kids are real kids, too."

"You know what I mean. Anyway, this brother, Michel, or something. Quite the handful. Into drugs, women, not going to school. Angry little man whose fist put him in contact with the juvenile justice system here. To hear the mother tell it, he had this girlfriend and both sets of parents were against it. She was black, he was lily-white, and no one approved. One fine day he and this girlfriend eloped, drove up to the Normandy coast and . . . that was that."

"They married and lived happily ever after?"

"Quite the opposite. Drove their car off a cliff into the ocean, holding hands all the way down."

"Seriously? They found them like that?"

"No, silly, they only found part of one of her legs and deduced the rest from the carnage. And a motorist saw the car go over the edge. It might have been an accident, but given that his mother had threatened to cut him off, well, there was also talk of a double suicide."

Hugo shook his head. "Crazy story. Does Paul know all this?"

"Dunno. You can ask him next time you see him."

CHAPTER THREE

On Monday morning Hugo worked from the dining table in his living room so he could enjoy the sun streaming through the main windows, which he opened just enough to allow in the sounds of a waking Paris. He made three pots of coffee, all of which were awful, and resisted the temptation to grab a book and enjoy a quiet, and decent, café crème in one of the nearby cafés.

At ten thirty Tom emerged from the spare room, rubbing his head and grousing about the sludge in the coffee pot.

"You're a man of many talents, Hugo," he said.

"Yeah, I know, making coffee isn't one of them."

"You need a wife. What's going on with Claudia and you?"

"I think they call it casual dating," Hugo said. "It's fine, we're both happy."

"Sure you are. Has she met Merlyn yet?" An edge in Tom's voice suggested there was more to the question than just the words.

"You know she hasn't; Merlyn just got here. And Merlyn's my friend, Tom, nothing more. She's just a kid."

"Almost thirty."

"Friend. Kid. And you're my age, so . . . you know."

"You don't have to worry—she seems like a nice girl, which means she might be a little vanilla for me."

Hugo burst out laughing. "Oh, Tom. You're a man of many talents. But reading women isn't one of them."

"Oh yeah?" Tom asked. "Go on."

"I've got to go—an appointment at the library. But I'm having dinner with Merlyn and Miki tonight, if you want to join us."

"What are they doing today?"

"Merlyn called about an hour ago to check in. She's going shopping and Miki's writing in some café somewhere. So unless you want to come to the library with me, you're on your own."

"Hotbeds of action and excitement, libraries. In my experience, anyway."

Hugo smiled and left Tom staring out of the apartment window, his elbows on the ledge as he watched the foot traffic on Rue Jacob below. Out on the sidewalk, Hugo looked up and gave him a wave before setting off toward the Eiffel Tower and the American Library, on Rue du Général Camou.

He walked slowly along Rue Saint-Dominique, sticking to the shaded side of the street, pausing to look into shop windows he'd not seen before and slowing to take in the smell of cooking as he passed the bistros. A tourist couple, given away by their sturdy shoes, backpacks, and camera, paused in front of him to stare at the wife's phone. As he reached them Hugo realized what they were doing, and that paper maps were obsolete now, little squares of glass giving the temporarily lost a precise and easy way to safety.

As he got closer to the Seventh Arrondissment the streets widened and became quieter, the shopping districts melting into residential neighborhoods, and the cafés became few and far between. But as he rounded the corner onto Avenue Rapp, he couldn't help but admire the view of the Eiffel Tower as it loomed over a narrow side street, visible between a pair of old stone buildings. The most iconic of Paris's tourist sites framed just for him.

The library sat a hundred yards off Avenue Rapp, a stone's throw from the Champ de Mars, the park that spread out like a grassy apron southeast of the Eiffel Tower, a perfect spot to picnic or just lie back and admire the tower.

He pushed the door open and stepped into the library, impressed with the number of people milling around. In front of him was the check-out desk, to his right the area set aside for the book sale, and to his left the reference-book area and a conference room that had glass walls that, Rogers had once told him, were virtually soundproof. He felt himself relax as he stepped inside, this place having the same effect all libraries had on him, with the quiet sounds of people leafing through books, the whispered conversations, and the almost-meditative state of the patrons as they devoted themselves to the written word. Hugo had often thought libraries were akin to places of worship, his version of church, where reverence and peace enveloped him like a blanket.

Hugo nodded to the two young men behind the check-out desk, then walked past them, his eyes peeled for Paul Rogers. It was almost 11:15, so his writing stint should have ended for the day. He kept going, entering the long, low room where the stacks of books began. This was the main part of the library, a deep, almost cavelike space whose second story meant a ceiling lower than in the entrance way, and also cut out all natural light. He walked slowly, looking down each row, but didn't see Rogers.

At the end of the room he glanced at the stairs that led down to the basement, a place closed to the public. To Hugo's left were the bathrooms, a spiral stairway up to the second floor, and the children's section. He could see through the glass door a dozen children sprawled on cushions and rugs in a semicircle, eyes glued to the young man reading a story from a picture book. He heard footsteps coming down the staircase from the floor above, and smiled when he recognized Nicole Anisse. They'd met on half a dozen occasions, and Hugo had always been impressed by the tall, attractive, and whip-smart brunette who was one of the library's two reference and collections librarians.

"Nicole, *bonjour*." He held out a hand, but she smiled and gave him the traditional two kisses. Her cheek was cool against his, the light scent of her perfume alluring despite the setting.

"Monsieur Marston, *comment ça va*?" *How are you?*

"Very well, thank you. I'm looking for Paul Rogers."

She looked at the clock on the wall. "He should be finished with his writing. You're welcome to go down and knock on the door."

"He didn't tell me exactly where he writes," Hugo said.

She nodded toward the basement stairs. "He converted the storage space that we call the *atelier*, put a chair, desk, and lamp in there. At the bottom of the stairs, turn right, you'll soon come to the last row of shelves. You wouldn't know it was there unless someone told you, but head between the wall and the shelves, it's at the far end, white door."

"Sounds like a great little hideaway."

"It's perfect for him, really. Tucked away in the corner, nice and quiet." She pulled a face. "Although it's a little creepy down there. If I was locked in that space for two hours every day, I'd go insane, so I have no idea how he manages to be creative in there."

"Insanity and creativity are closely linked, *non?*" Hugo joked.

"Maybe."

"He's always down there alone?"

"He likes the quiet, so yes." Anisse smiled. "Except for a certain lady who guards the door. You'll see who I mean."

Hugo thanked her and started down the steps to the basement. Almost immediately, the chattering from the front of the library was silenced, and as he descended the air around him felt cooler, and perhaps a little staler. There was something else there, too, though. Something reassuring in the dusty air, that inescapable book smell, and Hugo's fingers itched to start flipping covers, turning pages.

At the bottom of the stairs curiosity overtook him and he went into a short hallway to his left, which ended in a closed door. He knocked on it gently and, when no one answered, he opened it and went in. *Boiler room and storage*, he noted to himself. *Practical, not creepy.*

He retraced his steps, closing the boiler-room door behind him, and walked toward the large basement. At the base of the stairs, he found himself looking at maybe twenty rows of metal shelves, each filled with books, and in various places along the wall lay piles of books as tall as him. He moved to his right, to the last stack, which he rounded with care. To his right was a brick wall, painted white many years ago, and at the end of the row was a closed door. Paul's converted writing room.

Hugo remembered what Nicole Anisse had said about a woman

watching over the former *atelier*, but didn't see her until he got closer to the door. She gazed down from a four-foot-high painting, a woman in a white tunic and white turban with oddly rosy cheeks and a slightly bored expression in her eyes. As he looked at the painting, Hugo was glad Anisse had told him its subject was a woman; he might have wondered otherwise.

Hugo stood in front of the door and hesitated. He hated to interrupt a man busy with his work, his own form of art, but Paul Rogers had told him it would be OK to do so. Hugo knocked gently and waited. When he got no response, he knocked a second time, louder, but still heard nothing from inside. *Maybe he finished up and isn't in there?* Hugo tried the door, but it was locked. He knocked again.

"Paul, it's Hugo Marston," he said, then raised his voice a notch. "You in there?"

Silence.

Hugo retraced his steps and found Nicole Anisse still outside the children's section. "No reply from the dungeon. Did Paul reappear?"

"*Non*," she said. "At least, he didn't come past me."

"OK. I don't mean to worry you, but do you have a key to the room he's working in?"

"It's locked?"

"He probably locked it when he left."

"Monsieur Harmuth can get a key. Ah, there he is."

"Did I hear my name?" Harmuth approached them, a smile on his lips. "Telling him what a great boss I am?"

"*Bien sûr*," Anisse said with a playful roll of the eyes. *Of course.*

"Hey, you know I don't speak French," he said playfully, before turning to Hugo. "Not very well, anyway. Always learning. The embassy guy, Hugo, right?"

"Hugo Marston, nice to see you again." Hugo had met Michael Harmuth several times. He was Paul Rogers's right-hand man, the assistant director of the library for the past year or so, and the library's resident IT whizz. Harmuth had an open, friendly face and bright eyes. With white hair, he looked older than he probably was, but he had an energy about him that Hugo liked. They shook hands and Harmuth winced. "My bum elbow," he explained.

"Tennis player?" Hugo asked.

"Heavens no. A brisk walk is about all I manage these days. Elbow, back, and the right knee when it's cold. If I tried anything more than a stroll I'd fall apart."

Hugo chuckled. "I'm getting there myself. Still manage a run once or twice a week but it takes me days to recover."

"Don't you have to pass fitness tests and all that, as a secret agent?"

"I'm hardly secret. And no, nothing like that."

"I see. So here's something I've always wondered," Harmuth said conspiratorially. "Do you guys carry your guns with you at all times? FBI agents do, right?"

"They do. And I probably shouldn't answer that." He gave Harmuth a wink, answering him without words.

"Ah, I see. Very cool. With one of those under your armpit, I guess you don't really need superhuman fitness or ninja training."

"I'm a long way from my ninja days. Like I said, a run now and again makes me sore. Advil is my friend."

"Not me. Stopped using processed pharmaceuticals years ago. I use the natural stuff—you should, too, and I'd be happy to give you some pointers. There's some really good stuff out there, for general pain but also for more serious ailments."

"I may take you up on that, thanks." He paused, then continued. "So I was looking for Paul, had an appointment with him, you might say."

"He's probably still writing."

"I figured, but yesterday he told me to interrupt him if it got to be eleven. I just knocked on his door but there was no answer."

"He wasn't there?"

Hugo shook his head. "And it's locked."

"That's odd. Let's pop down there and see. If he's like me, he may just be taking a nap."

"I wondered if he had headphones on, some of the new ones are pretty good at drowning out the world," Hugo said. "But I knocked pretty loudly."

Harmuth patted his pockets and came up with a key, a look of worry on his face now. "You know, about a year ago Paul had . . . it wasn't a heart attack exactly, but he had some problem. Irregular heartbeat or something."

They started walking. "I didn't know that," Hugo said.

"You know what he's like, pretty private, so a lot of his friends had no idea. I'd only been working here a little while, I think he only told me because he had to, for time off."

A jolt of worry shot through Hugo and he started forward, quicker steps than before. "He'd call an ambulance if something was wrong, I'm sure," Hugo said. *Assuming he was able to.*

"Actually, no. We just put in this new technology, it jams cell signals. We wanted people to put their damn phones down and read books in here."

Hugo followed Harmuth down the stairs into the basement, which seemed smaller and tighter with two of them there. Harmuth advanced on the *atelier*'s door with the key in his hand, his pace suddenly slower, more hesitant. He glanced nervously at Hugo, who said, "You want me to do it?"

"No, I'm sure everything's fine. I'm fine." He pulled his shoulders back and stopped in front of the door. The key rattled in the lock. Harmuth took a quick breath, turned the door knob, and pushed the door open a crack. "Paul? You in there?"

Harmuth's head and right shoulder disappeared into the room, but he stopped short of going all the way in, his left hand still on the door knob as if for safety. He paused like that for a full five seconds, and Hugo was about to step forward to see for himself when Harmuth staggered back.

"What is it?" Hugo started forward, grabbing Harmuth's shoulders when it looked like the man might collapse. Harmuth nodded that he was all right, so Hugo pushed the door to the little room open and looked inside. Paul Rogers sat in a leather office chair behind a rickety desk that carried a water bottle, several books, a notepad, and an open laptop. He'd tilted to one side, his eyes wide open and his mouth gaping. But it was the color of his skin that gave it away, the gray tinge and the waxy pallor that Hugo had seen a hundred times before, in a hundred different places. The light from the bare bulb reflected off the walls, making him look almost blue, but one thing was for sure: Paul Rogers was dead.

Hugo moved into the room, his eyes scanning everything around him, careful not to touch anything. This looked like a natural event, a heart attack, and Hugo saw no signs of violence to Rogers's body. Out of habit and training, Hugo rounded the desk and put two fingers to Rogers's neck to confirm that the man was dead. *No pulse, skin cold. He's been dead an hour at least*, Hugo thought.

He took one more look around the room and then stepped back into the hallway. He pulled out his cell phone but saw there was no service. Harmuth was sitting on the floor, pale and wide-eyed. His mouth moved silently for a moment, then he asked, "Is he . . . is he dead?"

"I'm afraid so," Hugo said.

Harmuth's eyes dropped to Hugo's phone. "You have to go to the entrance. The cell-phone jammers."

"Right. Normally I'd approve," Hugo said grimly. "Can I leave you here for a moment while I call this in?"

"Umm, sure." Harmuth's eyes flickered to the door. "I'm sorry, I've not really seen . . . that before. I've been lucky, I guess."

Hugo reached back and closed the door to the little room, instinctively touching only the frame of the door and not the knob. "Just make sure no one goes in, OK?"

"No problem." Harmuth started to get to his feet, and Hugo gave him a helping hand. "Might frighten people if I'm sprawled out on the floor," he said with a weak smile.

"Just hang out here, I'll be right back."

Harmuth glanced at the door again and grimaced, then gave Hugo a quick nod.

Hugo watched his phone display as he walked briskly through the library to the front entrance. He realized that he didn't quite know whom to call. All of his encounters with death, including the ones on foreign soil, had been of the nefarious kind, where there was no doubt that police and forensics people were needed. As he neared the front of the building, Hugo saw the bars indicating service. He called up his list of contacts and dialed the only person he knew would be able to help.

"*Salut*, Camille, it's Hugo." Lieutenant Camille Lerens, his contact and friend in the Brigade Criminelle, the division responsible for investigating the city's most serious crimes, like murder, kidnapping, and terrorism.

"*Ah, mon ami, comment ça va?*"

"I'm well, and you?"

"The happiest woman in the force," she said.

Despite the circumstances, Hugo smiled. He knew full well what she meant. A few years ago, Camille Lerens had been Christophe Lerens, a good cop in Bordeaux whose bravery was sorely tested when he decided to make the full transition to the person, the woman, he'd always been on the inside. The macho culture of the police had challenged Camille's resolve, but supportive parents and the surprise allegiance of one of Paris's fiercest police chiefs had seen her through. As far as Hugo could tell, Camille's gender was now a nonissue, her abilities as a police officer having won over even the worst of her tormentors. Where living life as a successful woman, and one of color no less, had once been a dream, it was now her reality. She could have been bitter about the long, hard road, Hugo knew, but that wasn't her way.

"Glad to hear it," he said. "So I've got a situation, not sure how to handle it."

"Tell me."

"I'm at the American Library on Rue Général Camou. Someone who works here, a friend of mine, actually, was working by himself in a basement room and died."

"I'm sorry to her that. . . . Natural causes?"

"Looks like it."

"I hear something in your voice. You sure?"

"I'm not a doctor, Camille, I wouldn't want to say I'm sure. But it doesn't look like murder or suicide, so I'm not sure what else it could be." A sudden wave of sadness swept over him. For the last few minutes he'd been in work mode, tucking away any and all feelings to make sure the right people were notified and doing their jobs. But saying the words, bumping into that realization that his friend Paul Rogers had just passed away . . . that fact was no longer tucked away, and Hugo felt a hollowness in his chest at the loss of a good man.

"He was your friend, you said?"

"Yes. He's the director here, I've known him several years. We talked a lot about books, and he was supposed to show me some that the library is selling."

"*Je suis désolée*, Hugo. Do you want me to come out there?"

"No, I just didn't know the procedure for a death by natural causes."

"Normally, a doctor is called and he or she will certify the death and issue a *certificat de décès*, of death. You know what, I'll come out and bring a couple of crime-scene people with me. Things are slow and it's better to be safe than sorry."

"I don't think you need to, Camille. He was alone in a room, the door locked, and may have had a heart condition."

"It's no problem. The crime-scene woman I usually use has a new recruit, this is a perfect training opportunity for him. If it's natural causes, it won't matter if he screws up."

"If you're sure. I'll head back down to the room and make sure no one goes in. And there's no cell-phone service in the building, just so you know."

"Convenient, if you want to murder someone," Lerens said lightly, then quickly changed her tone. "Sorry, I didn't mean to be flippant."

"It's OK," Hugo said. "I thought of that, too."

Hugo found Michael Harmuth at the bottom of the steps to the basement.

"I didn't want to stay right there," Harmuth said. "It was too quiet, and that painting. I've never liked it."

"That's fine, as long as no one went in."

"No one's come down the stairs, no. Is someone coming?"

"The police. I'm pretty sure it was natural causes, but they want to come by anyway and double-check."

"Sure, OK. Do you need me still, or . . . ? I wouldn't mind getting some fresh air."

"Of course, I'll wait here for the cops."

"Thanks." Harmuth paused. "We have cameras, I think they're operational. Color ones, too. There's one that would cover the *atelier*, so let me know if they want footage from this morning. I'll have someone download it, or do it myself."

"They might, just to cover their bases. I'll ask." Hugo was impressed with Harmuth's dogged professionalism under the circumstances. The man even knew how to pronounce the word *atelier* properly, not easy for a foreigner. "Why do you have cameras in a library?"

"You'd be amazed the places people steal from. Libraries aren't immune, and some of the books down here are quite valuable." He shook his head sadly. "When I first started working here they told me they didn't lock the basement doors at night. They still don't during the day, too much hassle to keep getting the key. Staff come down here a lot, and members of the public could easily find their way down here, too, so cameras seemed like a decent idea."

Hugo watched as Harmuth shuffled up the stairs, slowly shaking his head as if he couldn't quite believe what was happening. A common reaction to unexpected death, as Hugo well knew.

It took thirty minutes for Camille Lerens and her two crime-scene specialists to arrive. Also with them was the medical examiner, whom Lerens introduced as Doctor David Sprengelmeyer. A wiry man with floppy, dark hair, Sprengelmeyer looked more Italian than French, or, as his name suggested, German.

"Former French national squash champion," Lerens said. "Now pokes at dead bodies for a living."

"Nice to meet you," said Hugo. "You go in first?"

"I'm probably the only one going in. I have to certify the death officially, but unless there's anything suspicious, these two head back to the office." He gestured to a short woman and her male colleague, and introduced them as Meike Stuedemann and Charles Allée. "I won't touch anything, don't worry." He said it with a friendly wink. "Done a lot more poking bodies than playing squash these past few years."

"Hey, if you're working with Camille, you know what you're doing. I have no concerns at all."

They watched as the senior technician, Meike Stuedemann, unzipped her bag and took out a clear packet containing white forensic scrubs. She handed the packet to Dr. Sprengelmeyer, and he dressed quickly and quietly. The scrubs on, he pulled a surgical mask over his mouth and then donned blue latex gloves. He nodded at the watching group, then moved alongside the metal bookshelf toward the door. He opened it and stepped inside. He left the door open, and all four of them shuffled closer to watch, but Sprengelmeyer looked back and his brow creased in what appeared to be a frown. When he spoke, his voice was muffled.

"This isn't a spectator sport, how about some space for me and some dignity for him."

Eight feet shuffled backward and Lerens muttered, "We're a little past dignity at this point."

Hugo smiled. "No one likes being watched while they work, so I get it."

"True," Lerens said. "*Dites-donc*, how did you manage to be here?"

"I spoke to Paul yesterday. He called me about a sale of books the library's having, some expensive but a few I could afford. He was holding one in particular for me, a signed Truman Capote."

"You knew him well?"

"Through a few events the embassy has held or attended here. A couple of visits here outside of work, but we didn't hang out socially or anything."

"*Bon.* So while he's working, tell me, how's everything else?" She smiled. "Still dating Claudia?"

"Off and on. Mostly off. You?"

"Enjoying being me still." She smiled. "Hey, you and I should go out one night," she joked.

"That'd blow Tom's mind," Hugo said. "Lucky I don't date colleagues."

"Lucky for whom?"

"Them, usually."

"With that attitude, I'm sure. Ah, here we are."

Doctor Sprengelmeyer stood in the doorway of the little writing room. He lowered his mask and stripped off his gloves. "*Il est mort.*" *He's dead.* "No doubt about that." He held up a warning finger. "But don't start asking me how long he's been that way."

Lerens gave him a wry smile. "It's my job to ask."

"And mine is to give you an accurate answer, not make wild guesses."

"Can't be that wild," Lerens said. "Hugo, how long did you say he'd been in that room?"

"He told me he starts around eight or nine, so just a couple of hours. The tape will tell us."

"What tape?"

Hugo indicated the security camera tucked high in the corner. "The tape from that camera."

"*Oui,* if it actually works," Lerens said, then turned back to Sprengelmeyer. "You're not going to give me any clue as to cause of death?"

"Would if I could. Nothing stands out, no visible trauma, no indication of anything other than his heart stopped working."

"No need for the CSU techs?" she asked.

"Not as far as I can see."

Hugo stepped forward. "Mind if I take a look?"

Sprengelmeyer glanced at Lerens, who shrugged. "You think I missed something?"

"I sincerely doubt it," Hugo replied. "I'm just curious, that's all." The doctor moved out of the doorway and Hugo walked past him into the room. He paused and turned back to the doctor. "His skin. Is it a little blue?"

"*Un petit peu,*" Sprengelmeyer said. *A little bit.* "I would imagine it's from a lack of oxygen, it affects people differently. And, of course, the room color will make the skin look bluer than it really is."

"Yes, of course," Hugo said. "Thank you."

He stood inside the room and took everything in. The body of his dead friend dominated the tiny space, of course, but Hugo knew to look elsewhere, knew that if something *was* wrong, any clues needed to be discovered before the room was disturbed. He looked at the desk where a laptop sat open in front of the dead man. A plastic water bottle sat on one side of the computer, next to a writing pad and a pen. On the other side of the desk, a large book lay open. Hugo stepped forward and saw it was a reference book, an encyclopedia of handguns. Beside it, another book, a mystery novel by Terry Shames. Hugo checked the notepad but could make little sense of the scribbled notes, the arrows and boxes Rogers had drawn. *Character names and plot points?* Hugo wondered.

A sound behind him made Hugo turn. Camille Lerens stood by the doorway, watching him intently. Hugo moved to the end of the desk. On the floor behind it lay a crumpled handkerchief. Hugo knelt for a closer look but saw no blood or any other kind of stain; it looked clean, if a little old.

"See something?" Lerens asked.

"Probably not. But maybe." He stood. "You said your crime-scene person needed training, right?"

"Yes. On an actual crime scene."

"You're all here now. Let's pretend."

"You wouldn't say that unless you thought something was wrong." She put her hands on her hips and looked at Hugo. "What is it? What makes you think this is a crime scene?"

Hugo shrugged. "Nothing. A feeling. And like I said, you guys are all here. You even have a real dead body to work around. As far as training exercises go, I would imagine this one's pretty good."

Lerens nodded. "*D'accord.*" She frowned and looked at Rogers.

"He does look blue in here, it's weird." She stepped out of the room and spoke to her crime-scene experts. "*Bon*, treat this as a murder scene. He's been poisoned by a jealous wife, for his fortune. Don't miss anything."

"*Bien*." Stuedemann smiled. "But poisoned because she's jealous or because she wants his money?"

"Both," Lerens said. "Smartass."

"And she poisoned him by passing through a locked door."

"She's the devil incarnate, so all the more reason to be extra thorough."

Hugo walked out of the room and stood beside Lerens as Stuedemann and Allée pulled on their white scrubs. Allée stooped and pulled a camera from their equipment bag and checked its settings. He nodded to Stuedemann, and they both snapped on gloves.

"*Bon, une question*." Stuedemann pointed to the room. "Did you touch anything? Did anyone else, as far as you know?"

Hugo thought for a moment. "*Oui*. I touched the door knob earlier, when I tried it and found it locked. Michael Harmuth touched it, too. He had to, to get in."

"Who's Monsieur Harmuth?" Lerens asked. She had a notebook open and pen poised.

"He works here, assistant director of the library."

Lerens wrote in her little book. "Anyone else?"

"Not that I know of." Hugo indicated the camera overlooking that corner of the library. "But if that thing's working, it shouldn't be hard to find out."

"Security cameras in a library." Lerens shook her head. "What's the world coming to?"

Meike Stuedemann smiled and then covered her mouth with a surgical mask. They all waited as Allée took half a dozen photos of the door, then knelt in front of the silver handle and dusted it with a small brush. Stuedemann watched as her colleague applied and then carefully removed tape, which he placed on a square card. He wrote the location and then nodded to Stuedemann who, after a brief and respectful pause, stepped into the little room.

Hugo and Camille stood quietly as Dr. Sprengelmeyer took off his scrubs and gloves, leaving them in a pile on the floor. He wasn't looking at them, and Hugo had the distinct impression that he wasn't happy about the crime-scene people going to work in the *atelier*. He'd heard them say it was a training exercise, but Hugo also knew that they wouldn't be doing it at all if someone didn't think something was amiss. And that called Dr. Sprengelmeyer's expertise into question.

"Who'll do the autopsy?" Hugo asked.

"I will," Sprengelmeyer said, without looking at him. "Why?"

"Just curious."

"No spectators," the doctor said curtly.

They could hear Stuedemann and Allée moving around the little room, hear the click and see the flash of the camera. Hugo moved toward the doorway, conscious of the painted lady in the turban, watching them all. Stuedemann stood by while her colleague photographed the desk from several angles. That done, Allée picked up the water bottle and dusted the outside for prints. The bottle was three-quarters full of what looked to be water, and, when Allée finished removing prints from the outside, he checked that the lid was on tight and slipped the bottle into a plastic evidence bag. He then moved around the desk and stopped in front of the handkerchief. He photographed it from several angles, zooming in and out, then put the square of cloth into its own evidence bag.

"People still use handkerchiefs?" Stuedemann muttered. "How quaint."

Allée chuckled, then looked up at her and asked: "I've photographed the books and dusted the open pages, but should I bag them as evidence?"

"Do they belong here, to the library?" Stuedemann asked.

Allée checked the spines for library markings and nodded. "They do."

"Then just photograph them. As long as there's no blood spatter or other substance on them, I don't think there's any need. The detectives will know where to find them."

"OK. What about his hands, bag those?"

"Might as well, for the practice," Stuedemann said.

Hugo moved back into the hallway, leaving them to their work. "I think I'll go grab that surveillance," he said to Lerens.

"Because watching hours of nothing is fun?"

"I assume you have an intern or lowly someone-or-other who can do that for us."

"'Us?'"

Hugo started down the hallway. "Yep. We're a team, remember?" He started back up the steps to the ground floor of the library, wandering to the front, where he found Nicole Anisse.

"Nicole, have you seen Michael Harmuth?"

"Someone called about the Severin collection. I think he's dealing with that."

"*Merci bien.*"

"*Monsieur.*" Her eyes were wide and she looked suddenly fragile. "Is everything all right? I saw the police arriving and Monsieur Harmuth is upset. Did something happen?"

Hugo knew it wasn't his place to tell her, but she'd already seen enough to be worried. "I'm afraid someone has . . . Let me find Monsieur Harmuth. . . . Is he really your supervisor?"

"*Oui*, he is." She hesitated. "Or Michelle Juneau, she's Paul's assistant, does all the human resources, payroll, that kind of thing. She's helping him with the collection so I'm guessing she's with Michael right now."

"Where is the collection kept, do you know?"

"In the basement. They've put in a cabinet for it, to keep everything together. If anyone wants to see all or part of it, they'll bring it up to the conference room." She pointed to a door behind the check-out desk. "That's the other stairway to the basement, the one we use most. They're probably down there."

"OK if I use it?" Hugo asked.

"Sure. I'm needed up here but I'll show you the way." She led him behind the desk, nodding to the three people manning it that all was fine, and held the door open for Hugo. As he passed her, he saw the worry in her eyes and tried giving her a reassuring smile. He wasn't sure it worked.

"It's just to your left downstairs," she said.

He trotted down the stairs and at the bottom could hear the muffled voices of Lerens and the CSU team at the other end of the basement. But the packed rows of shelves between them might as well have been walls, they seemed so distant; and, not for the first time, Hugo noticed the chill and stale air, and felt the hairs on his arms stand on end.

He moved to his left, into an open area littered with piles of books, carefully stacked to avoid collapse. A woman stood with her back to him as she studied the contents of a closed glass cabinet. As he watched, she rattled the cabinet's locked doors and put her hands on her hips in apparent frustration when they wouldn't open.

"Well, hello," Hugo said. "I didn't expect to see you down here."

CHAPTER FOUR

The woman stiffened, then turned slowly to look at Hugo, her eyes wide with surprise. "Hugo. What are you doing here?"

"Looking for Michael Harmuth and Michelle Juneau. You?"

Miki Harrison grimaced. "Trying to avoid Michelle Juneau."

"Why?"

"Let's just say I'm doing some unauthorized research."

"And possibly some criminal trespassing."

"Probably. But asking politely hasn't gotten me anywhere."

"Maybe. But you still shouldn't be down here—the signs are clear this is employees-only. I wasn't kidding that you're trespassing." Hugo softened his tone. "How did you get down here?"

She pointed toward the far side of the basement. "Followed someone down and then wandered this way."

"Didn't you see the police activity?"

"I saw some people, didn't know they were police. I was quiet and trying not to be seen. What's going on?"

"Nothing you need to worry about." The library was like that, Hugo was beginning to see. Full of narrow spaces and twists and turns, plenty of ways to sneak around and keep from being seen. A hide-and-seeker's delight. He pointed at the glass cabinet. "The Severin collection, I presume?"

"It looks like it. Some of it, at least," Miki said. "I didn't see any of her stuff elsewhere, so presumably whatever I want is in there."

"Ah, the secret papers. Although I don't see a dagger. Did you ever talk to Paul Rogers about those?"

"Not yet. I was told he's busy, so I thought I'd have a look for myself," Miki said.

"You've been at the library all morning?"

"For an hour. Getting the lay of the land, you might say."

He nodded and said, "Look, I'm afraid I have some bad news about Paul. It's not public knowledge yet, so please don't say anything, but there's no harm in telling you."

"Telling me what?"

"He passed away this morning. He was writing his novel and appears to have had a heart attack, right here in the library. Those people you snuck past were dealing with that."

Miki's mouth opened slightly but she didn't speak at first, as if she were unsure whether to believe him or not. "Right down here?"

"Yes. He'd created a room for himself over there." He indicated with a nod of his head.

"Oh no. And he's . . . he's dead?"

"I'm afraid so."

"Oh. That poor man. I'm really sorry."

"Yeah, he was a good guy."

"Does he have family?"

"A long-term girlfriend, yes. No kids as far as I know."

"How old was he?"

"Not very," Hugo said. "I understand he had heart trouble in recent years, though."

Miki nodded, then looked around her. "I suppose I should leave. I know I shouldn't be down here, and now it seems . . . well, I should leave."

"Probably a good idea." He indicated the stairway leading up to the circulation desk. "This way is best."

She gave Hugo a small smile and walked toward the staircase, stopping when she got there. She turned and said, "You're staying down here?"

"I may have to help out."

She cocked her head. "How come?"

Smart woman, Hugo thought. "The police were called just in case. A formality, just routine. But I was there when he was found and he's a dual citizen, so I may have to linger a little."

"That's weird. I mean, that someone called the police for a heart attack."

"That was me."

"Oh. Look, I don't mean to be nosy or inappropriate," Miki said. "But did something make you think it wasn't a heart attack? I mean, isn't that kind of your job?"

"It used to be my job, but not anymore," Hugo said. "And I only called them because it was a body in a library, an at-least partly American citizen in a foreign place. Just seemed like the right thing to do."

She gave him a little smile. "Sounds like a game of Clue."

That might be amusing in a week or two, Hugo thought. *But not today.* "I'll walk you upstairs," he said. "The circulation desk is up here. If we bump into Madame Juneau, we'll say you were with me."

"Can we tell her we were doing something exciting?"

"Not today." *Again with the insensitive comments*, Hugo said to himself. *Everyone deals with the news of death differently, of course, but some people . . .* They reached the top of the stairs and slipped past the librarians at the desk, moving into the area where the books were laid out for the sale. "Here we are, safe and sound."

"Thanks, Hugo," she said. "Maybe see you tonight?"

"I'm planning on it."

He followed her to the main doors, and Hugo held one open for her. He watched as she walked away, still not sure what to make of her. He made a mental note to look her up online, see if she had a body of work as a journalist, something credible and professional that might justify her intrusion into the library basement, and perhaps even her insensitivity. Although that seemed more like a personality issue.

A voice behind Hugo made him turn. "*Monsieur?* You were looking for me?" She spoke in French.

"Madame Juneau?" He'd seen her at the library in previous visits, but they'd never been introduced.

"Michelle Juneau, *oui*." She was an attractive woman, probably in her late thirties, with glossy, russet hair. Her green eyes and bright-red lipstick made Hugo think of Christmas. But there was a formality to her, one that Hugo thought hid either a fiery temper or an unusually gentle nature. Maybe both.

Hugo offered his hand. "I'm Hugo Marston, a friend of Paul Rogers."

"I recognize the name; it's a pleasure to meet you. How can I help?"

Hugo was suddenly aware of people passing by, close to them, and the curious eyes of Nicole Anisse. "Is there somewhere we can talk in private?"

"We have a large book sale this morning, Monsieur Marston, so I hope we can be brief." She gestured toward a nearby door. "We can use my office."

She led him past the circulation desk, alongside the main stacks. A third of the way down, she turned into a short hallway and led him through a door into a large and open administration area. Tucked around a corner, out of sight from anyone in the main library, sat a large safe. It was chest height, was roughly four feet wide and deep, and looked a hundred years old. Hugo's first thought was how much it must weigh, but he was also interested to see it was accessed by a key, not a combination. Past it lay Michelle Juneau's office and a second one, with Paul Rogers's name on the door. Juneau stood behind her desk, waiting for him. He went into her office and closed the door.

"I'm afraid I have bad news," he began. "I came here to meet with Paul this morning, for the sale. He was working on his book when I found him."

"*Found him?*" she repeated. "Why do you say it that way?"

"Paul is dead, madame. He appears to have had a heart attack."

A small hand fluttered to her mouth, but she never took her eyes from his. She squared her shoulders, composing herself. "Paul is . . . You are sure he's . . . he's really dead?"

"The police doctor is here, there's no doubt. I'm sorry."

She reached for the back of her chair and slowly sat down. She was quiet for a moment then looked up. "Police? Someone called the police?"

"I did. I'm not familiar with the reporting process here after a death, and I wanted to be safe rather than sorry."

Her shoulders slumped. "Yes, of course. I'm sorry. I can't believe this is happening." A thought seemed to strike her. "Is he . . . his body . . ."

"The police are still here, with him."

A pause. "You said a heart attack. Why are the police *still* here?"

He didn't want to tell her the truth, that they were using a man's death for training purposes. And he didn't want to tell her, either, that something didn't quite feel right to him, something he couldn't begin to put his finger on. Something about the body's position, or the odd way people were reacting. Maybe it was something about the little room itself . . . Hugo just didn't know. He smiled to himself. Or maybe it was just that pretty much every death he'd seen in the last twenty years had been a homicide, and he was just projecting his history onto the sad, but very natural, death of Paul Rogers.

"I'll go check," Hugo said. "I'll try and make sure they don't disturb the people here for the sale."

"*Merci bien*, I appreciate that." She shook her head sadly. "Poor Paul. And Sarah, oh my goodness, who will tell Sarah?"

"I hadn't thought that far ahead."

"I do hope it's not the police—I know she's not," she paused, clearly searching for the right words, "she's not very good with authority."

"It may have to be them, but if so I'll go with them. I'll be there, I promise."

Juneau frowned, but then nodded her approval. "That will be good, thank you." She started for the door, then turned. "You said you came to see him about the sale. That is my project. Is there something I can help you with?"

"Paul was holding a book for me, but it doesn't seem important now."

"Please, if it was important before, then it is now. Perhaps more so. Paul would want you to have the book, I'm sure. What was it? I will go look where we put special orders aside."

"It's by Truman Capote, a signed copy."

"The title? I'll go look now."

"Thank you. The book is *In Cold Blood*."

Hugo picked his way through the crowds on the Champ de Mars as he made his way toward where Paul Rogers lived with Sarah Gregory, less than a mile from the library and on the other side of the busy public green space. He'd offered to deliver the news, bearing Juneau's warning in mind, and Camille Lerens had reluctantly agreed. It looked like natural causes, they agreed, so her superiors might wonder why she was making it a police matter by visiting with the surviving kin.

As he walked, Hugo instinctively patted his pockets when the packs of tourists passed him, wary not of them but of the lone vendors tracking them like prey, their hungry eyes roaming over the groups, looking for a score. Their selfie sticks and shiny trinkets made them seem like fishermen trying to lure in willing customers, but in Hugo's mind they were more like the predators you'd see circling the water holes of Africa, practiced at spotting the weak, those least wedded to their cash—the gullible and the gaudy-minded.

The apartment was in a building on Avenue de Suffren, an apt name for today, Hugo couldn't help thinking. He pressed the buzzer and after a moment a disembodied voice came out of the speaker.

"*Allô?*"

"Ms. Gregory, this is Hugo Marston. I work at the US Embassy and am a friend of Paul's."

"Oh, yes, hi. He's not here right now, he's at work."

That moment, Hugo thought, *that brief moment on the cusp of despair, when someone's world has changed but they don't know it yet, have no sense of the pain and sadness they're about to suffer.*

"I just came from there. Can I come in for a moment?"

A moment's hesitation. "Yes, of course. Take the stairs up one flight, then first door on your right."

A buzzer sounded and Hugo pushed open the door. He crossed the small marble foyer and trotted up the stairs to her apartment, and knocked. A moment later, the door was opened by a tall, slender woman with her blond hair in a ponytail.

"Hugo, nice to see you again."

They exchanged *bises* awkwardly, Hugo still more accustomed to shaking hands with Americans than kissing them.

"You, too, Sarah." He gestured toward her apartment. "May I?"

"Of course. Is everything OK?"

The first tinges of worry. The start of the landslide.

Hugo didn't say anything, just stepped into the entryway as she moved back inside. He followed her through a doorway on the left, a large living space that opened into a modern kitchen.

A man rose from the sofa to Hugo's right. He was tall with coffee-colored skin and close-cropped hair, a good-looking man in his early thirties. He wore a white shirt tucked into blue jeans, an expensive watch on his wrist.

"I'm sorry, I didn't realize you had company," Hugo said.

"This is Alain Benoît, a friend of mine and Paul's," Sarah said. "He was just on his way out."

The man moved toward them, his hand extended. "*Enchanté*," Benoît said.

"Hugo Marston." Hugo looked hard at the man as they shook hands, looking for signs of … *anything*. It was odd that Sarah had emphasized that Benoît was a friend of them both, and given the age difference between Sarah Gregory and Paul Rogers … and this was Paris, the city of love. Or, perhaps, Hugo had been in law enforcement too long, suspicious of everything and everyone.

Sarah gave Benoît a gentle smile as he walked over and kissed her on each cheek. "See you tonight," he said in French. Sarah nodded and they waited for Benoît to let himself out.

"I'm sorry to interrupt," Hugo said.

"It's fine, like I said, he was leaving anyway and we'll see him this evening for dinner."

The weight of Hugo's mission pressed on his chest at the word *we*. The moment shortened even more, Hugo already forming the words to snap another person's world in two, change it indelibly and forever. Whoever Alain Benoît was, Paul Rogers was not going to have dinner with him tonight, or any other night.

"Can we sit?" Hugo asked.

"Sure." She gestured to an armchair as she sat delicately on the sofa, worry now clear in her eyes. "Is something wrong? Is it Paul?"

"Sarah, I'm so very sorry, but there's no easy way to say this. Paul appears to have had a heart attack at the library. I'm afraid he's dead."

Sarah gasped and a hand flew to her mouth. Her eyes filled with tears and she shook her head slowly. "No, he can't be. He was just here. He was fine."

"I'm sorry, Sarah, I know how much of a shock this must be."

"Are you sure? I mean, could there be some kind of mistake?"

"I saw him myself. I was there when he was found, and with the doctor who came."

"Oh my God." She sat quietly for a moment, her eyes searching Hugo's face as if for signs of hope. Then she whispered, "He's really . . . gone?"

"Yes," said Hugo. "I'm afraid so."

She stared at him for a moment, then her eyes drifted away, tears leaking down her cheeks. "My Paulie. I don't . . . I can't believe it. How can he be gone, just like that?"

"Sarah, is there someone I can call to be with you?"

Her eyes swiveled back to him. "Oh, God. His mother. This will kill her."

"Would you like me to tell her?"

"Yes." Sarah nodded, then stared down at her hands. "Wait, no. I should be the one. She won't be able to cope with it, though." A sudden sob wracked her chest. "I don't think I can cope with it. How is this happening?"

"Is there anyone else who can be with you right now?"

She raised her tear-filled eyes to him. "No. I don't have anyone else. It's just . . . it was just me and Paul. Just us."

CHAPTER FIVE

The following morning, Hugo walked back to the library, the usually bright sights and sounds of Paris dulled by the heaviness in his heart. He wanted to return to Sarah Gregory's apartment to check on her but felt it wasn't his place. He was also irritated with himself for doubting her, and yet wanted to go back, just a little bit, to see if Alain Benoît had returned. There'd been something about the interaction between the two that hadn't seemed natural. None of his business, he knew that, but meddling was his job, had always been his job.

And then, so was suspicion. Hugo was fighting the idea that Paul had died of natural causes. In a career filled with senseless and premature deaths, Hugo had learned that at least when a man or woman was murdered there was a bad guy to catch, a direction for the loved ones to look and a path for the world's helpers, like Hugo, to take.

Not so when there was no bad guy, though, when nature or chance was to blame. The last time he'd felt this way had been worse, of course, when his wife was killed by an old man who'd not spotted a red light. A death unavengeable, a death as senseless and premature as any, and one that devastated Hugo's life for a long time, its cold tendrils reaching him still. He and Sarah Gregory had this in common now, a directionless grief to overcome, an empty space with no one to blame.

The death of Paul Rogers had cast over Hugo's life an all-too-familiar, and very unwelcome, shadow.

He was a block away from the library when his phone rang. It was Camille Lerens.

"*Bonjour*, Hugo," she said. "Are you at work today?"

"Quiet day, I'm heading back to the library."

"What for?"

"I thought I'd take a peek at those video tapes."

"Again I ask: What for?"

"To pass the time," Hugo said. "Like I said, a quiet day."

"Hugo, what are you trying to do here?"

"Nothing. Nothing at all."

"Do you really think that Monsieur Rogers's death was suspicious?"

"No idea."

"See," Lerens said. "That's exactly my point."

"You haven't made a point."

"I have. There is no reason whatsoever to think he had anything other than a heart attack."

"Maybe he was poisoned."

"I think aliens did it."

"Funny. When's the autopsy?"

"Right now, actually. I was expecting Doctor Sprengelmeyer to have finished by now."

"Will he run a tox panel?"

"The same one he always does. But that's not even the issue. You have no reason to go poking around there, upsetting people."

"Who have I upset, exactly?"

Lerens paused. "I spoke with Michelle Juneau this morning. She's concerned about the police activity yesterday, says it turned some people away from the book sale. The wrong kind of publicity, she said."

"I thought there was no such thing."

"Not my area of expertise. But I assured her that Monsieur Rogers died of natural causes, and that other than a routine autopsy there'd be no need for any kind of police investigation."

"Great," Hugo said. "And me showing up to look at a video in a private room won't be a police investigation."

"Ah, you think she'll be happy to see you?"

"Well, I'm a good customer and I have a book to pick up. So sure, why not?"

"*Eh bien,*" Lerens chuckled. "And when you ask for the surveillance tapes, how will she feel about that?"

"I'll let you know."

"Look, Hugo. I know he was a friend, and I know in this business we look at things differently. But sometimes that means we see things that aren't there. Not everything surrounding a dead body has to be a clue, not in the real world."

"Just in ours?"

"Right. So do what you have to do to come to terms with his death, but remember that."

"I think you have this backward, Camille."

"How so?"

"I'm sick of death, and I'm sick that Paul's gone. But I'm not trying to prove this was murder, because I'm even sicker of that. I'm trying to prove to my suspicious self that this *wasn't* . . . well, anything but natural. Simple as that."

"I'd like to believe you," she said, and Hugo could hear the smile in her voice.

"I'll call you in an hour or so and report back, yes?"

"You mean you'll call to bug me about the autopsy."

"*Bonne idée,*" Hugo said. *Good idea.*

Inside the library, Hugo saw Michelle Juneau walking from the circulation desk into the main stacks, toward the administration room and her office. He followed her and put a hand on her door as she was closing it. She turned and it was clear she'd been crying, but she stiffened her back and cleared her throat, a tissue still clutched in her hand.

"Oh, Monsieur . . ."

"Hugo. Call me Hugo."

"*Je m'excuse.* Hugo, I'm sorry, you startled me a little."

"Sorry, I didn't mean to sneak up on you. I was hoping I could look at the surveillance video from the hallway outside the *atelier.*"

Her eyes narrowed. "That lieutenant told me there would be no more police, no more disruption. Why do you need to look at surveillance video?"

"For my own peace of mind, I assure you."

"That's not much of an answer."

Hugo flashed his most disarming smile. "It's the best one I have."

"*Bien*. As long as we don't have another horde of cops coming and going, we still have our sale going on."

"It's just me, I promise."

She gestured for him to follow her into her office. She sat in front of her computer and logged in. Hugo moved behind her and watched as the mouse moved in her hand and she brought up the library's surveillance software.

"I've only done this once or twice, so bear with me." A few more clicks and the hallway outside the *atelier* popped onto the screen. "Let me select the date and time . . . yesterday, starting when?"

"Let's start at eight." He waited while she used drop-down boxes to start the playback at the right time. "How long do you save these, do you know?"

"I think six months," Juneau said, "but we can download onto an external drive if there's something specific we want to keep. Do you want to do that?"

"I brought one in case. It'll depend on what's on there. Hopefully nothing."

She looked up at him with a frown. "Hopefully?"

"Presumably." He flashed the smile again and moved aside as she stood.

"I'll leave you to it. How long do you think you'll be?"

Hugo peered at the screen. "I see there's a fast-forward button, if I use that, maybe an hour at the most."

When Juneau had left, Hugo fished into his pocket for a small notebook and pen, then clicked the play button and watched for a few seconds. He checked the timer and clicked the fast-forward arrows, making the tape run at four times normal speed. He sat back to watch, eyes glued to the screen.

At 8:32, Paul Rogers walked under the camera and into the frame, and Hugo leaned forward to slow the action down. Rogers looked normal, healthy, and in his own world, slowly heading to the little room with a laptop under his arm and a water bottle in his other hand. Hugo thought back to the room as he'd seen it. He rewound the tape and let it play through Paul's appearance again, seeing nothing out of the ordinary.

He watched as Rogers unlocked the door, and made a mental note to find out who had access to a key to the little room. He hit fast-forward again, watching the screen, seeing nothing but the empty hallway. He was about to check his watch when movement caught his eye.

At the bottom of the screen, a head appeared, then a figure walked slowly down the narrow aisle toward the room where Rogers was working. Hugo sat forward, eager to see who it was, whether he'd recognize the person. He did. Right outside the *atelier*'s door, Michael Harmuth, with something under his arm, stopped. He turned away and put the object down, leaning it against the wall next to the door. *The book about weapons.* The picture wasn't clear enough to read the title, but the cover colors and the size looked right.

Hugo sat, barely breathing, watching to see what happened next. Harmuth straightened and knocked on the door, two taps. He didn't wait for a response, just turned and walked in the direction he'd come, back toward the camera.

Ten seconds later, the door opened and Paul Rogers poked his head out. He looked down the aisle, then to either side before spotting the book. He stepped out to retrieve it and went immediately back into the room, closing the door. That was at 9:19. Hugo watched the rest of the video, until he and Harmuth returned around 11:30. Nothing.

So, sometime between 9:19 and 11:30, Paul Rogers had died. No one had gone in or out of the room or, except for Michael Harmuth, so much as passed by. Hugo found it odd that Harmuth hadn't mentioned dropping off the book, but since he'd not seen or interacted with Rogers in any way, perhaps that was why. He must have assumed Rogers was working and didn't want to disturb him.

He left the tape running as he thought about the timeline, watching idly as he himself walked away, having given instructions to Harmuth not to let anyone enter. He sat up a little straighter when the assistant director went to the door and stopped. The man's hand rested on the handle, and then Harmuth opened the door, stepping halfway in.

What's he doing? Hugo wondered. Harmuth stood half in and half out of the doorway for about two seconds, then gently closed the door and walked up the hallway, shaking his head.

Hugo thought for a moment, resolving to talk to Harmuth as soon as possible. Then, out of curiosity, Hugo rewound his way to where the tape started that day, just after 8:00 a.m. He watched the thirty minutes speed by until Rogers appeared, but no one else showed up on the screen.

He then found the surveillance from the previous day, surprised but impressed that the library was open on Sundays. He scanned through the last hour. Nicole Anisse, Michael Harmuth, Michelle Juneau, and Paul Rogers all came and went from the little room, but nothing looked out of the ordinary to Hugo. *But then how would I know?* he thought.

Hugo took out the thumb drive he'd brought and, after a few false starts, figured out how to download the parts of the tape that he wanted. As he was finishing up, Michelle Juneau reappeared in the doorway.

"*Vous avez fini?*" she asked. *You've finished?*

"*Oui, merci bien.*" Hugo stood. "Tell me, is there someone in particular who closes up the basement at the end of each day?"

"*Oui.* Messieurs Rogers and Harmuth usually have that job." She looked down, as if embarrassed. "This will sound silly to you but . . . some of the women don't like it down there. It's so quiet and there are no windows. The last person down there has to use a flashlight because the switch isn't near the door, so . . . either Paul or Michael took on that job."

"Don't worry, Nicole said the same thing and I've been down there, it definitely has its own special atmosphere. Thanks again." Hugo offered his hand and then headed into the main part of the library. He stopped in front of the circulation desk, where Nicole Anisse was typing on her phone. She looked up and smiled.

"*Oui, monsieur?*"

"*Je cherche* Monsieur Harmuth," Hugo said. "Is he here today?"

"*Oui,* I think so. He should be restocking the teen lounge."

"You have a special area for teens? I didn't know that."

She smiled. "That's because grown-ups aren't allowed in there. Even staff here have a five-minute limit."

"I like that idea. I'd have appreciated that as a teenager."

"Me too," Anisse said. "It's on the second floor, above the children's section. There's a window by the door so you can look in and see if he's there."

"*Merci.*" Hugo started to turn away, but he had one more question for her. "Who would be responsible for the Severin papers now? Madame Juneau?"

"Her or Monsieur Harmuth, I'm not sure."

"Thanks again, I'll see if I can track him down," Hugo said. He walked the length of the main floor, wishing *Bonjour* to a couple of men shelving books, and then started up the short staircase to the teen lounge. He peeked through the window by the door and saw Harmuth standing with his hands on hips, looking at a dozen or so books piled on a cart. He looked up when Hugo walked in.

"Mr. Marston, how're you?"

"Fine. Please, call me Hugo." He looked around at the space, filled with more couches and bean bags than books. A large television screen was mounted to the wall, and two computers sat on a desk. "Am I allowed in here?" he asked, with a smile.

"Normally, no, but there are no kids here today so you're safe for a few minutes. Plus, it's pretty much soundproofed up here, so no one will know," Harmuth joked back. "Are you here for the sale?" He sighed, his eyes now sad. "Or something to do with Paul?"

"The latter. Quick question for you. I looked at the surveillance tapes just now."

"Oh, good. Anything interesting?"

"Not really," Hugo said. "The only people on them yesterday before I arrived are Paul and you."

"Me?" He looked surprised, then seemed to remember. "Oh, the book he wanted. Yes, I left it outside the room. Someone had checked it out and he asked us to let him know when it came in. He was using it as a reference tool for his own novel, and so when I saw that it was checked in, I thought he might want it."

"You just left it outside the door?"

"I didn't want to interrupt, make him feel like he had to chit-chat with me." He gave a sad smile. "My mother was a writer, or an aspiring one, and she'd get very annoyed if I interrupted her while she was working. Plus, you know, always busy around here. So yes, I just tapped on the door and left it outside for him in case he wanted it."

"Makes sense."

"I still can't believe it." Harmuth shook his head slowly, then looked up at Hugo. "Paul died of natural causes, didn't he?"

"If that's what the medical examiner says, yes. I've no reason to doubt it."

"Seems like you do, though."

Hugo gave him a wry smile. "Comes with doing my job for too long. Suspicious nature, I guess." He looked over Harmuth's shoulder as Nicole Anisse came through the door, and Hugo couldn't help but notice what a striking young woman she was. Worry was etched on her face, though, and she didn't seem to be noticing the people around her.

"Monsieur Harmuth, *un moment, s'il vous plaît.*"

"*Bien sûr*, what's going on?"

Her eyes flicked to Hugo but she didn't hesitate for long. "It's Laurent."

"What about him?" Harmuth asked.

"He's . . ." Her voice cracked. "I think he's dead."

Hugo's head snapped up. "Who's Laurent? Are you saying someone just died here?" *Someone else*, he thought.

Anisse looked stunned, but she replied: "He's the janitor, Laurent Tilly."

Hugo turned to her. "Tell me what happened exactly. Where is he?"

"He was helping Jorge reshelve some books. Jorge Tacao, he's a volunteer," Anisse said, "I went to help, too. He said he wasn't feeling well and went into the bathroom. I asked Jorge to check on him." Anisse covered her mouth to stifle a sob. "He was lying on the floor, not breathing."

"Is he still there?" Hugo asked insistently.

"We didn't know what to do. We called for an ambulance, but it's not here yet." Her eyes filled with tears. "But he's dead, I'm sure he is. I saw him through the open door and he looked . . . just dead."

CHAPTER SIX

Hugo followed Nicole Anisse and Michael Harmuth to the hallway by the bathroom, where Laurent Tilly lay inside. The door was closed, and when Anisse and Harmuth paused outside, Hugo pushed his way in. On the floor in front of him a stocky man crouched over Tilly, pressing repeatedly on his chest. Hugo assumed he was Jorge Tacao, the volunteer. When he looked up Tacao's face was red, and he was out of breath.

"Is he alive?" Hugo asked in French.

"*Je ne sais pas*," Tacao said. *I don't know.* "I thought I felt a pulse but I'm not sure. I thought I should do this just in case, until the paramedics arrive."

"Good." Hugo knelt beside the fallen man and put his fingertips on his wrist. "I think you're right—it's faint but there's a pulse."

The bathroom door opened and Michael Harmuth came in, his face pale and drawn. "Is he . . . ?"

"We're working on it," Hugo said.

The stocky Tacao grunted and paused to wipe his brow. He glanced at Hugo for a second and moved forward to continue pumping Tilly's chest.

"Let me," Hugo said in French, and the man nodded and moved back. Hugo shifted into position. He pressed his palms into Tilly's sternum and set into the rhythm of compressions as he'd been trained, his eyes on Tilly's face for any signs of life. After four minutes his arms were aching, sweat starting to break on his brow, but he was determined to keep at it. He'd seen people survive and recover after much longer resuscitation attempts. Three minutes later, his arms were burning and sweat dripped off his forehead. He was about to ask Harmuth or Tacao to take over when the door swung open and two men in blue uniforms came in. One of them knelt beside Hugo and nodded at him, a sign to move away, let them do their job.

Hugo stood and retreated to the doorway beside Tacao and Harmuth, wiping an arm over his forehead. The three men stood looking at the still-unmoving form on the floor as the paramedics went to work.

"Thanks for helping," Harmuth said to Hugo.

"You're welcome." He turned to Tacao. "What happened?"

"*Eh bien*, he was just shelving books, several of us were. He said he felt nauseous and headed in here. I went to check on him when Nicole asked me to, and found him on the floor." He shook his head. "*Merde*, I thought he was dead."

He might be, Hugo thought, but he said, "Let's go outside, get out of their way."

Tacao and Harmuth followed him out of the small space. Tacao pulled a packet of cigarettes from a back pocket and headed straight for the exit with a wave. Harmuth led Hugo to a small nook at the end of a stack, and sank into one of the two comfortable chairs.

"I need to sit down," he said.

Good, Hugo thought, settling opposite him. *In a minute, I have one more question for you.* "Are you OK?"

"I think so. This is all a bit much, though."

"It sure is," Hugo agreed. "Michael, do you mind if I ask you something?"

"No, what about?"

"The video. When I went to call the police, you opened the door to Paul's room."

Harmuth sighed. "Oh, yes, that. I'm sorry; I know I shouldn't have, you said to keep everyone out." He paused. "It's just that, standing there in the quiet, none of it seemed real. I mean, I've been in that basement, in and out of that *atelier*, many times. I know a couple of the girls find it a little creepy down there, but to me it's not; it's a serene and peaceful part of the building, and whenever I'm down there it brings me a real sense of calm. Standing there yesterday, with you gone and the quiet all around me, it didn't seem real. I guess I had to check, to see for myself that it was true." He sat up straight, worry in his eyes. "Oh, my goodness, I didn't contaminate anything did I? Like, screw up some kind of investigation?"

"There's no investigation—it's fine. I was just curious, that's all." Hugo suddenly felt bad for asking, reminding himself that his own reaction to death was inevitably different from most other people, especially civilians. Death was more foreign to them, more abstract, and when it happened in their midst their ways of processing it required sensitivity from people who'd become accustomed to seeing it. People like him.

They both turned their heads as a thumping noise came from the direction of the bathroom.

"What was that?" Harmuth asked.

"I think they're using a defibrillator, trying to restart his heart. Either it stopped or he didn't have a pulse after all." The sounds came again, then the muffled voices of the paramedics through the open door. Harmuth and Hugo sat in silence, their eyes on the doorway, waiting for something to happen. After a couple of minutes, the paramedics passed the end of the aisle where they were sitting, a wheeled stretcher between them. Laurent Tilly was strapped securely to it, a mask over his nose and mouth.

"Looks like he's alive," Hugo said. "Jorge probably saved his life."

"He is?" Harmuth stood and watched. "Thank God." He turned to Hugo and all the worry had washed away, relief on his face. "You know, I've never been good with medical things. Illness, even death. That's a little ironic because I used to work in a pharmacy, selling drugs and all this medical and life-saving equipment. I'm a lot happier amongst books, I can promise you that."

"Me too," Hugo said, standing. "I'm sorry those two worlds collided yesterday and today. Not pleasant for anyone." He paused. "You OK here? I need to go outside and make a phone call."

"Yes, I'm fine. Just fine."

Hugo made his way to the front of the library, then stepped out onto the street. He dialed Camille Lerens, who answered quickly. "Hugo, *salut.*"

"*Salut.* I hope you don't mind, I wanted to check on the results of the autopsy on Paul Rogers."

"Expecting anything in particular?"

"No. Just curious."

"I doubt that. But Doctor Sprengelmeyer said he died of natural causes, a heart attack."

"That so?"

"Yes, Hugo. Shocking result, I know."

"Did he run that tox panel?"

"Like I said before, same one he always does. Still natural causes. And if you're thinking someone poisoned him, not only was the tox panel clear but he had no puncture wounds between his toes, or anything like that."

"So he checked?"

"Of course he checked. I told you, he's one of the best." She paused. "Hugo, what aren't you telling me?"

"Another man just collapsed and almost died here this morning. Minutes ago."

"Are you serious? What happened?"

"Not sure, the paramedics took him away. Maybe a heart attack, but I'm no doctor so I'm just guessing."

"And you think this is related to Rogers's death."

"Quite the coincidence, don't you think?"

"That's why the word exists," Lerens said. "Because they happen."

"Maybe. I just get this tingling in the back of my neck sometimes. It's a feeling that doesn't explain itself, sometimes makes me ask dumb questions, and usually makes me look stupid."

"Oh yes?"

"Yes, for a while anyway. Thing is, it's usually right."

"Maybe something else triggered it this time, something unrelated but you're connecting it to your friend's death."

A vision of the suave Alain Benoît popped into Hugo's head, a man who may be sharing some kind of secret with Paul's fiancée. "You might be right. I don't suppose you know a guy by the name of Alain Benoît?"

"*Non*, I don't. Why?"

"Long shot." Hugo smiled to himself. "There are only two million people in Paris, sorry. One of those dumb questions, I guess."

"What does he have to do with this?"

"Probably nothing. He's a guy I met when I went to Paul's house to tell Sarah, his fiancée, about his death. Benoît was there with her."

"And? Or are we jumping to unfair and unreasonable conclusions?"

"Well, we are in Paris," Hugo said, a little sheepishly.

"You want me to run him through the system? If so, I'll need more than his name—must be two hundred Alain Benoîts in Paris."

"No, no need. I think I'll find a reason to go back there, see if I can find out a little more myself."

Lerens said nothing for a moment, then, "Hugo, I don't understand why. If they're having an affair, it's none of your business. I know Paul was your friend, but what will you achieve by confronting his grieving wife about an affair?"

"She's his long-term girlfriend, not his wife. And I'm not confronting anyone."

"No, you're just going to ask really stupid questions about something that's none of your business . . . questions that make it obvious what you're thinking."

"I can be subtle."

Lerens sighed heavily down the phone. "Explain it to me; tell me what you think you are looking for, what you think you might find."

"No idea," Hugo said. "Right now, I'm just trying get rid of that tingling sensation in the back of my neck."

Hugo reassured Lerens that he had a valid reason to visit Sarah. Two, in fact: the first was to let her know about the autopsy result; the second was to offer assistance with negotiating the French bureaucracy and complex funeral and burial procedures.

"How thoughtful of you."

"He was a friend, I'd offer that anyway."

"Just go easy on her, Hugo. Even if she is having an affair, Monsieur Rogers was still basically her husband; she's going to be devastated. Maybe even more so, with the guilt. Either way, don't go making things worse."

"It's me going, Camille, not Tom."

Lerens laughed softly. "Good point. All right, I have work to do."

They hung up, and Hugo started in the direction of Sarah Gregory's apartment. Ten minutes later, he stood on the steps to the building and rang her bell. He waited a full minute, then rang again. The door buzzed without anyone answering, and he pushed it open, walking quickly across the foyer and up the stairs to her apartment. The door swung open, a pale Sarah Gregory almost leaning on it for support.

"Hugo. Come in. The place is a mess, I'm sorry. I haven't had the energy."

He followed her into the living room. "It's not a mess," he said. "And even if it were, I certainly wouldn't care."

"Sit down." She didn't wait for him to do so, sinking into the sofa. *Lerens was right*, Hugo thought. *Whatever else is going on, this woman is most definitely a grieving widow.*

"I wanted to let you know, I spoke to the authorities just now." He knew not to use the word *police*, it always added anxiety to these situations. "They had to conduct an autopsy, but they confirmed that Paul died of natural causes, a heart attack."

Sarah Gregory nodded, as if the news was expected, obvious.

"I also wanted to offer my help," Hugo went on. "Things are always harder when you have to deal with foreign regulations and customs. We have people at the embassy who are trained to assist when an American citizen dies here. That includes dual citizens like Paul."

"Thank you. I may take you up on that. Our . . . my friend, Alain, has offered to help, too."

"Good, the more support you have, the better."

"Michelle Juneau, from the library. She called me this morning, too. Said she went through this recently when her father passed away. She said she'd help, that the people at the library wanted to do something."

"Good." Hugo took out a small notebook and wrote down some numbers. "Call any of these and explain who you are. I'll let folks at the embassy know what happened, give them a heads-up."

"Thank you."

"Of course. Is there anything else I can do for you, Sarah?"

"Yes, actually." Her voice was almost a whisper. "Would you check on Paul's mother? She's directly below us. You've met her before, right?"

"Yes, a couple of times. Paul brought her to some of the library events."

Sarah nodded. "She may not remember you, in the last few months her memory has gotten awful. I don't know if it's Alzheimer's or just dementia, but . . . well, I'm not sure she's even properly accepted Paul's death." She sighed. "I'm not sure I have, to be honest."

"I know, me neither," Hugo said. "I'll go see her now."

"Thanks, I just can't deal with her right now. We've never been close, I don't know if you know that. That's made this so much harder."

"She doesn't blame you, surely?"

"She can't, can she? But yes, I think she does anyway." She stood and gave him a weak smile. "And thank you, really."

"Of course, anything I can do, just let me know."

Hugo stood to leave, and Sarah followed him out to the front door. She lingered in the doorway as he went down the front steps.

"Hugo."

He turned. "Yes?"

She looked at him for a while, her expression unreadable. "Just, thanks. I wanted to say thanks."

He nodded. "You're welcome." He waited, just for a second, in case she had more to say, but with a soft smile she moved back into the entryway and closed the door.

He took the stairs to the ground-floor apartment and knocked on the door. As he waited for an answer, he pictured the robust woman he knew as Paul's mother. Claire Rogers was her name. Striking even in her seventies, she wore her hair as red as it was when she was younger, and lipstick to match. A smoker until her forties, she had a deep, infectious laugh that she broke out whenever possible. Hugo wondered if her brashness covered the sorrow of losing her first son. She'd clung to her adopted son, Paul, at public functions like he was her lover, not a child. But despite her outgoing personality, she was known to spend hours in her small back garden, a perfectionist who wouldn't brook any help and wouldn't let anyone out there unless she accompanied them.

The woman who opened the door shocked Hugo with her appearance. The coiffed red hair had disintegrated into a mess of dirty gray, and, devoid of makeup, she looked every day of seventy. Even her posture seemed to have crumbled.

"*Oui, monsieur?*" Watery eyes looked up at him, unrecognizing.

"*Bonjour, madame. Je m'appelle Hugo Marston.* I am a friend of Paul and Sarah. I wanted to come by and express my condolences, see if there's anything I can do for you."

Her eyes narrowed as she fought to remember Hugo, but a quick shake of the head denoted failure. She waved a wrinkled hand for him to follow her into the apartment.

"Have we met before?" she asked, lowering herself into an overstuffed armchair.

"We have, but a while ago." Hugo looked around and picked a chair that would be easy to get up from.

"No one has told me how he died," she said.

"It was a heart attack, I just found out for certain myself."

"A heart attack? But he was young."

"I know, it's a terrible thing," Hugo said. "I'm so very sorry for your loss."

"I don't have anyone left."

"You have Sarah, upstairs. I'm sure she'll take care of you."

"I didn't mean that." There was a hard edge to her voice, as if the Claire Rogers of old was striking back. "I don't mean her."

"Your other son," Hugo ventured. "You mean your first and his girlfriend."

"Yes." She was wistful now, and her change in tone took Hugo by surprise. "His girlfriend. We didn't approve of that girl."

Just like you don't approve of Sarah Gregory, Hugo thought.

She sighed and sat back. "I'm next. My doctor said it, or something like it."

"Surely not, you look fine," Hugo said. "Do you still work in your garden?"

Her eyes flashed and she started to rise. "You stay out of there, that's my place. Mine!"

Hugo raised his hands in a calming gesture. "I wasn't planning to go out there, Madame Rogers, I was just . . . Would you prefer me to leave?"

She sank back into her chair, anger replaced by look of confusion on her face. "Didn't you just get here?"

Hugo was surprised by how far she was gone, mentally. He knew it was hard for those close to someone with dementia to recognize the sharp slides in coherence when they happened, but he felt sure she wouldn't be able to look after herself here much longer. And with her poor relationship with Sarah, it seemed unlikely they'd team up now that Paul was gone.

Hugo stayed for another ten minutes, bringing Madame Rogers a glass of water and listening to her ramble about her family, her sons. She lamented the lack of grandchildren, but at one point raised hopeful eyes to Hugo. "Perhaps it's not too late, people are having kids later these days. Especially the boys, *n'est-ce pas?*"

"They are," Hugo told her. "They certainly are."

When she walked him to the door, he bent to kiss her cheeks, but she grabbed his hand. "You are a policeman, *non*?"

"I used to be, in America," he said.

"I remember that. What day is today?"

"Tuesday."

"Will you come back tomorrow? Tomorrow evening, because I sleep in the afternoons. At night I don't sleep so well."

"Yes, of course." He groaned inwardly, wondering if she'd even remember the invitation. But he could hardly refuse the old woman. "I'll be back around six o'clock, when I finish work."

Hugo set off toward the nearest metro station, École Militaire, trying to turn his mind back to work. But it was the slow season in Paris, and therefore at the embassy, and he had no pressing matters to occupy his thoughts. He looked into the shop windows as he walked, staying in the shade even though the day was cooler than the past week had been. He paused at a small boutique selling old books and realized he'd not collected his copy of *In Cold Blood* yet. Somehow he didn't much want it anymore.

He shook his head and started walking again, barely registering the handsome face and athletic figure of Alain Benoît striding in the opposite direction, toward Sarah Gregory's apartment building. Hugo noticed his passing too late to say anything, only in time just to watch him walk away. And then, in a split-second, Hugo made up his mind.

He set off after the Frenchman, keeping a full thirty yards behind him and ready to duck into a store if the man stopped or turned.

Benoît didn't. He kept up his determined pace all the way to his destination, where he punched in the front-door code and disappeared inside.

The code that led to the apartment of a grieving woman.

CHAPTER SEVEN

The next morning, Hugo set off early for work. He bought two croissants to eat at his desk and was grateful that his secretary, Emma, was there to make coffee. Like everything else she did, her coffee was brewed with efficiency and to perfection.

"Why are you even here?" she asked when she brought his first cup.

"I could ask you the same question."

"It doesn't make sense that we work in a country with so much vacation time, yet we get so little."

Hugo smiled. "And you think complaining to me will change the vacation policy of the entire State Department."

"Gotta start somewhere."

"Then start with the ambassador, he's got more pull than I do."

"I did. He said to complain to you."

Hugo closed his eyes as he inhaled the rich coffee aroma. "If it wasn't for this nectar, I might give you extra time off regardless of what the State Department says."

Emma raised a chiding eyebrow and went back to her desk. Half an hour later, Hugo was deleting e-mails and wondering where to eat lunch when his cell-phone rang. It was Merlyn.

"What're you doing?" she asked.

"Working hard, how about you?"

"I'm going to the Rodin Museum and gardens. Miki's headed to the library." She paused. "Actually, she has a favor to ask."

"Sure, fire away."

"Here she is."

Hugo heard the phone change hands, then, "Hi, Hugo, this is Miki."

"Morning. How can I help?"

"I'm sorry to ask this of you, but Merlyn and I only have about ten days here, which isn't long for researching a project like this."

"Go on."

"Thing is, I don't mean to sound insensitive or . . . you know. But with Paul Rogers gone, I feel like my access to the Severin papers just closed off."

"I'm sure someone there will help you, no? Michael Harmuth or Nicole Anisse. Have you talked to them?"

"I went by yesterday afternoon. Harmuth wasn't there and I get the feeling that Anisse chick doesn't like me."

"How about Michelle Juneau?"

"She doesn't seem to like me, either." She sighed. "Look, the thing is, it's more than just the letters and diaries and all that. I know you think it's silly and maybe there's not as much to it all as I'd like to think, but I'm absolutely certain there's a really great story here. And I don't get why they're covering it up, keeping it quiet. No one looks bad if it's true she helped the Resistance. Right?"

"I can't see a downside if that's the story, agreed."

"So I was hoping to get a meeting with Isabelle Severin myself."

"That sounds like a great idea."

"Yeah, well, it's a great idea all right. But I have no clue how to contact her."

"And that's where I come in."

"Merlyn said you might be able to help. She said you could find anyone."

"With the exception of Jimmy Hoffa and Bigfoot, she's probably right."

"Jimmy who?"

"Look, I'll have to think about it. I know Ms. Severin is an icon, here and at home, so I'll need to run it by my boss."

"Thanks, Hugo. How long will that take?"

"I'll call him right away and get back to you."

He disconnected and dialed his boss, the former spook and always-affable Ambassador J. Bradford Taylor.

"Hugo, what's going on?"

"Nothing, a nice quiet summer. Next thing on my schedule is driving you to the airport on Friday."

"Forget about it, I'll take the bus. So what can I do for you?"

"I'm calling about Isabelle Severin."

"What about her?"

"Well, I have a friend who wants to meet her. I'm sure Severin has an agent or personal assistant or something, but I've no idea how to get in touch. I also wanted to make sure it was appropriate; I know she's a national treasure, so I didn't want to upset anyone by connecting my friend without due process."

"Is this a social call your friend wants to make?"

Hugo chuckled. "Hardly. It's a friend of a friend and she's planning an article or book. She thinks Severin was some kind of spy during the war, wants access to her supposed secret papers."

"I thought everything went to the American Library."

"The nonsecret ones did, yes."

"And do the secret ones even exist?" Taylor asked.

"No idea. That's what young Ms. Harrison is trying to find out. She wants to go directly to the horse's mouth, so to speak."

"So she's a journalist."

"Yes, freelance."

Taylor snorted. "That's another word for *unemployed*."

"Maybe. Which is probably why this is so important to her."

"I suppose it'd be fine to ask for a meeting, as long as she doesn't harass Ms. Severin into it. Why don't you act as go-between?"

"I can do that. Do we have her contact information?"

"Check with Maureen, she should have it."

Maureen Barcinski was the embassy's Cultural Affairs attaché, a ball of energy with a memory for names and faces that surpassed any Internet search engine for range, depth, and speed. One of seven kids, she was as good with people as anyone Hugo had ever met, and every Christmas she baked the most delicious chocolate cakes, one for every department at the embassy, which furthered her popularity. She answered her phone on the second ring, the familiar sing-song voice making Hugo smile.

"Maureen, it's Hugo. Question for you."

"Hugo, it's been too long! You never come to the functions I organize, what's that about?"

"I never get your invitations, Emma must keep losing them."

"Emma's never lost anything in her life, you lying toad. And here you are wanting my help."

"Very thoughtless, I know. How about I come to the next one?"

"Oh, hush. What can I do for you?"

"Isabelle Severin. How do I get in contact with her? Or her assistant?"

"Oh, I know we have that information somewhere. We used to see or hear from her several times a year, but I don't think she's been in touch for quite some time. A year or two at least. Can I call you right back?"

"Sure, thanks."

Hugo stared at his computer as he waited, looking up when Emma let herself into his office with more coffee. She frowned at the croissant crumbs on his desk but didn't offer to clean them up. Not her bailiwick, as Hugo well knew. When she'd gone, he gazed out of the window, fighting the urge to research someone in particular, but halfway through his coffee his eye fell on a book by Oscar Wilde. He took it as a sign.

He smiled to himself as he quoted the famous writer: "The only way to get rid of temptation is to yield to it." He leaned forward and typed the name Alain Benoît into the computer, coming up with nearly five thousand results. He clicked on the Images button to see if he could spot his man, find out which Alain Benoît he was. He scrolled through several pages of results and then saw him, that distinctive handsome face. He was pictured with a Tour de France stage winner, each holding a glass of champagne and smiling. The caption to the photo indicated that Benoît was a journalist.

Another one, Hugo thought. He added *journalist* to his search terms and came up with several articles the man had written, but very little personal information. Hugo read between the lines as best he could and put his feet on his desk to think. From what he'd seen, Benoît had tried early in his career to write more serious articles, then moved into sports. *A change of interest, or maybe an opportunist who goes where the money is?*

A moment later, the intercom on his phone buzzed and Emma's voice came through.

"Green alert."

"Thanks," Hugo said. "I'm ready as I'll ever be."

A moment later, Tom Green burst through the door, a frown on his face and his thumb jerking toward Emma.

"Does she warn you when I show up?"

"We have a special alert system. If you come in and I'm not here, it's because I disappear down the escape hatch."

"Screw you, too." His face brightened. "Hey, at least that means you wanted to see me this time."

"Nope," Hugo said. "Escape hatch is stuck."

"Good, I'm bored. Buy you lunch?"

Hugo let his feet drop to the floor. "Wait. You're buying lunch. For me."

"Miracles do happen."

"Sure, but it's not even ten."

"Oh, right. I can't buy you brunch, I never spring for brunch."

"Shocker." Hugo turned his computer screen toward Tom. "You ever seen this guy before?"

"Handsome devil."

"That's a no?"

"Correct," Tom said. "Who is he?"

"Alain Benoît, a friend of Paul Rogers. And of his fiancée."

"I don't like the way you said that. All suspicious-like."

"Nope," Hugo said. "I was just curious about him."

"Why would that be?"

"Not much to do here in the summertime." Hugo shrugged. "He was at Paul's place the other day, when I went to tell Sarah the news. There was something odd about them, something . . . conspiratorial."

"Nice to know someone's getting a little action."

"He was there yesterday, too. He knows the code to the building."

"Maybe he lives there."

"I don't think so," Hugo said. "His name's not on the list of residents."

"So you resorted to a little Internet searching?"

"Just to pass the time."

"And what did you find?"

"Not much, actually. He's a journalist, looks like a freelancer, mainly sports. But nothing much on him personally, he's not active on social media."

Tom's eyes narrowed. "But you found something. Or made some Hugo-esque deductions."

"The latter. If I had to guess, I'd say he comes from the north, Brittany or Normandy, and comes from money."

"And pray tell," Tom said, "how Sherlock comes to those conclusions."

Hugo winked. "Elementary, my dear Tom. Those pictures of him online, he's wearing nice clothes, expensive ones. And three different watches, all more than I can afford. But for a journalist his work is sparse and not very high-profile, so he has disposable income but isn't married and isn't a big shot."

"Hence, family money."

"Right, but that's just a guess."

"And he's from the north because . . . ?"

"His accent. That one was easy."

"I'm still not clear on why we care?"

"Like I said, I was just curious and had time to kill. Hang on." Hugo picked up his phone as it rang. "Hi, Maureen. Tom's here, I'm putting you on speakerphone."

"Hi, Tom Green," she said. "How's Mr. Handsome?"

"Dandy, my dear. You?"

"Fine. Got some info for your boyfriend."

"Wouldn't touch him with a twenty-foot barge pole," Tom said. "I know where he's been, and it's not pretty."

"Hypocrite," Maureen laughed. "Anyway, Hugo. I found Isabelle Severin's contact information, but it's not been updated for two years. So I checked and she's not living at that address anymore."

"Is she still in Paris?" Hugo asked.

"No. I spoke to the concierge of her old building who said she moved into an incredibly high-priced retirement home. He didn't know the name but he said it's the kind that movie stars and former presidents live in when they don't have family."

"When was that?"

"Over a year ago. She had to let her personal assistant go, which is a shame because they were together for fifteen years."

"Did the concierge say why she moved to the home?" Hugo asked. "I mean, is she physically or mentally unable to live alone?"

"I have no idea, but possibly neither. My mom moved into one because she was bored living alone and wanted the company. And, you know, to get her spot at the home before she went cuckoo."

"But in Severin's case, we don't know?"

"I have the name of her former assistant, I can give you that. Maybe you can track her down and ask."

A simple favor was seeming like a lot of work suddenly, but Hugo conceded that he didn't have much else on his plate. "Sure, why not," he said. "If she's easy to find, I can check and see what she knows."

"Cool," Maureen said. "Her name is Juneau. Michelle Juneau."

CHAPTER EIGHT

Hugo headed back to the library by himself, as Tom claimed to have errands to run, and found Juneau in her office, frowning at a computer on her desk. She looked up when he let himself in without knocking.

"Monsieur Marston, you're back?"

"*Bonjour.*" He sat down, unasked, in the chair opposite her. "*Oui,* I'm back but on a more personal mission. Trying to do a favor for a friend. First, I assume you speak English."

She looked surprised, then amused. "Of course. How would I get a job here if I didn't?"

Hugo smiled. "Fair enough. I suppose Madame Severin wouldn't have hired you if you spoke no English."

"Actually, she requested that I speak only French to her. She wanted to learn and then become fluent."

"How long since you stopped working for her?"

"Right before I came here, just over a year ago. I used to come here with her, incognito usually. She liked to sit and read, and hear the activity going on around her."

"No one ever recognized her?"

"Occasionally, but I don't remember anyone approaching us. It was a safe place for her." She smiled at the memory. "Anyway, I started volunteering here and then became full-time a year or so ago."

"When Madame Severin moved into the retirement community."

"That's right." Juneau cocked her head. "Are you trying to find her?"

"Yes, for a friend. She wants to interview her."

"Mademoiselle Harrison, I assume."

"Right again," said Hugo. "She's wanting to write an original and exciting book about your former boss."

"Which I don't plan to help her with."

"Why not?"

"In my experience, journalists like Mikaela Harrison dredge up the past when they think they can add to it. And, also in my experience, they're very liberal with the truth of their new facts."

"All the more reason for you to cooperate, surely," Hugo said. "I mean if you refuse to help her, can you really complain when she gets facts wrong that you could have corrected?"

"The onus is on her to get them right, or not publish. I have no obligation at all to help her or oversee her work."

"I think she feels differently, seeing as you're a library employee."

"I will provide her the same access everyone else gets," Juneau said. "No less, no more."

"OK, but why all the cloak-and-dagger? Everyone here must know you worked for Isabelle Severin, but no one mentioned it to Miki Harrison when she was looking over the collection."

"Paul knew. But Michael, he got here after I did and I don't think I ever told him. The folks here know that on this topic I prefer them to be discreet."

"Why?"

Juneau sighed. "Isabelle Severin is more than just a movie icon, she's an amazing woman. She's been exceptional all her life and, more personally, she was very good to me at a difficult time and I owe her a great deal."

"Go on."

"You would be amazed, *monsieur*, at the number and range of people who try to see her. Gossip writers, fan-club members, and in fifteen years about four men who claimed to be her long-lost sons."

"I hadn't thought about that."

"She is a generous and kind person, but she is also very private. And in recent years she has reached that point where others could take advantage of her. The transition to a retirement community was planned and executed with great care, and at her behest."

"Would you make a request on Mademoiselle Harrison's behalf, at least?"

"No, I will not. Whatever she is writing, she will have to use the papers that Isabelle donated."

"She seems to think that the donation was bigger than the library's viewable collection."

"Meaning?"

"That some part of what she gave to the library is being kept secret."

"Ah. Is that what *you* think?"

"I have no idea," said Hugo. "I've heard the rumors about her involvement in the war, and given how hush-hush everyone's been, I certainly wouldn't blame Miki Harrison for thinking there might be something else to see."

"Let me guess." Juneau gave a small smile. "The famous dagger."

"Does it exist?"

Juneau's smile turned into a laugh. "Think about how this works, *monsieur*. If it exists, then clearly it's not something she wants revealed, which means I am sworn to secrecy and will lie and tell you it doesn't exist. If, on the other hand, it *doesn't* really exist, I will say so."

"Either way, you give me the same answer."

"And Mademoiselle Harrison."

"She's going to be very disappointed."

"I'm sure, but that is not my concern." She looked down. "I'm sorry, that sounded harsh, I did not mean to be."

"I'm curious. If Isabelle Severin helped the Resistance, if it's true she killed a Gestapo officer, then why would she want to hide that? Wouldn't it only serve to boost an already-incredible reputation?"

"You are an American. Have you studied our history, the French history of the Second World War?"

"To some degree I have, yes." Hugo thought of his old friend Max, the bouquiniste who'd been deeply affected by the war but never said anything. Affected enough that afterward he became a Nazi hunter, and never spoke of that either. At least not to Hugo.

"Then you will know that it's not like in the movies, where there are good guys and bad guys, and everyone wears the right color hat. In a real war, in *that* real war, the truth was more complicated. People did what they had to do to survive. People did things they were later ashamed of, but at the time maybe they had no choice. If the stories about Isabelle are true, then I expect they are only partly true."

"Some people might be embarrassed if the whole truth came out?"

"Assuming there is substance to the rumors. Yes, I would think embarrassed would be a mild way of putting it."

"I understand. So, now that Paul is gone, are you overseeing the collection?"

"In truth, I was before. Which means I will continue to be, and I'll have Nicole Anisse and Monsieur Harmuth help me. Would you like to see it?"

"Just the dagger," Hugo said with a wink.

Juneau smiled again. "*Bien sûr*. I'll have it brought right up, wrapped in the Shroud of Turin."

"Now that would be a scoop," Hugo said. He stood and thanked her for her time, letting himself out of her office into the larger administration room. Harmuth sat at a desk with a cup of coffee, looking at a computer screen.

"Hugo," he said. "What are you doing here?"

"Running into brick walls."

"Sorry to hear that. Wait, is this about Paul?"

"No, a personal matter. Speaking of which, I saw Madame Rogers yesterday."

Harmuth sat back and shook his head. "That poor woman. How was she?"

"Not well, honestly. I'd not seen her for a while but she looked like a different person."

"Dementia and the loss of a son will do that, I'm sure."

"True," Hugo said. "I'm just not sure she should live there by herself much longer."

"Ah, on that front we're working on a solution."

"A solution?"

"Yes. Before Paul died we'd talked about moving her from the apartment to a nursing home. The plan is for me to move into her place, and my rent will go toward the fees."

"That sounds like a great idea. Is she on board with it?"

Harmuth grimaced. "She was. I talked to Paul about it six months ago, and according to him she was very much in favor. Naturally, I'll wait a little before mentioning it. Although I can't wait too long, my own living situation isn't settled."

"How long has she been . . ." Hugo hesitated, looking for the right words. "Not herself, I guess?"

"Paul said it started about a year ago, slowly at first and then all of a sudden she was forgetting things, or making crazy statements. You know, getting paranoid that people were out to get her."

"That's how dementia works, I think," Hugo said. "Very sad."

"Do you know her well?"

"We've met a few times but I wouldn't say I know her well, not really. And she didn't really seem to remember me last night. But in my mind she's quite a force of nature, a tough and funny woman."

Harmuth smiled. "That's what I've heard. Well, I hope this works out, it'll be good for us both."

"If it seems right, I'll mention it tonight."

"Oh, you're going over to see her?"

"She asked me to. Said she had something to show me, though I half wondered if she knew what she was saying."

"Or if she'll remember tonight that she invited you."

"Possibly not. But I'll stop by and check on Sarah, too, see how she's doing." Hugo paused, wondering whether he should really ask his next question. "Do you know Alain Benoît?"

"No. Who is he?"

"A friend of theirs. Of Paul and Sarah. It doesn't matter."

"Never heard of him."

"No problem." A thought struck Hugo. "How is Monsieur Tilly?"

"Thank heavens, he's fine. Apparently it was a cardiac event of some sort, but he's being released from the hospital tomorrow."

"I'm very happy to hear it. Nice to get some good news for a change."

"That's for sure." Harmuth checked his watch, then picked up a book from the desk. "Well, I better go find something to eat. Believe it or not, I hardly ever get a chance to read while here. Lunchtime is a sandwich and a patch of grass on the Champ de Mars, so I can people watch between chapters."

"One of my favorite pastimes," Hugo said. "But I have an office and some paperwork awaiting me." *And some disappointing news to deliver to Miki Harrison.*

The sun cast long shadows over the streets as Hugo made his way from the Cambronne metro station toward Madame Rogers's home. He kept to the west side of Avenue de Suffren, enjoying the cooling air and the activity around him, smiling at the couple drinking champagne in a horse-drawn carriage and admiring the ingenuity of a workman giving an empty storefront a fresh coat of lavender paint. The man knelt on a large square of bubble wrap that he'd taped to the ground, protecting his knees from the hard cement and the sidewalk from careless brushstrokes and splattering paint.

On the steps of the apartment building Hugo pressed the buzzer to Madame Rogers's apartment and waited. When he got no reply, he pressed it again, wondering if maybe she had a hard time hearing the bell. He tried Sarah Gregory's buzzer next, but again got no reply.

He looked around, as if he might see one or the other approaching, then walked over to a bus stop and sat down. It only took four minutes, an elderly couple returning from an evening stroll, perhaps, but all too happy to let the well-dressed gentleman through the main door behind them. He watched them disappear arm-in-arm up the stairs before knocking on Claire Rogers's door. When no one responded, he knocked again and pressed his ear to the door. He tried again, and waited.

Not wanting to waste a trip, he turned and went up the stairs to see if Sarah Gregory was home. He got no response there, either, but as he was about to turn away, Hugo thought he heard a noise inside. He listened closely, a tingle of concern creeping up the back of his neck. He put his hand on the doorknob and turned it slowly. The door squeaked as it opened.

"Hello?" Hugo called.

No reply.

He opened the door all the way, then stepped into the entryway so he'd have a view of the lounge to his left. It was empty. "Sarah?" he called again. The apartment was quiet but for sounds from the street drifting through an open window, a sheer white curtain waving gently in the breeze.

Hugo paused in the doorway to the main bedroom, uncomfortable with the violation of privacy, but he had to make sure she wasn't there, that the feeling in the back of his neck was wrong. He walked past the king-size bed, neatly made, his eyes fixed on the partially open door to what he assumed was the bathroom. When he got there, out of instinct he used his elbow to nudge open the door.

Neither instinct nor experience prepared him for what he saw.

Sarah Gregory lay face-up in the bath, pale and naked, her blond hair splayed across the back of the ceramic tub. The water covered her legs and hips, which were almost invisible to Hugo, mere shadows in the red liquid. Blood striped her breasts and shoulders, too, streaks of crimson on a pure-white canvas. Hugo moved forward, glancing down to make sure he didn't step in her blood.

"Sarah, what have you done?" he whispered, as his fingertips pressed against her neck. He tried not to look, but his eyes were drawn to the gashes on her wrists, the vertical cuts that had split her veins and allowed her life to flood out forever.

A sound from the apartment made Hugo straighten.

He listened, unsure of what he'd heard, if anything. *A door closing?* He looked down at Sarah Gregory, her eyes open but seeing nothing, and a great sadness swept through him. He allowed himself to feel it, for just a moment, then pushed it down, pressed it into the compartment of his mind where it needed to stay for now. He turned and stepped quickly out of the bathroom, through her bedroom to the living room. His hand dipped inside his jacket, hovering close to his gun as he stopped and listened.

Nothing.

Behind him, the front door was closed. *Didn't I leave it open?* he wondered. He opened it and stepped onto the landing, but it was empty and no sound came from the stairs. Then he heard it, the rattle of the front door to the building as it closed, as if someone was trying to do it quietly.

Hugo took the steps two at a time, his boots slipping on the tile of the landing as he spun to take the lowest flight. He hit the ground floor at a run, crossing the empty foyer as fast as he could. He pulled open the door and stepped out into the street, remembering at the last second to stick his foot back into the building to keep the door from locking him out.

He looked left and right, then across the street, but saw no one he recognized—just half a dozen people alone or in pairs, strolling in the balmy evening. He calculated how long it'd taken him to get there after hearing the noise and chided himself for being too slow, estimating that someone in a hurry could have turned a corner or ducked into a store in the time he'd taken. And with no access key to the building, he had no choice but to abandon the chase. If that's what it was.

He stepped back into the foyer and took out his phone.

"Camille, it's Hugo," he said as soon as the police lieutenant answered.

"*Bonsoir,*" she said. "You sound out of breath."

"I'm sorry to bother you, but I think you and your team need to pay a visit to the Seventh Arrondissment again."

"The library?"

"Not this time. The man who died, Paul Rogers. He lived in a nearby apartment with his girlfriend, Sarah Gregory. I just stopped by there to check on her, and to see Paul's mother."

"Are they OK?"

"Sarah's dead. I don't know about Paul's mom, she wouldn't open the door. Or couldn't, I don't know which."

"Dead? Are you saying she was murdered?"

"She's in the bath with her wrists slit."

"She killed herself. *Merde*, that poor girl."

"There's something else," Hugo said.

"What?"

"I thought I heard someone. I'm sure I left the front door open when I went in, but after I found her, I think someone snuck out of the apartment and closed the door behind them."

"Are you sure?"

He paused. "Honestly, no. But I stood at the top of the stairs and I'm pretty damn certain someone went out of the building as quietly as possible. The front door makes a racket, but someone closed it with barely a rattle."

"Hugo, that's . . ." Her voice trailed off, but Hugo knew what she was thinking. The same thing he'd be thinking if someone had told him all this.

"Look, I get it. But think about this, Camille. Paul Rogers dies, then a day later someone else at the library almost dies, and now Sarah. I'm fine with coincidences up to a point, but this feels wrong."

Lerens's voice was gentle. "Paul died of natural causes. Sarah Gregory wouldn't be the first broken-hearted lover to commit suicide after losing the love of her life. It's textbook."

"When I spoke to her, she was wondering how to deal with everything. But she was planning to; I could tell by the way she was talking."

"Maybe she changed her mind. Maybe it all seemed like too much."

"Yeah, maybe. But how do you explain the person in her apartment sneaking out?"

"The one you're not sure exists?" She sighed. "What do you want me to do, Hugo?"

"Get a crime-scene team down here. And break down Madame Rogers's door if you have to."

"Fine, I'll send a team. Sit tight and wait, will you?"

"Sure. But I'm giving your boys five minutes, then I'm breaking down that door myself."

CHAPTER NINE

The city came back to life the next day.

Hugo left his apartment just before eight in the morning, and he felt the uptick in vibrancy before he reached the end of Rue Jacob. The traffic was busier, too, as he crossed the busy Boulevard Saint-Germain, heading toward the quieter, more residential, Seventh Arrondissment and the American Library.

Claire Rogers had been fine, claimed she was asleep and hadn't heard Hugo knock. Nor did she remember why she asked him to come and see her. The old woman sat on her couch and cried when Hugo told her, as gently as he could, about Sarah Gregory's death, shaking her head in disbelief and mumbling quietly to herself. A police counselor had stayed behind with her, to help her to bed and maybe provide some gentle pharmaceutical relief from her distress.

Now Hugo was on his way back to the library. He wanted to deliver the news of Sarah Gregory's death to the staff himself. Out of common decency, of course, but also because he wondered. Wondered how people would feel, how they might react.

On every street, people leaned out of open windows to clip open their shutters, letting in the morning summer breeze to blow away the vacation dust and stale air. The stores that had been closed on his previous walks to the library were now opening, small trucks idling by the curb as their drivers ran in and dropped off stock for the shelves. He passed the proprietor of a small art shop, a gray-haired man of around fifty wearing blue jeans and a tattered denim jacket over a crisp white shirt, and sky-blue tie. The man lounged in his doorway with a cigarette in his hand, and his voice cracked when he exchanged *Bonjour*s with Hugo.

He headed down Rue Saint Dominique, one of the busier streets that could take him in that direction, a vein of commerce running between the more residential streets. He slowed to read the words on the side of a post-office vehicle that trundled past him: *Smile. There could be a love letter for you in this van.* The van stopped outside an Irish pub, and as he got close Hugo read the chalkboard out front, proudly advertising the finest burgers and "cocktails of the choice."

His view opened up as he entered the Esplanade des Invalides. To his left, the green lawns extended to the impressive collection of military and medical buildings, with the chapel dome dominating the long façade. Closer to him, as if intentionally spoiling the view for tourists, a homeless man sat on a park bench, straddling it as he shared a loaf of bread with twenty or so fluttering and cooing pigeons.

As he got close to the library, Hugo took out his phone and called the main number, asking for Nicole Anisse.

"Would you be able to help me with something?" he asked her.

"Sure. But . . . is this Hugo asking, or the police?"

"Just Hugo."

"For now, anyway, right?" Her voice was light, as if she were making fun of him. Or flirting.

"True. I'm on my way to the library right now, but sometimes I feel like Madame Juneau isn't wild about having me here."

"It's not you she minds, I don't think. It's that the police seem to follow you around."

"She doesn't like the police?"

"I don't think any businesses like having the police around, do they?"

"I just wondered if it was something personal with her."

"Not that I know of." A pause. "I guess I don't know her that well, but I don't think so. So what was the favor?"

"I'm curious about Paul's account history, books he checked out. Would you have access to his history the same as you would a regular customer?"

"Yes, I think so. I'll have a look and print it out. When will you be here?"

"About fifteen minutes, if I don't stop for coffee."

"See you then."

She was waiting for him at the circulation desk. As he came in, she gestured for him to follow her to his left, past the conference room, into a space with two desks. She went behind one of them and picked up a manila folder.

"Here. Not very interesting, I don't think. His check-out history for the past year."

Hugo pointed to a chair. "May I?"

"Yes, of course."

"Thanks." Hugo sat and opened the folder. It took him a moment to sort out the columns and rows, orient himself to what the page was saying, but he got there quickly. The book on weapons was the most recent request, not surprisingly. Before that, a string of novels, from science fiction to steampunk to crime fiction. In the middle of the list, a nonfiction title caught Hugo's eye, checked out about two months ago. *The Crime Writer's Guide to Killing with Poison.* He showed Anisse the page. "What's this notation?"

"It looks like he checked that book out and paid off a late fee at the same time. We often ask our customers to do that, pay any fines while they're checking books out, so they don't pile up. It's a habit we staff members fall into ourselves."

"Very sensible," Hugo said. "May I make a copy of these?"

"Keep them, I can reprint if I need to."

"Thanks. Do you know if Michael Harmuth is here?"

"He wasn't about twenty minutes ago. Something I can help with?"

"Who's the senior person here?"

"'Senior'?" Anisse smiled. "This is a library, not the police or military. But probably Michelle Juneau. I expect she's in her office—do you know where it is?"

"Yes, thank you." He waved the papers. "And thanks for these."

He wandered past the circulation desk, along the side of the stacks, until he reached the short hallway and door into the administration area. He let himself in, tapping the top of the safe as he passed it and wondering idly if an infamous dagger lay within. He knocked on Michelle Juneau's door.

She looked up from her computer and gestured through the glass panel by her door for Hugo to enter. Her eyes were wary, as if she'd resigned herself to his constant appearances, hoping only that he didn't bring the police with him. Or bad news. For his part, Hugo knew he was going to disappoint on the latter.

"I'll get straight to the point, Madame Juneau," he began, as soon as he'd sat down. "I have some very sad news."

"Monsieur Tilly?" She leaned forward. "Did he become sick again?"

"No, it's not about him. It's about Sarah Gregory. I was at her home yesterday and found her in the bath tub. It looks like she committed suicide, I'm really sorry."

"*Mon dieu*," she said, a hand covering her mouth. "Sarah? She really did that?"

"She'd been very upset over Paul, of course. I can only think that she . . ." Hugo shook his head. "She didn't want to live without him."

"That's terrible. Oh, my goodness, that's just so terrible." She sat back in her chair. "One week ago they were both here, both so alive, so happy. And now both are gone. Forever."

Hugo's phone buzzed in his pocket. He slid it out and glanced at the screen. "Excuse me a moment, I have to take this." He stood and stepped out of her office. "Camille, how're you?"

"*Bonjour*, Hugo. I suppose you could say that I'm intrigued at this point."

"What does that mean, exactly?" He turned into the stacks and found a comfy chair at the end, a comforting wall of books on either side of him.

"It means that I have the results of Mademoiselle Gregory's autopsy."

"It's done already?"

"Doctor Sprengelmeyer has a squash tournament to attend, so he started work early today."

"What did he find?"

"That she died from exsanguination."

"Yeah, thanks Camille, I could've told you she bled to death. You're not in the habit of calling to state the obvious, so what else?"

"She had a lot of medication in her system, painkillers. And I do mean a lot."

"That seems pretty consistent with someone who's just lost their partner, and who's contemplating suicide."

"True. And I suppose someone as distraught as she was might also take flunitrazepam, but on the other hand . . . ."

"Are you serious?" He didn't try to hide the surprise in his voice. Flunitrazepam was also known as Rohypnol, sold as "roofies" to desperate and depraved men who drug women in bars and take them home to assault. The press referred to it as a "date-rape drug" but as far as Hugo was concerned it was a rape drug, with no qualifiers.

"Very. It's technically a sedative so we have a call in to her doctor to see what she was prescribed."

"Good." Hugo thought back to his encounters with her. "She didn't seem high or out of it in any way when I was at her place."

"She may have been saving them for the big exit."

"Glad you're being thorough." He hurriedly corrected himself. "I mean, I know you're always thorough, but . . ."

"I get it." Lerens chuckled. "You're glad I'm open to this being more than just suicide."

"I would expect no less."

"*En fait*, there's a little more to it, I should admit."

It was Hugo's turn to laugh. "Come on, Camille, what else?"

"She had some bruising on her chest and neck, her throat."

"She was strangled?"

"No, not that. It could be from anything, but there are no identifiable patterns or marks consistent with strangulation. Sprengelmeyer said those bruises might be consistent with Sarah being pushed and held down."

"But it's not definitive."

"He said it could simply be evidence of her falling, bumping into something, or maybe rough sex."

"Bumping into something with her neck?" Hugo said, incredulous.

"Hey, I'm just telling you what Sprengelmeyer said. You can leave the cross-examination to the lawyers."

"Will you send me the report when he's finished?"

"If there's anything criminal, this will be a police matter, Hugo."

"Ah, the familiar jurisdictional dance."

Lerens laughed. "I know. I can't even pretend to pull that stuff with you. Of course I'll send you the report, and you're welcome to give me all the opinions you have."

They disconnected and Hugo walked back into Juneau's office, leaving the door open behind him.

"You looked worried," she said. "Everything all right?"

"A little early to say." He brightened his voice. "My job makes me a worrier, I expect that's all there is to it."

She studied him for a moment, then got up and closed the door. When she sat down again, she looked at her hands. "This is going to sound silly," she began. "It's just, something's been bothering me and it's basically nothing, but with all that's been going on, Paul and now Sarah, and you with that look on your face . . ."

"What is it?"

"I didn't say anything to the police because . . . because there's nothing really to say."

"Slow down, Michelle, and tell me what's bothering you." He gave her a reassuring smile. "If it's nothing, then there's no harm. If it's something, then I probably ought to know."

"*En effet*, that's true." She took a deep breath. "About a week ago, maybe two weeks now, I was closing up the library. I went down to the basement to make sure all the lights were off."

"Which staircase did you use?"

"The one behind the circulation desk."

"OK, go on."

"Well, I got to the bottom of the stairs and I thought at first all the lights were off. Then I thought I saw light at the far end of the basement."

"Where the *atelier* and the rear stairs are?"

"Yes, exactly. Anyway, I looked again and realized it was the light above me reflecting off the side wall because all the other lights were, in fact, off. But then I thought I heard voices, so I turned on more lights." She looked down for a moment. "I admit, I was a little scared. The basement is cryptlike at the best of times, but at night . . ."

"So I've heard," Hugo said gently. "Did you see anyone?"

"As soon as I turned the lights on, the voices stopped. I didn't want to go investigate, but it was like I couldn't help myself. I started to walk down that way. I kept telling myself either no one was there or it was a staff member who'd lost track of time. I had to check because if it was, I didn't want to lock them down there."

"You usually lock the basement at night?"

"We do now, since we keep some valuable books down there, and since there's only the front and back doors to it, it's easy to do. And, of course, now we have the Severin collection." She shivered. "I couldn't imagine being locked down there overnight, I'd go mad."

"Tell me what happened then?"

"I called out three or four times, I felt silly because it suddenly seemed like I was alone."

"No one responded?"

"No, so I kept going. I was looking, too, but didn't see anyone until I got near the end and then, out of nowhere, he just stepped out in front of me. Just appeared, I guess, from between the stacks. Just like that, he was there. I actually screamed, can you believe it?"

"Who was it? Who was there?"

"I haven't screamed like that since I was a kid." She shook her head, as if trying to free herself of the memory. Then she looked up and answered Hugo's question. "It was Paul. Paul Rogers."

CHAPTER TEN

Hugo sat back and thought for a moment. It could mean nothing, Paul Rogers in the basement where he liked to write, in the library that he ran. But why hadn't he responded to Michelle Juneau when she asked if anyone was down there?

"He would have heard you calling out?" he asked.

"He should have. It was quiet, so yes, I'm sure he would."

"Did he give a reason for being down there?"

"He didn't need to and I didn't ask." She shrugged. "It's his library. Was."

"And you didn't see anyone else with him?"

"There wasn't anyone, no."

"How can you be so sure?"

"Because I'd already locked the door to the basement from the back of the library. The only way out was the way I'd come. Paul followed me back upstairs and we locked the door and left."

"Could someone have stayed behind the stacks, maybe in the *atelier*?"

She frowned in thought. "But why? I mean, it's possible, I suppose, but I could see through the shelves that the door to the *atelier* was closed, and if the light had been on, I expect I would have seen that, too, under the door."

"So, if someone was down there, you locked them in?"

"Definitely. And I guess Paul could have come back later and let someone out, but I saw him walking away, he seemed normal and not . . ." She searched for the right word. "Not anxious, I guess. He was happy and joking with me, like always."

"And if he was down there, why would he bother being secretive?"

"*Précisément.* No reason at all. Perhaps if he was having an affair, but Mademoiselle Gregory had left the library about thirty minutes before." She waved a dismissive hand. "Quite apart from that, he adored her. I would bet everything I own he wasn't having an affair."

"And she adored him, too?" Hugo couldn't help but ask.

She held his eye for a moment, and when she spoke her voice was soft. "Monsieur Marston, I told you about that incident because . . . I am not sure why, now. You seem convinced that something is amiss at the library right now. That night I thought something was wrong, too, at least for a few minutes. I don't know why Monsieur Rogers was down there, I don't have any idea what he was doing or why he didn't reply when I called out. Perhaps he was off in his own world, thinking about his novel."

Hugo knew he was being chided. "You're right, I didn't mean . . ."

She held up a finger. "I had the utmost respect for him, and I still do. I can assure you, he was not having an affair, and his relationship with Mademoiselle Gregory cannot possibly be of concern to you or any other policeman."

Hugo nodded to show he understood. "I meant no offense. Paul was a friend of mine, too, and I'm struggling to make sense of his death, and now Sarah's. Please, forgive me." The strength of her feeling had taken him by surprise, making Hugo feel genuinely chastened but at the same time raising other, rather ugly, thoughts in his mind. Specifically, did Michelle Juneau herself have feelings for Paul Rogers? Was it possible that she'd been the one in the basement with him, and this story was her way to explain away anyone seeing them leave the library together?

And then again, maybe it was all nothing. A colleague of his at the FBI had once told Hugo that if all you had were questions and no answers, you were looking in the wrong direction, seeking the wrong thing. Right now, he sure was heavy on questions and light on answers.

For now, he thanked Michelle Juneau for her time, and stepped out of her office and into the main library. To his left was the entrance, with the circulation desk and conference room, the busiest part of the library. To his right it was quieter, and Michael Harmuth stood between two stacks, nose tipped in the air as he looked through his glasses at the spines of some books. He looked over as Hugo moved toward him.

"What're you doing back here?" Harmuth asked.

"Bearer of sad news, I'm afraid. Somewhere we can talk?"

"Jesus, what now?" Harmuth shook his head and led Hugo to the nook they'd occupied previously. "I guess I should sit down."

Hugo did as well, and told him as gently as possible about Sarah Gregory, leaving out as many details as he could. Including the possibility she'd been murdered. Harmuth paled as Hugo spoke, his shoulders visibly drooping.

"That poor girl," Harmuth said.

"She must have loved him very much," Hugo said quietly.

"She did. And I suppose I should find some comfort in the idea that they're together now," Harmuth said. "But I don't. Maybe that'll come later."

"I think I should go see Paul's mother. Someone will need to arrange the funerals. She'll almost certainly need the assistance of the embassy."

"No." Harmuth straightened. "We'll do it. It's the least we can do. We may not have the know-how but we have the funds, and with Sarah gone now, too, there's no need to burden Paul's mother. Absolutely not." He stood, as if the possibility of a specific task had taken him over, pushing the despair aside and allowing a surge of energy and resolve to sweep over him. "I shall start immediately."

Hugo didn't have the heart to tell him the bodies probably wouldn't be released yet, hoping he'd focus on the process before trying to contact the police or medical examiner. He watched Harmuth walk away, then walked to the front of the library and dialed Tom.

"Hugo, you quit your job?"

"Funny. I'm working from home."

"In that case, bring me a sandwich, I'm in the bathtub."

"Didn't need that image. And by 'home,' I meant library."

"I see. What can I do for you?"

"I need you to find someone." Hugo gave him the name, and Tom let out a low whistle.

"Sounds like fun," Tom said, "but I gotta find one other thing first."

"What's that?"

"The soap." Tom said, as the sounds of splashing came down the phone. "I dropped it so I know it's in here somewhere. Maybe under my—."

Hugo shuddered and quickly hung up.

That night he had drinks with Merlyn, Miki, and Tom, but he abandoned them at eight to have dinner with Claudia, a formidable four-course meal at Il Vino on Boulevard de la Tour-Maubourg. Hugo hadn't known what to expect, accepting Claudia's late-afternoon invitation without knowing anything about the restaurant. In truth, it had been more of an insistence than an invitation—she'd wanted the scoop on Merlyn and Miki Harrison, and she wouldn't take no for an answer.

The waiter greeted her like an old friend, and Hugo smiled to himself as he caught the young man admiring his customer's figure. Hugo didn't blame the man; she looked gorgeous in her black skinny jeans, a silvery blouse, and a fitted black blazer.

As they settled into their booth, the waiter handed them small, leather-bound menus but Claudia waved them away.

"*Comme d'habitude*, Henri."

"Same as usual?" Hugo asked. "You're a regular?"

"Regular enough. Trust me, you won't regret it."

"So how does it work?"

"They'll bring us a glass of wine for each course, and pair it with something or other."

"Something or other?"

"Chef's choice. You like surprises, right?"

"Sure. I'm not a picky eater. Bring it on."

The first serving of wine came in a black glass to disguise its color, and the waiter left them to enjoy, and guess, what they were drinking. The puff pastry filled with foie gras that accompanied it, he was more than happy to announce.

"This," Hugo said after swallowing a morsel, "is absolutely amazing. Fantastic."

Claudia smiled. "Told you. Now guess the wine."

"Not my forte."

"Oh, come on. Try."

"Fine." Hugo took a sip. "It's white, I can tell you that much. Very light, so not a chardonnay, but it doesn't have that grassy taste of sauvignon blanc. I don't know, I really don't."

"Me neither," she laughed. "But isn't this fun?"

"It really is," he agreed. "Kind of like Christmas for hungry grown-ups."

The waiter returned after fifteen minutes and smiled kindly as they tried to guess the wine.

"A Riesling," he said finally, "and this one is from the Basque region."

The meal took them another ninety minutes, four courses plus the *amuse-bouche* and a sorbet to cleanse the palate before dessert. It was only at the end that Claudia mentioned Miki and Merlyn.

"I'm sure I told you about Merlyn ages ago," Hugo said. "You remember hearing about my adventure with the crazy hangman in England?"

"Oh, right, something about going undercover at a kinky party."

"That's the part you remember?" Hugo laughed. "But of course it is. Anyway, Merlyn was my . . . tour guide, I guess. She helped me out a lot."

"And her pretty friend?" Claudia said it with a twinkle in her eye, but Hugo felt that she was watching him closely, curious about his reaction to the question, and the girl in the question.

"Pretty, indeed," Hugo scoffed. "She's gorgeous. Stunning. Have you seen her legs? Like an athlete's, I've never seen a pair like them."

"You won't make me jealous, Hugo."

"Perhaps, but I can have fun trying."

She reached over and squeezed his hand. "I know the chef. For me, he'd put a little cyanide in your dessert."

"That so? And would you wear black at my funeral?"

She gave a casual shrug. "Sure, if I could find time to attend."

"Tom would hunt you down, you know that, right?"

"Oh, for sure. He'd hunt me down and marry me."

Hugo raised an eyebrow. "You're the marrying sort all of a sudden?"

"I could make an exception for Tom."

"We could have a double wedding—me and Miki, you and Tom."

"Nope." Claudia shook her head. "You're dead in this scenario, remember?"

Hugo laughed. "I forgot." He raised his glass to her. "Here's to cyanide-free dessert."

She clinked her glass against his. "For now, anyway."

The mention of cyanide had made him think of Paul. Not that his friend had been poisoned, only that if he *had* died of unnatural causes, poison seemed like the most likely way. Except, of course, the lack of puncture wounds and clean tox screen. But Hugo decided to tell Claudia about it, get her impressions and maybe rouse the journalist into helping him poke around the foggy corners of events.

First, he finished telling her about Merlyn and Miki, the latter's interest in the Severin collection. Claudia had heard the rumors about Severin's involvement as a spy, but she hadn't heard about the dagger, the Gestapo story.

"Speaking as a journalist, proving that story would be quite a scoop," Claudia said.

"Agreed." Hugo then laid out the facts as he knew them, Paul's death followed by Sarah's and the bruises on her neck and chest. And, most significant to him, the figure in Sarah's apartment at the time she died.

"Definitely murder," Claudia concluded.

"I spoke to Camille yesterday. She's still not convinced. No evidence in Paul's case and the marks on Sarah are inconclusive."

"And the stranger in her apartment?"

"As Camille pointed out, maybe someone innocent who found her and panicked." He shrugged. "Or maybe I didn't hear anyone at all, I certainly didn't see anyone."

"Your instincts and senses are pretty good." Claudia nodded, thinking. "Perhaps the first, someone was there and panicked. After all, you wandered in and found her, I suppose someone else might have."

"Maybe, but I'm not buying it."

She paused, her lips pursed in thought. "Why would someone kill Paul and Sarah?"

"I can't help thinking it has to do with the Severin papers, the dagger, and that great scoop."

"That's assuming it even exists."

Hugo smiled. "That's what I intend to find out tomorrow."

"How?"

"I asked Madame Severin's former personal assistant and couldn't get a straight answer." Hugo took a measured sip of wine. "So tomorrow I'm going straight to the source."

"Wait." Claudia sat up straight. "You're going to see Isabelle Severin?"

"I sure am."

"Is she expecting you?"

"Not exactly. Tom located her and I plan to use my wiles and charm to get in to see her."

"I'm sure it'll be a worthwhile visit, handsome." A smile spread slowly over Claudia's face. "And I'm coming with you."

"Actually, no. You're not," he said mildly.

"Give me one good reason why not?"

"Because civilians should never be part of any investigation. And because I don't want to crowd the woman and scare her."

"First of all, this isn't an investigation. You basically just told me that you have no evidence of any crime, so this is a fishing expedition at best."

"Well, as a matter of—"

"And second of all, two's company, not a crowd. And I'm hardly an intimidating presence, especially when compared to a hulking brute like you. In fact, I should go interview her while you sit in the car."

"Hulking brute?"

"Compared to delicate little me," she said. "Plus, I'm a journalist and know how to get people to talk."

"Yeah, I didn't get any training or experience at that in my years at the Bureau," Hugo said. "Silly me for thinking that a profiler might be able to wrangle an answer from an old lady."

"Now you sound like a cowboy," she laughed. "A mean one, wrangling old ladies."

They fell silent as the waiter arrived with their desserts. "This is a variation on an English trifle. We have a light sponge base that normally would be a little dry and . . ." He seemed to struggle for the word.

"Unexciting?" Claudia filled in.

"*Exactement.* But the base of the dish is a shallow pool of rum, which the sponge absorbs and transfers to the custard on top. Even into the thin layer of strawberry preserves, which we make here." He held up a reassuring finger. "But don't worry, it's not all about the rum. I think you'll find the balance of flavors just right."

"Sounds delightful," Hugo said. "*Merci bien.*"

"But wait until I bring your next wine. I will not make you guess, it is a very good Sauternes."

When he'd left them alone, Claudia poked her fork into the dessert, a little dubious. "I never would have imagined a French chef emulating an English pudding."

"Maybe, but I will say," Hugo said, savoring a bite, "in this case, be glad. Be very glad indeed."

CHAPTER ELEVEN

The drive took them a little less than two hours. Once out of Paris it was a straight shot northeast, a fast and picturesque drive along the E50, about 150 kilometers along a road that ran for more than five thousand, from the French port of Brest through five other countries and ending in Makhachkala on the Caspian Sea. Claudia sat beside him, buzzing with the energy of an excited schoolgirl. Or, in this case, a journalist with the tip of her nose in a potentially huge story.

The retirement home lay south of the main road, a wide-open property made up of manicured lawns and one-story cabins. Hugo was surprised to find the entrance ungated, and said so.

"We had this discussion when you first came to my house," Claudia said. "Crime happens but we're not paranoid about it. No fences, no guns."

"But she's one of the most famous movie stars in Hollywood history," Hugo said. "And God knows who else lives here, probably politicians and sports stars."

"None of whom want to pay a lot of money only to live behind bars, I expect."

"I guess." Hugo peered through the windshield. "There's the office, let's start there."

He parked and they let themselves into the administration building that looked more like a French country house. The receptionist smiled and looked behind them, as if they were a loving couple about to donate their mother to the place. She was an attractive woman in her late forties, and the nameplate in front of her read *Janelle Cason*.

"*Bonjour*," Hugo said, and continued in French. "My name is Hugo Marston, I'm with the American Embassy in Paris." He slid his credentials onto the desktop as he spoke, and ignored Claudia's fidgeting. Maybe it wasn't an official investigation, but two dead Americans was justification enough for the badge to come out. "I was hoping to have a quick talk with one of your . . ." He hesitated, unsure how a retirement community might refer to its own inhabitants.

"One of our residents?"

"Yes, exactly. Madame Isabelle Severin."

"Oh. Is she expecting you?"

"No, madame, she's not."

Cason frowned. "I will have to see if she's available. It is usually advisable to make an appointment, especially for someone as eminent as Madame Severin. She does not like to see new people."

"It's very important," Hugo said gently.

"Can I tell her what it's about?" Cason asked.

"*Bien sûr.* It relates to the generous donation of her papers to the American Library."

They sat and waited as Janelle Cason disappeared into a back office and made contact with someone, presumably the supervisor responsible for access to their residents. Hugo flicked through a fashion magazine without seeing the pictures, only noticing what he was reading when he saw Claudia smiling at him.

"Put that away, Hugo, you dress fine."

"Thanks for the vote of confidence."

"Sure. Do you mind if I record our meeting?"

"If it happens, be my guest. But be subtle and make me a copy."

"Deal."

Cason reappeared a minute later. "I'm sorry, we were unable to reach her."

"Unable to reach—?"

Cason smiled. "She's fine. Taking her morning nap, is all."

"We can wait," Hugo said.

"Her nurse would rather you didn't."

"She has a nurse?"

"The community is made up of a hospital, a recreation center, a dining room and lots of individual cottages, all fitted for the elderly. For every five cottages there is a nurse, who is more than just a medical provider. She's like the residents' caretaker."

"More like gatekeeper," Claudia muttered.

Cason shot her a look. "People come here for privacy and to live out their years in dignity. I've yet to come across someone in their late nineties who welcomes a surprise visit from complete strangers, especially when those strangers carry badges. Now, if you make an appointment, maybe you can see her."

"How do we do that?" Hugo asked.

Cason went to her desk and opened a drawer. She took out a folder and extracted a sheet of paper. "If you fill this out, I will give it to her nurse, and she will discuss it with Madame Severin. If she wants to meet with you, one of us will call."

"Very good," said Hugo, taking the paper. "Thank you." He filled it out hurriedly and left it with Janelle Cason, giving her his warmest smile. "We're grateful for the help, really. And hope to see you again soon."

Claudia said nothing, just followed him out to the car. When they reached it, she said, "You're not giving up that easily, are you?"

Hugo gave her an innocent smile. "Whatever can you mean?"

"Do you know which cottage is hers?"

"Let's just say that I found her here thanks to Tom."

"Which means you know which cottage is hers, and probably which side of the bed she sleeps on."

"The man has his uses."

"Which is why I'd consider marrying him."

Hugo winked. "Sure you would. Hop in the car, her place is at the back of the property."

He drove slowly, avoiding the golf carts used by groundskeepers and the residents themselves. The shiny, black embassy car drew plenty of lingering looks, but, using his phone, Hugo managed to locate Isabelle Severin's wooden cottage without being stopped. The front door was painted light blue and either side of it large ceramic pots bristled with yellow and orange flowers.

Hugo and Claudia stepped out of the car and looked around, but the nearby cottages were as quiet as this one. The only sound was a lawnmower some distance away, and the gentle put-put of someone's golf cart. Hugo knocked softly on the front door and they waited. He was about to knock again when the door opened and he found himself looking down at the smiling face of one of the world's most famous actresses.

She looked nothing like her movie posters, of course, but Hugo was struck by how beautiful she still was. At almost one hundred years old, her skin was pale and clear, smooth like a child's. And her blue eyes sparkled, just like they did on the silver screen. She was tiny, though, and Hugo stepped back instinctively, not wanting to tower over her, intimidate her. And he had no idea whether to speak in French or English.

"*Bonjour, Madame*," he began, before switching to their native tongue. "My name is Hugo Marston. This is my friend Claudia de Roussillon."

Her brow knitted together as she looked back and forth between them, seeming to study their faces and especially Claudia's.

"De Roussillon?" she asked finally. "Are you Gérard's wife?"

Claudia stepped forward. "No, madame. I am his daughter."

"Oh, my," Severin said, smiling. "How you've grown. How is Gérard?"

"I'm afraid he . . . he passed away not too long ago," Claudia said.

The smile fell from her face. "I'm sorry. I didn't know. You better come in."

They followed her into the little house, and Hugo looked around once inside. They were in the main living room, carpeted and comfortable with heavy furniture built to last. To their left was a breakfast bar and, behind it, a small kitchen. To the right, a closed door, which Hugo assumed led to Madame Severin's bedroom and bathroom. Large windows filled the room with light, and opposite him were French doors leading onto a small patio, also bordered with potted plants and flowers. The place was small but had a cozy, warm feel to it.

Isabelle Severin gestured for them to sit on the couch, while she perched on the seat of an armchair. Hugo wondered whether, if she sat back on it, her feet would even touch the floor.

"You were telling me about your father," Severin began. "How is he?"

Claudia exchanged glances with Hugo. "Well, I'm afraid he passed away."

"Oh, no!" Severin clasped her hands together. "Was he ill?"

"He had dementia, I'm afraid." Claudia was telling the truth, although it wasn't the disease that had killed her father.

"I can't tell you how many good people I've lost to that darned affliction." Severin shook her head sadly. "Too many, simply too many."

"I wasn't aware that you knew each other," Claudia said.

"Quite well, really. When I used to be a little more social I'd see him at various functions. And I think he bought some of my books when I sold off a lot a few years back. Maybe five years ago?"

"He had a wonderful collection, I still have it."

"Oh, I'm so glad. Not really room for books here. I don't read much anymore, anyway. My eyes aren't as good as they once were."

"True for all of us," Hugo said with a smile. "We don't want to take up much of your time, do you mind if I ask you about a couple of things?"

"Remind me who you are, dear. This young lady's husband?"

"No," Hugo said. "We're good friends. I work at the American Embassy, the head of their security."

"Oh, I see. What on Earth could I help you with?"

"Well, you donated your papers to the American Library recently."

"Yes, I did. Very good of them to take all that stuff."

"How did that come about?"

She frowned in thought. "Gosh, let me think. I don't recall. I really have no idea."

"Did it have anything to do with Michelle Juneau, your former assistant?"

"Such a lovely girl, I do miss her. But why would she have anything to with it?"

"I just wondered," Hugo said, "because she works at the library now. It crossed my mind that you arranged a job for her there as kind of a favor."

"If I did, I'm afraid I don't have any recollection of it. A super young lady . . . how is she?"

"She's fine, I just saw her yesterday."

"Do give her my love, she was such an angel to me."

"I will," said Hugo. "Can I ask, was there—"

"Do you happen to have her address? I've taken up letter writing, just like in the old days. My doctor tells me it's good exercise for my eyes, my hands, and my mind. And I've never much liked computers. So, if you have her address, I'd like to write her."

"Let me look it up for you," Hugo said.

"Thank you. There's a pen and paper on my desk." She turned to Claudia. "I paid for nice paper, a lovely pen, I even have a letter opener for when people write back."

"I'm glad they do."

"Mostly, yes. But I don't have all that many people to write to, that's the problem. Most of my friends have passed away or are in no condition to write letters. And, of course, people just use computers these days."

As she spoke, Hugo pulled up the library's address. He went over to her roll-top desk, which was open with a clean blotter, capped Mont Blanc pen, and hefty letter opener. In a wooden slot, thick writing paper and envelopes sat together snugly, awaiting use. He slid out a sheet of paper and used his own pen, a cheap embassy ballpoint, to write down Michelle Juneau's name and the address of the library.

"Thank you, dear."

"You're welcome." Hugo was on his way back to his seat, his mind grappling with how to ask about the secret papers, maybe even her history with the Resistance, when someone knocked at the door.

"I am popular today," Madame Severin said. "Would you mind getting that?"

"Of course." Hugo moved to the door and opened it. The woman opposite him had her hands on her hips and a furious expression on her face. "Ah," Hugo said. "Madame Cason."

"Monsieur, I do not appreciate you deceiving me and ignoring my very explicit instructions."

"Yes, well." Hugo tried a disarming smile. "Turns out Madame Severin and Mademoiselle de Roussillon here are old friends."

"That may be so, but Madame Severin has a medical appointment in fifteen minutes."

"Right, if we'd made an appointment then we'd know that." He turned to Madame Severin. "Just a couple more questions?"

The old lady suddenly looked confused, uncertain. "Well, I don't . . . What about? I should get ready for my appointment. I had no idea."

Cason moved past Hugo into the little house. "These people are just leaving, madame, I will take you. There's no rush, so please don't worry yourself."

"Oh, well, then." Severin stood and moved to Claudia. "It was lovely to see you. Please do give my regards to your father." Her face brightened. "If I have his address still, I'll write him. How about that?"

"Yes, sure, that would be lovely," Claudia said. "So nice to . . . see you again."

Hugo took Severin's hand when she offered it, as gently as he'd ever held anything. "Thank you for your time, madame, perhaps I will come back when you're less busy."

"Such a handsome, charming, man," Severin said with a smile, "I can see why she married you."

She turned and walked toward the bedroom, and Janelle Cason gestured toward the open door. "Please remember that this is private property, monsieur. We are very protective of our residents, and if you return without permission, I will be forced to call the police."

"I quite understand," Hugo said. "My sincere apologies for the inconvenience."

Cason watched them from the doorway as they climbed into Hugo's car.

"Think she'll pass on our request for an appointment?" Claudia asked, as she pulled on her seatbelt.

"I don't know. You think it's worth my while to come back?"

"She clearly has dementia, to some degree anyway."

"Yeah, a lot of that going around. And once I realized that, I felt like kind of an ass peppering her with questions."

"But you have to come back, surely? If her collection has anything to do with what's happened at the library, you need to know if there is some kind of secret someone's keeping." She shrugged. "And today, you didn't find out anything."

"Not entirely true," Hugo said. "Did you see what she uses to open her mail?"

"No, I didn't notice."

"I did. And it looked a little too heavy, and a little too stabby, to be a mere letter opener."

Claudia gasped. "You think that's the infamous dagger?"

"No idea."

"Oh, *merde*, I wish I'd seen it. Why didn't you say something?"

"I was trying to when we were interrupted."

"No, to me, about the dagger. I want to see it."

"Oh, well, in that case." Hugo reached into his pocket and took out his phone. He pulled up his photo stream and clicked on a picture. "Here you go."

"You took a photo of it?" Claudia snatched the phone from his hand and studied the screen. "That could absolutely be a dagger. *The* dagger."

"It could also be a vicious letter opener."

Claudia reached over and squeezed his leg. "Yes, but now we can show this to an expert or two and maybe find out which. You clever, handsome, sneaky, charming man."

"Why, thank you." Hugo put the car into drive and pulled slowly away from Isabelle Severin's cottage, and the watching eyes of Janelle Cason. "Clever, handsome, sneaky, and charming enough for a pretty lady to buy lunch?"

"*Bien sûr.*" Claudia laughed. *Of course.* She gave his leg another squeeze, a little higher up this time, adding, "And maybe dessert."

CHAPTER TWELVE

Camille Lerens called as they neared Paris, and Hugo put her on speaker phone.

"*Salut*, Hugo," she said. "Are you busy?"

"*Bonjour*. Not busy, out and about with Claudia. How can I help?"

"I'm at Sarah Gregory's apartment, doing a more thorough search."

"It's murder after all?"

"Still trying to figure that out," she said. "Can you come by and look at a few things that are in English?"

"Sure, anything in particular?"

"Some papers of hers. Or Paul Rogers's. Both maybe. And generally, it'd be good to have your profiling experience here in case I'm missing something." He heard a smile in her voice. "I've heard you're good at that stuff."

"Thanks, but I doubt you've missed anything."

"Come anyway. You knew the guy, and her too, so . . . you know. Can't hurt, right?"

"*Absolument*. I can be there in," he checked the car's clock, "let's say forty minutes. Save me a parking spot out front."

"Don't be silly," she said. "You're on police business, you can park on the sidewalk if you need to."

"*Entendu*. See you soon." He disconnected.

"You going to let your favorite journalist tag along?" Claudia said, batting her eyelids dramatically.

"You should've asked Camille; this one isn't my call. So probably not this time, sorry."

"Didn't think so. That's OK, I have stuff to do anyway."

"Just to be clear, you're not writing anything about this yet, right?"

She shot him a fierce look. "Hugo, come on. I told you I won't write anything until the story's complete. Are you seriously asking me that?"

"Sorry. Just . . . you know."

"Yeah, I know. You being a jerk."

"Not for the first time. Where would you like the jerk to drop you off?"

"Any metro will do. How about Gare de Lyon?"

"Sure thing. I'll let you navigate, though."

"Great, thanks." She put her hand back on his leg. "Jerk."

Hugo ducked under the yellow crime-scene tape, stopping in his tracks when a uniformed officer put one hand to his holster and held out the other as a warning for Hugo to stop. Hugo had his credentials ready and held them up, breathing a sigh of relief when Lieutenant Camille Lerens appeared behind the *flic*.

"He's with me," she assured him, and the policeman nodded his acquiescence. "Come on in."

"Find anything?" Hugo asked. "I'm wondering whether she had a prescription for those roofies."

"No sign of those, but let's see what you think. We made a point not to disturb the place—I figured that might throw you off."

Hugo smiled. "I'm not Sherlock Holmes, you know. I think you overestimate my capabilities."

"Well, see what you can see. If you see nothing, you'll be on the same page as me."

Hugo moved slowly through the apartment, and despite Lerens's assurances, it was clear that a lot of Sarah's and Paul's things had been moved and put back in the wrong place. Not by much, and God knew by whom, but by enough that anything truly out of place would be disguised. Eventually he stepped into the room they used as a study. It was the same in there, drawers almost closed, papers in untidy stacks.

"I'll be honest, Camille."

"Please do."

"If you really want me to do my thing, call me before you guys go through it all. I can't tell you anything, except that I hope you all took more care looking at things than you did putting them back in place."

Lerens eyed him for a second. "We messed it up?"

"People tend toward tidy or messy. Not always in the same areas, either." He waved an arm toward to the apartment. "This place is neither one nor the other, which suggests to me it was tidy when you started but now . . ."

Lerens sighed. "Pushed for time. But you're right, I'll make sure to call you first, next time. Sorry Hugo."

"Hey, no worries. You said you found some papers?"

Lerens moved past him into the study. "Here, I put a few things on the desk. See what you think."

Hugo leaned over and looked at four stacks of papers. He leafed through the first to read a few lines on different pages, and said, "These are drafts of his novel. Some nice turns of phrase here."

"Literary genius?"

"I'm not the one to judge that, but I know a nice metaphor when I read one." Hugo replaced the papers and looked at the next stack. "Architectural plans?"

"Looks like it, for this address, too." Lerens poked a finger at the top of the first paper. "Which is odd because how do you add to a second-floor apartment?"

"Maybe it's internal, structural changes," he suggested.

"What few talents I have don't include reading architecture plans, so maybe."

Hugo unfolded several sheets of paper and leaned over them. "You know, I think this is for the ground-floor apartment, Paul's mother's."

"Oh, that makes more sense." She looked over Hugo's shoulder. "Yes, you're right, the apartment number there is hers."

"Finally, we solve a mystery," Hugo said with a smile. He looked at the third pile of papers.

"That one I figured out. It's the information about the retirement community Madame Rogers is going to. Looks nice."

Hugo pulled a color brochure from the small stack and looked through it. "Saint Joseph's in Amboise. Paul was a Catholic?"

"No idea," Lerens said. "He was your friend, you should know. Or maybe just his mother is."

"Maybe." Hugo inspected a stapled sheaf of papers. "This is the contract, looks like five hundred Euros a month for all expenses. Nice price."

"In my limited experience, the religious homes are the cheapest and usually the best. Hardest to get into, as well, for those reasons."

"Well, she managed it." Hugo looked at the first page. "Move-in date is not filled in."

"With all that's happened, you think she'll still go?"

Hugo shrugged. "Probably makes even more sense, to be honest. She doesn't have anyone here to take care of her anymore."

"*Ah, oui, c'est vrai,*" said Lerens. *That's true.* "One other thing I've not found anywhere."

"What's that?"

"A will," Lerens said. "Do you know how they work here?"

"Actually, no."

"One of three ways. First, drafted in front of witnesses and a *notaire*, who sends it to the central registry of wills. Second, you draft your will, hand it over to a *notaire* in a sealed envelope, and the *notaire* sends it to the central registry. I called over there and checked; they have nothing for either Paul Rogers or Sarah Gregory. Which means the only other option would be a holographic will, one that you write entirely by hand and hold on to. I went through their drawers and filing cabinets and didn't see any copies of a will, or a living will. I didn't even find a safe where that stuff might be."

"What about passports?" Hugo asked. "People usually keep their important papers together."

"*Oui*, I found those in a file folder, in the cabinet. They were together in a manila envelope with the passport expiry dates written on the outside."

"Yeah, Paul was organized," Hugo said. "It sounds like if there was a will, it'd be in a folder. And I'd put money on there being one."

"Right. I mean, it's possible he didn't have one but seems unlikely. Especially since he did have life insurance—I found that in another properly labeled folder."

"Interesting. How much?"

"Half a million Euros. Sarah was the primary beneficiary, then his mother."

"Well, there you have it. Both killed by a senile old lady, it's perfect."

Lerens chuckled. "You and your black sense of humor."

"It's the only way to survive sometimes."

"It is. But back to the subject at hand, why would they have the passports and life insurance, but no will?"

"No idea," Hugo said. "Perhaps we should go down and talk to Madame Rogers about that, since we're already here. Also, I've not heard anything from Michael Harmuth about funeral plans, maybe she knows about those."

"*C'est possible.* How senile is she?"

"Not too far gone, I think, not yet anyway." Hugo smiled grimly. "Perhaps we'll catch her on a good day."

"Why don't you call Harmuth, see if he'll come over. He knows the old lady pretty well, right?"

"He's only been at the library for a year, I think, so I doubt it. Although, he said he was helping Paul make all the arrangements for the retirement home."

"*D'accord.* We can be sure he knows her better than we do, how about that?"

"True. I'll call him." Hugo took out his phone and dialed the library. "*Bonjour*, is Michael Harmuth available, please?"

A moment later, Harmuth's voice came down the line. "Hello?"

"Michael, it's Hugo Marston. I'm calling to ask you a favor."

They loitered at Paul and Sarah's apartment, waiting for Harmuth to arrive. He'd called Madame Rogers to make sure she was home, and to ask if they could come by. She'd accepted, Harmuth said, but who knew if she'd remember that when they got there.

As he waited, Hugo alternated between wandering through the rooms and stopping to look more closely at books, pictures, anything that caught his eye. At one point, he returned to the desk carrying Rogers's papers and looked at everything a second time. The only thing he learned, though, was that the architectural plans were for a small sunroom and tile patio where Claire Rogers's precious garden lay. Hugo doubted that a sunroom would get too much use in Paris, but one with a glass roof could be made cozy with a blanket, a mug of hot chocolate, and a good book on a rainy afternoon. Not that Madame Rogers would approve of her special place being destroyed.

Harmuth rapped on the apartment door as Hugo stood in the doorway to the bathroom, trying to both re-create and forget the scene he'd encountered so recently, poor Sarah tinged red with her own blood, either murdered or dead by her own hand. Hugo welcomed the interruption.

"Let's go down," said Lerens. She watched as Hugo and Harmuth stepped out of the apartment, then she locked the door and put back the strip of crime-scene tape. "Probably no need for that at this point, but policy says it stays for a week."

Harmuth knocked on Madame Rogers's front door, with Hugo and Lieutenant Lerens giving him a little distance, so as not overwhelm the old woman. She answered at the second knocking, peering out from behind the door. Her eyes narrowed for a moment, then something flashed in them, recognition of Harmuth, and she looked past him to his companions.

"You know Monsieur Marston," Harmuth said. "He's a friend of Paul and Sarah."

"Police?" Madame Rogers said. "Is that a policewoman?"

"Yes. May we come in?" Harmuth asked, his voice gentle, soothing.

"Yes. Yes, of course." Madame Rogers turned and shuffled into her apartment, leaving the door open for them. Hugo again marveled at the change in the woman, and her home. Once elegantly furnished for dinner parties, it was now a disorder of clothing, boxes, and blankets. It looked like she'd set up a bed on the couch, a nest of pillows and quilts. She headed straight for it, sitting awkwardly on the edge. The others found seats around her.

"Madame," Hugo said, "how are you feeling today?"

She looked at Hugo for a moment, then gave him a warm smile. "One of the good days, thank you." Hugo was about to speak, but she cut him off. "I remember you from the other day. Paul spoke highly of you. Did you also come here for parties?"

"Several, yes, and some events at the library, too."

"Yes, I remember a few of those." She held her smile for a moment, then a cloud seemed to pass over her eyes, and she looked around the room as if lost. Her gaze settled on Michael Harmuth, and then she turned away, her eyes now filled with tears. "My son. My poor son."

Harmuth shook his head gently. "We're so very sorry for your loss, madame, it must be very hard for you. But these people have a couple of questions . . . is it OK for them to ask you right now?"

"Questions about what?" she said, her voice faltering.

"We were wondering about two things, madame," Hugo said. A thought striking him. "First, whether you had a spare key to Paul's apartment."

She blinked and two tears ran down her cheeks. "A key? I don't . . . if I do, I don't know where it is. I'm sorry."

"That's quite all right," Hugo said reassuringly. "The other thing, do you happen to know if he had a will?"

"Yes, of course. We met with a *notaire* and he did mine, I didn't want to write it out by hand. But Paul did, the *notaire* was right there, too. I remember because we did it all together last year. When I, you know, started to be less well."

Perhaps two years ago, then, Hugo thought. "So the *notaire* sent yours to the registry, but Paul kept his?"

"I imagine it's in his file cabinet. Does he have that still?"

"The cabinet, yes," Hugo said.

"In there. He keeps everything important in there."

"He didn't have a safe?"

"No," she said. "He kept everything in there."

"Do you recall the name of the *notaire* who helped with the wills?" Lerens asked.

Madame Rogers shook her head. "No. But I think I have his card with my copy." She waved a hand toward a desk in the corner. "Bottom drawer on the left, the key is in the lock."

"Thank you." Lerens got up and went to the desk. She slid the heavy drawer open and stood, looking down into it. Then she stooped and picked up a business card. She studied it for a moment, then placed it back into the drawer, which she left open.

"Did you say a copy of your will is supposed to be in here?" Lerens asked gently.

"Yes, that's where I put it."

"I'm sorry, madame, but it's not there. The card is the only thing in the drawer."

Madame Rogers knitted her brow in confusion. "Maybe I moved it? Perhaps Paul took it." She looked up, eyes wide like a helpless child. "I don't know where it is." She turned and looked at Michael Harmuth. "Did you take it?"

Harmuth shook his head, but his voice was gentle, kind. "No, madame, I didn't. I promise."

"If it doesn't turn up in a day or two, let me know," said Lerens. "I can come look for it, but it's just a copy so it being lost wouldn't change anything."

"Even if it was the real thing, I don't have much to leave behind," the old woman said. "Just this place, so it doesn't matter."

"Let us know if we can help," Lerens said. She closed the drawer and took her seat, nodding to Hugo almost imperceptibly.

Hugo was curious as to the old woman's attitude toward leaving her home, so he gestured to the boxes. "Are you moving soon, madame?"

She leaned over to a side table and plucked a tissue from a box. She dabbed at her eyes and nodded toward Harmuth. "My . . . I'm sorry, I get confused. Michael and the nice lady from the library have been helping me. They've been very kind."

"Madame Juneau?"

"Yes, I think that's her name."

"That's right," Harmuth said. "Actually, Nicole's been over, too. She's stronger than all of us put together. Michelle and I lift one box, she lifts three."

"Yes, Nicole," Madame Rogers said, her voice distant. "I think I remember her."

"Will you have a garden where you're going?" Hugo asked. "I know you've always been so fond of yours, kept it up so well."

"My garden?" She sighed, as if the idea of a garden was all too much, or she just didn't care anymore. "I don't know. Perhaps."

Hugo caught a look from Camille Lerens, one accompanied with a slight head tilt toward the door.

Hugo stood. "Well, we've taken up enough of your time, madame. Thank you." He decided not to say anything about the funeral service; she seemed emotionally fragile enough at that moment.

Harmuth and Lerens stood, too. "I'll be back in the next day or two to help you with the packing, OK?" Harmuth said gently.

The old lady nodded but didn't seem to be listening, so Hugo led Lerens and Harmuth out of the apartment and closed the door gently behind them.

"She's not doing so well," Hugo said.

"You can't blame her," Harmuth said with a sigh. "Everything in her world is disintegrating. Her son, Sarah, her own health."

"And her living situation," Lerens added. "Hugo said you're moving in here."

"Yes. The plan was for my rent money to go toward her retirement fees."

"Makes sense, for you both," Lerens said. She turned to Hugo. "So, do you want to hear the name of the *notaire* who drew up their wills?"

"Someone I know?"

"Yes, and no," Lerens said with a smile. "A man by the name of Alain Benoît."

CHAPTER THIRTEEN

Hugo drove Harmuth back to the library to spare the man a walk in the still-hot afternoon. On the way, Hugo thought about the incident between Michelle Juneau and Paul Rogers, their encounter in the basement of the library.

"Michelle told me that you and Paul were the ones who close up the library at night."

"Yes, that's the only reason I'm going back now, to help with that."

Hugo smiled. "A scary basement?"

"Yes." Harmuth laughed. "I wasn't going to make fun of the girls, but they don't like to go down there at night. I can see how it'd be a little creepy but I think they've talked themselves into a frenzy over it."

"Did Paul stay late to write down there, in the *atelier*?"

"At night? I don't think so, no. He only used to write in the mornings, then do library business the rest of the day."

"You never saw him down there when you were closing up?"

"No, never." Harmuth looked over at Hugo. "Why do you ask?"

"Just curious. And there's only the front stairs, behind the circulation desk, and the ones at the back of the building?"

"As ways to get into the basement? That's right." Harmuth held up a finger. "Well, yes and no."

"Yes and no? Explain."

Harmuth chuckled again. "You don't know about the secret door?"

Hugo glanced over to see if he was joking. "Seriously?"

123

"Yes, actually. If you go down the back stairs, instead of turning right at the bottom into the main storage rooms, you can turn left."

"Where the boiler room is."

"Exactly. But beside the boiler room is another door."

"I didn't notice it when I went down there."

"You wouldn't unless it's pointed out. It's not hidden or anything, it's just painted over and never used. And locked, of course."

"But it leads somewhere?"

"Oh, yes, absolutely."

"Are you going to tell me where?" Hugo asked. He merged into the traffic on Avenue de la Bourdonnais, the Eiffel Tower soaring over them to his left.

"Next to our library is the library of American University. It takes up the majority of the block we're on. It leads into that."

"You're telling me you have a secret door into the American University's library?"

"You make it sounds so dramatic, Hugo. It's a locked door that we never use, and are not allowed to."

"Do you have access to a key?"

"Well, sure, I guess we do."

"Who's 'we'?"

"We keep a set of all the keys in the administration area. Specifically in a red box behind the photocopier."

"Is the box itself locked?"

"No. There's no need. Only staff and volunteers are allowed back there."

"All of whom would have access to those keys?"

"Yes, I suppose so."

"And how many staff and volunteers does the library have?"

"Well, we have eleven employees and a revolving number of volunteers. Over the course of a year, probably a hundred." He cleared his throat. "Look, you're making it sound like we're being careless with those keys, but we've never had a problem."

"Not one that you know about, anyway."

"You think someone's been using those keys? To get into the university next door?"

"I think someone did at least once, yes."

"Who?" Harmuth demanded.

"Now, that I don't know."

"What happened, then, can you tell me that?"

"I really don't know if anything did happen. Anything illegal, that is. But if you'll forgive me, I need to let Lieutenant Lerens know about it, and I should be telling her before I tell anyone else, don't you think?"

"I guess," Harmuth said grudgingly. "But I'm in charge of the place right now, so if there are nefarious goings-on, I'd like to be kept informed."

"Absolutely." Hugo tried a joke. "I promise, you'll be the second to know."

Harmuth smiled. "Fair enough. Next left, if you didn't know."

"I did, but thanks." Hugo turned left, then eased the car to the curb in front of the library's main doors. "Thanks for your help today, much appreciated."

"Sure thing. I feel so bad for the old lady."

"You said you guys were handling the funeral arrangements. Any word?"

"Yes, actually. We have to wait for the police to release the bodies, but when they do we have a crematorium lined up to handle things."

"Cremation?"

"Sure, of course. Paul and Sarah were both real hippies about recycling, being green and leaving a small footprint. They were starting to get into the alternative-medicine stuff, too, which Michelle and I were glad to see."

"Michelle Juneau?"

"Yes. She's the one who steered me toward most of this stuff. Didn't I mention that before? Anyway, cremation's not ideal but it's better than the whole burial circus."

"But aren't Paul and his mother Catholics?"

"I know, so what?"

"I was under the impression that Catholics were opposed to cremation. Did you run this by Claire Rogers?"

"Well, no. I mean, originally Michelle asked the old lady if she had any requests or requirements, but she told us to handle everything, have us at the library decide. If she was opposed to cremation, that would've been the time to say so."

"Maybe she didn't consider that it was an option."

"Hugo, I know you're not meaning to be difficult but, look. This has been a nightmare for everyone involved, Madame Rogers and everyone at the library who knew Paul and Sarah. I'm just trying to keep everything together right now, and I'm not going to second-guess Michelle's booking of the crematorium on the basis that a senile woman might object."

"That senile woman is Paul's mother." Hugo held up a pacifying hand. "I'm just saying someone might want to run it by her, that's all."

Harmuth opened the door. "I'll do that next chance I get." He gave a tight smile. "Thanks for the ride."

Hugo watched as Harmuth pushed his way into the library, and he wondered whether he should park and check out that secret door. If Michelle Juneau really had heard someone else down there with Paul Rogers, that seemed the most likely avenue of retreat for the mysterious companion. His thought process was interrupted when his phone rang. It was Lerens.

"Camille, miss me already?" Hugo asked.

"*Absolument.* I thought you'd be interested to know that I had an analyst take a look at the two computers Paul Rogers used. His laptop and his desktop at the library."

"They let you?"

"Yes, and it's a simple process nowadays. Our people can basically insert an external drive and mirror everything on the computer. Not download, but mirror."

"Not my forte, but sounds impressive," Hugo said. "What did you find?"

"Not much of interest on his home computer, but on the work one he'd been doing some research on poisons."

"For his book, probably."

"*Non*, I did a search of the manuscript. Nothing in it about poisons."

"So what are you thinking?"

"He looked at one in particular. Curare."

Hugo frowned. "Isn't that a South American root or something?"

"It's a plant extract, but yes. I'd heard of it but didn't know much about it, until now. Apparently Indians in South America use it on the tips of their arrows. It takes effect immediately and paralyzes the muscles so the animal, or person, suffocates. The effects don't last long, though, and if you get artificial respiration you can survive."

"Fascinating stuff," Hugo said, "but I assume you're not suggesting Paul was shot by a bow-and-arrow-wielding Colombian tribesman."

"No. But it's possible to test for it, and I wouldn't be doing my job if I didn't test his remains."

"Well, you can, but I watched the video surveillance. No one went in or out, no one saw or touched him, or gave him anything to eat or drink. If the effects start immediately and wear off quickly, he wasn't poisoned before he went into the *atelier*." He sighed. "What I'm trying to ask is, How do you see this as a possibility?"

"No idea," she said lightly. "I'm just ordering the test, Hugo, not claiming it as a fact."

"Test that water bottle for it, then, too."

"*Merci bien*. No way I'd have thought of that," she said.

"Sorry, I did it again, didn't I?" Hugo said. "I love the investigation process, but I do like to be in charge of it."

"That's OK, I'll get over it," Lerens said. "Doctor Sprengelmeyer is doing the preliminary test this evening; I'll call with any result. What's your plan?"

"I was thinking about paying a visit to our journalist friend, Alain Benoît. Do you need to come with me?"

"Yes, definitely. We've gone beyond the point of you poking casually around to see what you can turn up. With Sarah Gregory's bruising and now this poison twist, I need you to include me on everything. Preferably, I'll be the one deciding whether to include *you*."

"They both qualify as American citizens, remember."

"I know, but let's put it this way: If you interview a witness without me present, it'll need to be in accordance with our procedures. Which means it's recorded, and afterward you have to type up a report to go in the investigation file."

"I'm not about to drown myself in paperwork, so I'll wait for you to be available. Shall we say seven tonight?"

"No. I have a date. I'll pick you up at your apartment at nine tomorrow morning."

"A date? Who with?"

"I don't kiss and tell, Hugo. And if you send Tom to follow me, which I know he'd love to do, I'll shoot you both."

CHAPTER FOURTEEN

The next morning, Hugo waited for Camille Lerens on the sidewalk, ignoring the curious eyes of the passers-by who watched as he climbed into the police car. Their plan was to drive out to Alain Benoît's house in Vincennes and ask him about his friendship with Sarah Gregory and Paul Rogers. They'd discussed doing the interview over the phone or asking Benoît to come to the police station, but Hugo had insisted that the element of surprise might be useful. If Sarah's death was indeed murder, Hugo pointed out that Benoît was about the only real suspect they had, and they'd need every advantage possible.

Hugo felt his stomach rumble as he buckled his seatbelt, cursing Tom for cleaning out the fridge, again, and not restocking it. He nodded to Lerens that he was ready but just as they were about to pull away, Merlyn turned the corner into Rue Jacob.

"Hold on," Hugo said, and lowered the window. "Hey, you. Not looking for me, are you?"

"Yes, actually," Merlyn said. She stopped, waved, and smiled at Lerens. "*Bonjour, je suis* Merlyn."

"This is Lieutenant Lerens," Hugo said. "I've told you all about each other, good bits and bad."

"Uh-oh," said Merlyn with a smile. "You guys coming or going?"

"We're just heading out, what's up?"

"Heading out where?" Merlyn demanded. "I've barely seen you. Don't tell me you work weekends, too."

"Occasionally. How about we have dinner tonight, my treat."

"In that case, I want to eat at Les Deux Magots, where Hemmingway used to drink and write."

"That's a little touristy, isn't it?" Hugo said. Merlyn frowned, so he added, "But still fun, it's a neat place. Meet you there at seven?"

"Sure. Where are you guys going?" Merlyn asked.

"To see a man about a horse." Hugo winked. "Or whatever the Parisian version might be. What about you, any plans?"

"Thought I'd wander around, maybe stumble into a museum."

"Where's Miki?"

"I don't know. She was gone when I woke up this morning. She was on the phone with some guy last night, then went out to meet him and I didn't see her all evening. But she should be back by dinner."

"Invite her, if you want. How's her story coming along?"

"Not well," Merlyn said. "She's a little frustrated, I think. Or desperate, if you'd rather put it that way."

"Sounds bad."

"Well, no one's helping her. Not a criticism, don't take it that way. But with what's happened at the library, no one has the time or inclination to talk. I mean, they'll bring her the collection bit by bit, but it's the back story she wants."

"Still assuming there is one."

"She's sure of it. She found letters between Isabelle Severin and Josephine Baker."

"Oh, yes? The singer?"

"Seriously, Hugo? She was more than a singer. She was a spy, too, or so Miki says. Traveled around Europe gathering information on German troop movements and stuff like that. She used to pin notes inside her underwear, and because she was famous, she wasn't searched." Merlyn shrugged. "Miki thinks Severin did the same kind of thing, used her status to get access and information."

"Plus stab Gestapo officers. Or was it SS?"

"Are you making fun of her, or of me?"

"Neither. So what was in the letter?" Beside him, Camille coughed unsubtly.

"She didn't say exactly, although I got the impression she was a little disappointed. There was some sheet music in there, too, but apart from that, I have no idea."

"Original sheet music, eh?" Hugo said. "That's kind of cool. I'll let her tell me about it tonight. Need a ride anywhere?"

"In the back of a cop car? Been there, done that. Actually, I like this part of the city so I'm happy to walk." She waved at Hugo and Camille Lerens, then turned back the way she'd come, a slow saunter in the direction of the flower sellers on Rue de Buci.

Lerens pulled away from the curb and drove them east across Paris toward Vincennes, the roads relatively quiet on a Saturday morning. As she drove, she talked.

"So I asked you before but didn't get much of an answer. What's going on with you and Claudia?"

"Why does everyone keep asking me that?"

"Because you two are good together. You're happy when you're with her."

"Am I usually unhappy?"

"No, you're just Hugo. Slightly serious Hugo, who needs lightening up and a good woman to love."

Hugo looked out of the window. "Yeah, you may have something there."

"When did you last see her?"

"Yesterday, as it happens."

"Yesterday?" Lerens punched him on the arm. "Why didn't you tell me?"

"I'm not Tom, I'm more like you. I tend to keep my love life to myself. Such as it is."

"Yeah, that's like Hugo Lloris not bragging about the goals he's scored for France."

"What now?"

"He's a goalkeeper. They don't score, so he's got nothing to brag about." She looked over her shoulder and changed lanes. "Like you."

"You know, I've been following football for several years now, so no need to patronize me." Hugo heard huffiness in his tone, so lightened it. "What about you, how was the date?"

"Don't change the subject."

"You just told me I have nothing to talk about." Hugo shook his head in mock disgust. His phone rang, and he answered, glad to dodge any more questions. "Hugo Marston."

The voice on the other end snapped with anger. "Monsieur Marston, this is Janelle Cason. From Madame Severin's place of residence."

"*Bonjour, madame,* how can I help you?"

"I told you to make an appointment. I was very clear about that indeed."

Hugo kept his voice calm. "And that's what I did yesterday, I requested an appointment and left my contact details. I presume that's how you have my phone number."

"Maybe you did, but I've called the police, and if they see you here you'll be arrested."

"Arrested? I don't—"

"Poor Madame Severin was quite upset this morning, she rarely likes to see people and never first thing in the morning. I mean, goodness, have you never had an elderly relative or friend? Mornings are *never* good. And after I told you to go through the proper channels, it's an outrage."

"I'm still not understanding."

"Perhaps you will when the police speak to you. I told you, I've called them and they don't take kindly to people trespassing here. We have any number of well-known residents and the local police are *very* good at keeping us safe and free from harassment."

"I'm glad to hear that," Hugo said. "But are you saying someone tried to visit Madame Severin this morning?"

"Don't act like it wasn't you—you're not fooling anyone."

"I wasn't out there early this morning, Madame Cason. In fact, I'm spending my morning with a police lieutenant. She's sitting right next to me if you'd like to confirm that."

Janelle Cason snorted with derision and then, without another word, cut the connection.

Hugo stared at his phone for a moment as Lerens glanced across at him. "What was that about?"

"I'm not entirely sure. Claudia and I took a trip out to visit Isabelle Severin yesterday."

"The actress?"

"Yes, the one who gave her papers to the library."

"What for? You think her collection has something to do with Paul's and Sarah's deaths?"

"I don't know. Honestly, Camille, partly it was out of curiosity. This was the most beautiful woman in the world, the most glamorous, the greatest actress. She worked with Alfred Hitchcock, my favorite director."

"*Alors*, so partly the case and partly curiosity."

"Pretty much."

"And how did it go?"

"It was going fine until Madame Cason busted in. That's the lady who just called. When we showed up she insisted we make an appointment and not just drop by."

"Ah, but you dropped by anyway, didn't you?"

"Yes, and Madame Severin seemed fine with that. Like I say, until Cason showed up and chased us off."

"Well, to be fair, they need to be careful; they can't just let people wander around, knocking on doors over there."

"I know—it was a spur-of-the-moment thing. Maybe not the best idea, but not entirely the worst."

"And she called just to yell at you again?"

"No. She called to yell at me for going back there this morning."

Lerens threw him a puzzled look. "You didn't have the embassy car this morning, that's why I'm driving. How would you have . . . ?"

"Quite apart from the fact that I fell out of bed about thirty minutes before you showed up. Which reminds me, if you see a *boulangerie*, pull over and I'll buy croissants."

"I will. Why did she think it was you?"

"She didn't say. I guess she just assumed that it was after what happened yesterday."

"How odd. Look up the number for the nearest police station to the retirement community. I'll call them and see if that woman really made a report." Lerens signaled right and brought the police car to a halt in front of a row of shops, one of which was a bakery. She waited as Hugo found the number and handed her the phone. She clicked on the number to dial it and said, "I'll take a regular croissant and a chocolate one. And coffee, too, if they have it. Black, no sugar."

Hugo smiled and climbed out of the car. He heard Lerens starting to talk just as he slammed the door, earning himself a dark look from the lieutenant. The warm, buttery smells enveloped him as soon as he stepped into the *pâtisserie* and he breathed it in, getting the same feeling of happiness as always at the sights and smells of the pastries and cakes all around him. He never minded waiting in line at places like this; it gave him time to tempt himself with which delicacy he might like for dessert that night.

Only about forty of them, he thought.

Five minutes later, he climbed back into the car with their still-warm breakfast in paper bags, and handed Lerens her order.

"No coffee—if you want something in a paper cup, we'll have to find a Starbucks."

"Over my dead body," Lerens muttered.

Hugo smiled and pointed to her food. "Then just enjoy those. The place smelled amazing."

"*Merci.*" She stuck her nose in the bag and inhaled. "*Vive la France.*"

"Amen," said Hugo. "Any luck with the local *flics*?"

"Yes, actually. And I can see why Madame Cason is mad at you."

"Because I'm a time traveler? Or because I have a magic carpet?"

"I spoke to a captain there, Mariel Bard. The officer who responded to the retirement community didn't file his report yet, but Captain Bard was able to pull up the call text, what the operator types into the system when the call comes in. It's the information that the first officer on scene has."

"Sounds like the same system back home. Go on."

"The call text said that two people had knocked on Madame

Severin's door and basically forced their way in. Not hurting her, but just being a little too assertive."

"Two people?"

"A man and a woman."

Hugo immediately thought of Tom. Subtlety wasn't his greatest strength, but he also wasn't the type to bully ninety-year-old movie stars. "Was there a description?"

"Tall, good-looking man and an attractive woman. Severin was unsure of their ages, she'd just woken up and was very confused."

"I bet." *Tall and good-looking rules Tom out*, Hugo thought. "Anything else?"

"The captain said the couple was in the house for only a few minutes, asking questions and upsetting the old lady. A groundskeeper happened to drive by and see the front door open. He called security and they called the police. By the time the officer arrived, the couple was gone."

"Sounds like me and Claudia, but it wasn't." *Had Claudia gone back with someone else? But why?*

"One more thing," Lerens said. She pulled a croissant from the bag and made Hugo wait as she slowly chewed her first bite. "They stole from her."

"Stole? Like, money?"

"That's the odd thing," Lerens said. "No money or jewelry, just something of sentimental value, and Madame Severin is apparently very upset about it."

Dread filled Hugo's chest as he pictured the old woman's desk. "What did they take?"

"It's strange. All they took was an old letter opener." She took another bite and nudged Hugo with an elbow. "Dig in before they go cold. Delicious." She looked up. "Why the hell would someone steal a letter opener?"

CHAPTER FIFTEEN

They parked outside Alain Benoît's apartment building, which sat on a quiet street in Vincennes, a clean and tree-lined pocket of eastern Paris. They stayed in the car for a moment, just to see who was coming and going. Hugo watched as a sanitation worker in green overalls and a yellow reflective jacket wielded a brush that had green, plastic bristles. The man swept at the gutter in a gentle but constant rhythm, pushing along the stream of water that flowed past his feet from a hydrant fifty yards away, ushering discarded cigarette butts toward a grill in the curb with the measured patience and precision of a painter.

"You don't think we should have called before coming out?" Lieutenant Lerens asked. "At least had someone come by and see if he's here?"

"You have other plans for today?" Hugo asked.

"You do. Your friends from England are in town."

"I'll see them tonight. You should come out with us."

"I have plans."

Hugo glanced at her face but he couldn't tell whether she was making fun of him or was serious. "Look," he said, "it's not a surprise if we let the guy know we're coming."

"Surprises are overrated. In my experience, the badge and uniform are more persuasive."

"Well, today we have all three."

"Assuming he's in."

"Let's go find out." Hugo checked his watch, 10:00 a.m., then pointed to a woman who was pushing a stroller laden with shopping bags and was headed toward the main doors to the building. Hugo and Lerens climbed out of the car quickly and hurried in that direction, timing their arrival so that Hugo could hold the door for the harried woman once she'd punched in the code. The woman was surprised at first but seemed reassured by the police uniform, flashing them a smile as they followed her inside. She headed for the elevator as they angled off to the right, toward Alain Benoît's ground-floor apartment.

Lerens raised her fist to knock, but they both turned when the building's door buzzed and opened, and Benoît walked in. He didn't see them at first, his head down as he scanned the headlines of the newspaper in his left hand, which also held a to-go cup of coffee. A set of keys jangled in his right hand.

He was ten feet from his front door when he looked up and stopped in his tracks. His eyes darted between Hugo and Lerens, and he shifted his body back, either an unconscious response to their presence or the first step of flight.

"Monsieur Benoît," Lerens said. Her voice was low, forceful, letting him know they were there for a good reason and not about to let him run away.

"*Oui*," he said. "*Je suis Alain Benoît.*"

We know who you are, Hugo thought, *the only question right now is whether we have to chase you.*

Benoît stared for a moment longer, then his shoulders relaxed, as if he recognized Hugo or realized that they knew who he was and where he lived, so running would be pointless. "What do you want?" he asked in French.

"I'd prefer to talk in private, would you mind?" Lerens stepped away from his front door, giving him a path to it. Benoît moved forward, sliding his key into the lock and opening the door.

"What's this about?" he asked.

They followed him down a short hallway into a small apartment furnished with gray and white pieces, and too much stainless steel. *Clean lines but not very homey*, Hugo thought.

Benoît gestured for them to sit on the couch, and he perched on the edge of a low, white chair. "Well?" he asked.

Lerens pulled a digital recorder from her pocket and set it on the table between them. "Policy, I have to record this, do you mind?"

"*Non, pas du tout*," he said. *Not at all.* "But please, tell me why you're here."

She switched on the recorder and spoke in French. "This is Lieutenant Camille Lerens along with Hugo Marston of the United States Embassy at the home of, and speaking to, Alain Benoît." She looked at the display of her phone and read out the date and time, then paused and looked at Benoît. "We're here about Sarah Gregory and Paul Rogers."

"Sarah!" Benoît leapt up. "Where is she?"

Hugo and Lerens exchanged glances.

"When did you last see her?" Lerens asked.

"Last Tuesday. Where is she? I've been over there and tried calling, but she won't return my calls. Is she OK?"

Lerens took a breath. "Sit down, *monsieur*. Please."

Benoît lowered himself into the chair but leaned forward, elbows on his knees, a worried look on his face. "What is it?"

Lerens said, "I'm sorry to be the one to tell you this, but Sarah Gregory is dead."

Hugo leaned forward, too, knowing this moment was coming, his eyes glued to Alain Benoît. It took a moment for the words to sink in, but when they did, the blood drained from the Frenchman's face and his mouth opened as if to speak, but no words came out. "She was found on Wednesday," Lerens continued, "at her apartment."

Benoît shook his head, refusing to believe it.

"Right now it looks like suicide," Hugo said gently, still studying Benoît.

"There's no way," Benoît said, his voice cracking. "She loved Paul, of course, but there's no way she'd . . . she'd do *that*."

"How can you be so sure?" Lerens asked.

"No, she was too full of life, she was . . . it's just not her personality."

"You realize what the alternative is, *monsieur*?" Lerens asked.

It took a few seconds, but Benoît eventually did. "But who . . . ?"

"That would be up to us to find out," Lerens said.

"Everyone loved her, there's no way she had any enemies," Benoît said emphatically. "Absolutely no way. How did . . . how was she found?"

"In the bath, her wrists cut."

"*Non, ce n'est pas possible.*" His eyes were wild again, his tone adamant. "She was terrified of anything to do with blood. Or needles. Paul made fun of her for being so scared, asked how'd they'd ever have kids if she couldn't even get a flu shot."

Interesting that you'd know that, Hugo thought. He sat back and let Lerens continue to question Benoît, saving his questions for the end.

"That's good to know," Lerens said. "You said it wouldn't be her personality to commit suicide. How well did you know her?"

"Well enough to know that."

"How long had you been friends?"

"A few months, maybe three."

"And how did you meet?"

"I met them at the library. When they had an event related to the Severin collection."

"That was three months ago?"

"They've had it for longer, of course, but the event was, yes. Something like that," Benoît said. "It took a while for them to actually get everything. I think the old lady moving slowed things down."

Lerens nodded. "So you met at the library and became friends . . . how?"

"I don't understand."

"*Alors*, do you speak English?"

"Yes, fluently."

"I didn't know that."

"You didn't ask," Benoît said.

A little defensive there, Hugo thought.

Lerens kept her tone neutral. "I was just wondering how a chance meeting at the library resulted in you three becoming close friends."

"We had a lot in common. Liked the same books, movies. Sometimes people just get on well, become friends quickly. Hasn't that ever happened to you?"

"Not since I was a child, no."

Benoît sat back and his eyes flashed with anger. "Are you accusing me of something?"

"*Non*, absolutely not. But I do need to ask you some questions that in other circumstances would be considered impolite." Lerens held up a placating hand. "Please understand, I am just doing my job, trying to find out what happened to your friends."

"What do you want to know?"

"Again, I apologize for being forward. But were you and Mademoiselle Gregory having an affair?"

Benoît's eyes widened, and he burst out laughing, but quickly stifled it. "Are you crazy?"

"A simple yes or no will do."

"Then no. *No.* Why would you even think that?"

"I'm not sure that I do," Lerens said. "But you can't think it outrageous that I would ask. A handsome young man like yourself becomes friends with a beautiful girl like Sarah. She has an older fiancé or boyfriend who, as evidenced by that status, may not to want to commit to her. And this is Paris, after all. Would it really be so shocking that the two of you would fall in love?"

"I can assure you, Lieutenant, if that's your theory, you are very, very wrong."

"You were not in love with her?"

"I loved her." His body slumped, and Hugo knew the news was only now sinking in. "*Oui*, I loved her. But not that way. I loved Paul, too."

"*Bon*," Lerens said. "I have another difficult question. Do you know if there were ever any physical altercations between Paul and Sarah?"

"Physical . . . ?" Benoît looked confused for a moment, then said, "Are you asking if he abused her?"

"Did he?"

Benoît laughed again, a short, sharp sound. "That's even more ridiculous, he worshipped her. And believe me, if he'd laid a hand on her, she'd have beaten the hell out of him and then left him for good. She was tough, and there's no way she'd put up with that."

"Can you tell me where you were on Wednesday?" Lerens asked. "That afternoon."

"I was here, at home. I'm a freelance writer . . . I was working on a piece about the next rugby world cup." He sighed. "I imagine you want to know if anyone saw me."

"Yes, please."

"I doubt it. I had lunch here around midday and didn't leave until around six."

"Did you use your cell phone?"

Benoît frowned with thought. "I don't remember. I don't think so."

Lerens looked down at her phone as it rang. "Excuse me, it's the lab. Hugo, if you have any questions, go ahead."

"*Merci.* In case you're wondering, *monsieur*, I'm the RSO at the embassy and am involved because two Americans died."

Benoît nodded. "I remember meeting you at Paul and Sarah's. But what's an RSO?"

"Regional Security Officer." Benoît said nothing, so Hugo continued. "Do you know other people at the library?"

"A little. But mostly I heard about them from Paul and Sarah."

"Any one in particular?"

"Michelle and Michael, mostly."

"What about them?"

"May I ask why?"

Because if Paul and Sarah were murdered, Hugo thought, *and you happen to be innocent, then someone who knew them is guilty. Most likely, someone at the library.* But he smiled and said, "Just trying to get as full a picture as possible of all the people who knew them."

"Paul liked them both a lot. I don't think they'd been at the library long, but I know he was impressed with them. And liked them. I met

Michelle a few times and always thought she looked a bit like Paul's mother, with all that red hair and fiery personality."

"I hadn't thought of that similarity, but you're right," Hugo said. "What about Michael?"

"Paul liked him. Was grateful for the work he did at the library and thought he was very diligent." He paused. "Sarah wasn't such a big fan."

"Why's that?"

"I wasn't sure. I thought at first she was worried that he was trying to undermine Paul. But it's a library, not a multinational corporation, so I can't imagine there was any kind of power struggle, not really. No, I think it had more to do with Harmuth wanting to move in to Paul's mother's apartment."

"There was conflict over that?"

"That's putting it too strongly. It may have been nothing more than Sarah preferring to have the ground-floor apartment, and Michael wanted it, too. I gather he has a bad leg, or back or something, he probably didn't want to walk the stairs every day."

"Fair enough. Why did Sarah want the ground-floor apartment?"

Benoît shrugged. "We really didn't talk about it in any depth, I'm sorry."

What about Nicole Anisse, do you know her?"

"A beautiful girl," Benoît said. "I've spoken with her a few times, but I wouldn't say I know her."

"Did she get on well with Paul and Sarah?"

"Yes, as far as I know, they had no problems with her at all."

Hugo looked up as Lerens came back into the room, a frown on her face.

"All done?" she asked.

"I think so," Hugo said.

Lerens bent over the table and put her hand on the recorder. "Terminating interview." She clicked it off, and put the device in her pocket as she straightened up. "Monsieur Benoît, thank you for your time. If we have any more questions, may we come back?"

Hugo stood and Benoît followed suit, and said, "I guess so. Or call me, either one."

They walked down the hallway, and Lerens pushed open the door. They shook hands with Benoît, but Lerens had one more question.

"This may sound odd, and I could check independently, but it seems easier to just ask. Have you traveled lately?"

"Traveled?"

"*Oui.* Out of the country."

"Not for a couple of years, no," Benoît said. "Why do you ask?"

"And you're not planning to?"

"No, I'll be here. I'm not going anywhere."

"And would you consent to a search of your computer by the police?"

Benoît bristled. "My personal computer? What for?"

"Would you consent?" Lerens pressed.

"No, I certainly would not. I have private information on there, bank information, and . . . personal stuff."

"I understand," Lerens said. She gave him a tight smile. "We'll be in touch if we need anything. Thank you for your time."

Hugo followed her out of the building, and as soon as the front door closed behind them, he said, "Paul Rogers was poisoned, wasn't he? The curare."

"He most certainly was. Let's talk in the car."

She unlocked it remotely and Hugo sank into the front passenger seat as Lerens got behind the wheel. He turned to her. "So, what did Sprengelmeyer say?"

"The initial test for curare was positive. He's sending a second sample for independent testing, just to make sure. But right now . . ."

Hugo shook his head. "That's crazy. Wait, did he test Sarah, too?"

"He did. No curare in her system."

"But positive for Paul. I just don't see how or why." Hugo frowned, deep in thought. "The water bottle, did he test that? The water in it?"

"Yes. He's sending it for retesting, too, but not only was it clear of curare, but apparently it's not effective when ingested. If you eat or drink it, or just touch it for that matter, you're safe. It's not that kind of poison, it has to be absorbed into the blood more directly. Basically, straight into the blood stream."

"Like a poisoned dart."

Lerens laughed gently. "I don't recall seeing one of those at the scene."

Hugo nudged her with his elbow. "True, but I bet you're glad we had the crime-scene unit go to work there."

She rolled her eyes. "Fine. I'll let you have credit for that. But you got lucky. Every cop on the planet would have called that natural causes."

"Yeah." Hugo sat back, his mind working. "But it wasn't, was it?"

"*Non*. And I know what you're thinking; I'm wondering the same thing."

"That's the million-euro question, isn't it? The big mystery we're now left with," Hugo mused. "As unlikely as it seems, did Paul Rogers commit suicide? Or, almost as unlikely, did someone murder him?"

CHAPTER SIXTEEN

Lerens drove them back into Paris, the weekend traffic flowing like the Seine, a slow but steady roll toward the city center. They didn't talk much, and Hugo assumed his lieutenant friend was doing the same thing he was: processing what Alain Benoît had told them, and trying to get a grip on the toxicology finding.

She parked the car in front of a café on a street Hugo didn't know, and waved a hand distractedly when he pointed out it was a no-parking zone. "You think someone will ticket my police car?"

"You're setting a bad example," Hugo said.

"I'm leaving a regular parking space for someone else, is what I'm doing."

"Hadn't thought about it that way."

"You're welcome."

Hugo gestured to the café. "You know this place?"

"*Non.* But anywhere will do for an omelet, which is what I want right now."

"Fine with me." Hugo unbuckled his seatbelt.

"We need to talk about what the hell happened to Paul Rogers, because if he was murdered . . ." her voice trailed off and she shook her head. "I don't know how, why, or where it leaves us with Sarah Gregory's death. Did she kill him somehow and then commit suicide out of remorse?"

"I agree. We need to start with Paul." They climbed out of the car

147

and walked to the café door, which Hugo held open for her. They made their way to a table in the corner, by a large window overlooking the street. They sat quietly as a waiter arrived with menus and a carafe of water, pouring out two glasses.

"*Quelque chose à boire?*" he asked. *Something to drink?*

"*Un café, s'il vous plaît,*" Lerens said.

Hugo nodded. "*Moi aussi.*"

They looked at the menus, and Lerens mused over the ham-and-mushroom omelet, tempted, too, by a chicken-parmesan sandwich. When the waiter returned with their coffees, they both went with the omelet, then made small talk until the food arrived, Hugo picking at the basket of bread even though he wasn't very hungry.

"Even though it seems ridiculous, it has to be suicide," Lerens said when their meals arrived.

"Go on."

"He was definitely poisoned. Curare is quick-acting and, thanks to those cameras, we know he didn't come into contact with anyone before his death. There's no way anyone else poisoned him."

"I'd have to agree so far."

"The water wasn't poisoned, and even if it was, that's not how curare works, you can ingest it without harm."

"Did he have any injuries on him at all, places where the poison might have gotten into his blood?"

"No, Sprengelmeyer insisted he didn't. Not even a bruise."

"It's possible the good doctor missed a pinprick, something he could inflict on himself in a hard-to-spot place, but it's less likely the doc would miss an injury someone else gave him while administering the poison." Hugo took a bite of his omelet and washed it down with a sip of water. "So if no one else did it, he must have done it himself. But I honestly can't see why he'd commit suicide. That seems so far-fetched, I mean who kills himself with a rare, South American poison?"

"I agree, but you knew him, I didn't."

"And then there's Sarah. I find it hard enough to believe that Paul killed himself, but when you add Sarah's death into the mix . . ."

"Remember, we have his computer searches."

"Someone else could have used his work computer; that's not very persuasive to me."

"But who? And why?"

They ate in silence for a while, both mopping up the remains of their food with hunks of bread.

"Another coffee, I think," Hugo said, when he was done.

"Agreed." Lerens ordered them when the waiter came to clear their plates. When the coffee arrived, Hugo unwrapped a sugar cube and dropped it in.

"What's your plan now?" he asked.

"I want to check in with the detective looking into the unexpected visitors to Madame Severin."

"You think that was connected to Paul's death?"

"Don't you?"

Hugo shrugged. "Maybe. Paul was in charge of her collection. He'd likely have known if there was stuff being held back."

"He and Michelle Juneau, I agree."

"The younger version of Paul's mother," Hugo said with a smile. "I already talked to her, but unofficially, so maybe you'll have more luck."

"Another working weekend," Lerens said with a wry smile.

"So no dinner with us tonight?"

"I'm occupied this evening, remember? But thanks anyway. You have afternoon plans?"

"Yes, I'm going to do some research. On curare and whatever else pops into my mind."

"Now you're being coy."

"You know me," Hugo said. "I don't like to show my cards until I'm sure they're good ones."

Lerens sat up straight. "You have an idea of what's going on?"

"No, definitely not. If I did, I'd tell you."

"You better," Lerens said. "Else I'll swap you out for Tom. That man wouldn't keep secrets from me."

"No?"

She laughed. "I'm not sure he's even capable of keeping secrets."

"Oh, is that what you think?" Hugo drained his coffee. "In that case, you'd be in for a big surprise."

Hugo spent the afternoon at his office, glad of the peace and quiet and that he didn't have to ask Emma to intercept his calls. He fired up his computer and began his research with a look into the poison, curare, reading as much as he could about it. Lerens had been right, for it to kill Rogers it had to be absorbed into the blood, possibly injected or stabbed some other way. It didn't take much at all to paralyze a man's respiratory system, but even a cup of the stuff in Paul's water bottle wouldn't have been effective.

And yet there was no injury, no cut or graze or injection site. Hugo wondered if Sprengelmeyer would really be able to spot a tiny pinprick, but whether he could or not, no needle was found in the *atelier*. And with the quick reaction time of the drug, there seemed little doubt that the curare had entered the blood stream of Paul Rogers while he was in his little writing room.

But how?

Unable to solve that puzzle, and learning nothing more revealing about the drug, Hugo sat back and thought about the interview with Alain Benoît. He couldn't put his finger on anything the man had said that was a provable lie, yet he couldn't escape the feeling that Benoît had not been telling them the whole truth, had been hiding something. If this *was* murder, and Hugo believed both Paul and Sarah had indeed been murdered, then where did Alain Benoît fit in all this? The only two things distinguishing him from the other potential suspects were that he had been close to both Paul and Sarah, and the fact that he didn't work at the library.

But so what?

If Paul had been the only one to die, then Hugo could've seen a motive, an Alain Benoît in love with Sarah Gregory and unwilling to let Paul stand in the way. It was possible, he supposed, that Benoît killed Rogers and was subsequently rejected by Sarah, and he killed her in a fit of rage. Or maybe she knew or guessed he'd killed Paul, and was going to turn him in, leaving Benoît with no alternative but to murder her to avoid being caught.

Hugo swung his feet onto his desktop as Tom knocked and let himself in, dropping into a chair opposite Hugo with a grunt.

"Actually working?" Tom asked.

"One of us should."

"On the library murders?"

"That what we're calling them?"

"If they're murders." Tom frowned. "I got your message, obviously."

"Quite the conundrum, we have."

"You're smarter than me, big fella, so maybe you can explain either a motive, or how the hell Rogers got himself poisoned behind a locked door."

"I can come up with a motive, though it's a bit of a reach. What I don't have, is an answer to your second question."

"Where's Miss Marple when you need her, eh?"

"Making tea and crumpets, I imagine." Hugo shook his head. "We're missing some important parts of the story, but I'm not even sure which direction I should be looking."

"Toward Saint-Germain-des-Prés, I believe. At least, for the fore-seeable future."

"All about the stomach, eh?"

"Hey, we have guests to show a good time. And it's the damn weekend, lighten up for an hour or two." Tom gave him a lingering look. "After all, you know what today is, right?"

"It always seems like you shouldn't be the one to remind me about that."

"I know. Some sense of guilt or appreciation or some shit like that."

"And like I always say, you have no reason to feel either. But if it makes you feel better, just buy me a drink like you always do." Hugo winked. "Come to think of it, that's about the only time you ever pay for drinks. Including your own."

"Yeah, yeah." Tom shifted awkwardly and changed the subject. "Hey, I know, you can do your Sherlock trick for our new friends."

"Oh, I don't think there's any need for that."

"Hell yes, there is."

"You'd really make me do that?"

"And you're really gonna pretend you hate doing it?" Tom slapped the desktop as he stood. "Come on, it'll be fun. You know it pisses me off how good you are, and this time I'm giving you advance notice. That makes it easy."

Hugo swung his feet to the floor. "If it's easy, why don't you do it for a change?"

"Because, dummy, then I couldn't get mad." He lowered his voice to an almost-mutter. "And even though I'll never admit it in public, it's a pretty cool trick that I don't think I could pull off."

"Well, there's a rare admission," said Hugo, eyeing his phone. "And would you look at that, I think I was accidentally recording that conversation."

Hugo had not been to Les Deux Magots for over a year, and his last visit had been on embassy business. It had been the café of choice for the intellectual elites and writers of years gone by, people like Simone de Beauvoir, Albert Camus, Earnest Hemmingway, and Jean-Paul Sartre. The café lived off that history, and its location in Saint-Germain-des-Prés, but even with its tables filled with tourists rather than writers, the place still impressed.

Its tiled floors and polished tables, the shining brass handrails and immaculate wait staff, all gave the impression of a café in its heyday. As Hugo sat beside Tom, he found it easy to look past the backpacks and cameras and imagine this as the haven Ernest Hemingway settled into with his two pencils and writing journals, and maybe a libation to unlock the creative mind.

"This place is so cool," Merlyn said, her eyes shining. She sat opposite Hugo but her head swiveled from left to right, taking it all in.

"It looks like it's not changed for fifty years," Miki said. "And I mean that in a good way."

Once they were settled, a waiter approached the table, a slender man in his forties dressed impeccably in black pants, a white shirt, and a black vest. He took out his pen, which slipped from his fingers and fell to the floor. Hugo noticed the man wince as he stooped to pick it up.

The waiter straightened, pen in hand, and smiled. "*Bonsoir messieurs et mesdames. Quelque chose à boire?*" he asked.

Merlyn and Miki opted for champagne, Hugo went for an Americano, and Tom, ignoring Hugo's curious gaze, settled on a scotch with lots of ice.

"Moderation is more realistic than abstinence," Tom muttered when the waiter had gone.

"I'm with you on that," Hugo said. "No worries here."

Tom grunted and then slowly smiled at Hugo, an evil glint in his eye. "Say, ladies, I have a treat for you."

"Oh, yes?" Merlyn replied.

"Well, it's not my treat really, it's Hugo's. Have you ever read any Sherlock Holmes, seen the movies or the BBC series?" The two women nodded. "You know where he does that thing, where he can tell someone had just come back from the battlefield by the color of mud on his shoes, or deduces that someone's an aspiring magician from the one worn knee in his pants."

"Trousers, if Sherlock's doing it," Hugo said mildly.

"Whatever. Anyway, Hugo can do the same thing. Better, even."

"Is that so?" Miki asked, doubt in her voice.

"Yep. Pick someone in here, and Hugo will tell you something about them."

Merlyn immediately looked around, settling on a tall couple in their fifties by the main window. "How about them?"

Hugo shook his head, laughing. "It has to be someone I'd pay attention to, not someone I can barely see."

"Fine. Our waiter."

"Our waiter. All right." Hugo cleared his throat dramatically, then stared at the table for a moment. "He plays soccer in his spare time, or used to, and probably plays as a striker, although I could be wrong about that. He's injured right now—I'd say his right hip. Probably a strain to the hip capsule itself, or more likely the upper quads. And he's healing quite nicely."

Merlyn and Miki swapped glances, as if unsure whether they were being pranked. "Are you serious?" Merlyn asked.

"I am," Hugo replied.

"You get that from the way he holds his pen, I suppose?" Tom said.

"Actually, yes. But more from the way he tied his shoelaces."

Merlyn tilted her head and stared at Hugo. "No. Now you're kidding."

"Ask him," Hugo said. "See if I'm right."

"My French isn't good enough."

"Oh, I forgot to add that despite him feigning otherwise, he speaks decent English."

"Wow, really?" When Hugo nodded, she raised her hand to catch the waiter's attention. When he came over, Merlyn asked him in English, "*Monsieur*, do you play football?"

The waiter hesitated, then smiled and replied, also in English. "Yes, why do you ask?"

"I was just curious. You play every week?"

"Usually, but right now I'm injured. I hope to play again soon."

"Oh, you are? I didn't see you limping," Merlyn said.

"It's getting better. I strained my . . ." he paused, searching for the word. "The leg muscle by my hip, running for the ball."

"That'd be his quad," Hugo said smugly. "Upper quad."

"What position do you play?" she asked.

"Midfield or forward. Usually forward. You are a fan?"

"Yes," she said. "West Ham all the way."

"*Bien*." He smiled again. "Can I get you anything else?"

When the waiter walked off, Tom shook his head. "Damn, Hugo. Every time you get me. Every damn time."

"Yeah, that was amazing," Merlyn said. "Tell us how you knew."

"I can't do that," Hugo said. "That's like a magician showing the rabbit up his sleeve, or the false top in his hat."

Tom groaned loudly. "I forgot to warn you girls. A mandatory part of this little sideshow is Hugo making his audience beg him to tell how he did it."

Hugo sipped his wine and settled back in his seat. "Pretty poor job of begging, I have to say."

"Fine, I'll do it." Merlyn took his hand and batted her eyelashes. "Please, Mr. Hugo, we so admire you, will you kindly tell us how you knew all that stuff?"

"That's better," Hugo said. "I'll think about it."

"Oh, come on!" Miki said. "I'll beg, too, if I have to."

Something about her offer made Hugo uncomfortable, but he couldn't decide whether her tone overflowed with shameless sincerity or glib insincerity.

"Fine," he said. "He's wearing the bracelet of his favorite team—"

"Wait, you didn't say anything about that," Merlyn protested.

"Too easy. Anyone can spot a bracelet, even if you people didn't." He held up a hand to silence Merlyn's impending protestation. "And I know it's his favorite team, because they're playing right now and he keeps checking his phone, I imagine to see the score."

"So how did you know he plays?"

"Ah, that was a lucky guess," Hugo said. "He's at least forty but in good shape, so he obviously exercises. I combined his love of soccer with his injury and presumed. Some luck, I'll admit."

"And what about that injury?" Miki said. "You're not serious that you could tell from his shoelaces?"

"Actually, I am. Here's the thing," Hugo went on, "he's right-handed, you can see that when he writes down orders. But when he dropped his pen, he bent over and picked it up with his left hand. I looked at his shoelaces, and his left one is tied directly in the center of the shoe, over the tongue. But his right one is off center, way to the left. What do those two things tell you?"

"Not a fucking thing," Tom muttered. Both girls shrugged.

"That he is unable to lean directly over his right foot. When he bends his leg, his knee bends fine but goes out to the right and his foot tilts. Hip injury, on the right side."

"Unbelievable," Merlyn said. "And his position on his football team."

"Well, you don't get a hip injury from waiting tables, so it was likely to be playing socc . . . football. I've learned a lot about the game over the years, enough to know that the position requiring the most sprinting is the striker. So, there you have it."

"Lucky guesswork, all of it," Tom said.

"Yeah, but he was right, wasn't he?" Merlyn's tone was defensive, which made Hugo smile.

"Tom says that every time," Hugo said. "And maybe he's right."

"Maybe," Merlyn said. "But that shoelace thing was cool."

"How did you know he speaks English?" Miki asked.

"I can answer that one," Tom said. "He's a waiter in the most famous and touristy café in Paris. Speaking four languages is more important than being able to carry a tray without dropping it."

"Precisely," Hugo agreed. "Good job, Tom, you'll make a decent detective yet."

Tom raised his whiskey glass and mumbled something into it, and Hugo was pretty sure he knew what.

The two young women laughed, and kept laughing as Merlyn's phone buzzed and she shared a series of funny pictures with her girl-friend. Hugo watched them, as did Tom next to him. Hugo glanced at his friends and for a moment Tom held his eye, then he stood and went to the bar. He returned a moment later with two glasses of scotch. He handed one to Hugo, and they clinked glasses.

"Happy anniversary," Tom said, his voice low.

"Yes, that." Hugo raised his glass to eye level. "And to Paul and Sarah."

"Damn straight. And may that other son of a bitch roast in hell."

"I'm sure he is." Hugo checked to make sure the women weren't listening. "But about that stuff."

"Hey, you're not the bad guy, Hugo, and neither am I. The real bad guy's in prison still, remember that."

"That's what I'm trying to tell you. He's up for parole."

Tom shook his head. "Won't happen. Not a chance."

"You can't know that."

"Yes, I can. He'll get out one day, but not now. No way."

Hugo felt a foot nudging his shin under the table. "What're you boys being so serious about?" Merlyn asked.

"Oh, nothing," Hugo said. "Just talking about the good old days. The FBI. You know how geezers like us get, reminiscing."

"In that case, I have a question," Merlyn said.

"Fire away."

"Why did you leave the FBI? Seems like such a cool job."

Miki Harrison perked up. "You didn't tell me he worked for the Bureau, Merlyn." She turned to Hugo. "What exactly did you do for them?"

"A regular field agent for a few years, then I was with the Behavioral Sciences Unit based out of Quantico, but we zipped all over the country. All over the world, really."

"You were a profiler?"

"Yes, essentially. They have four units, one for counter-terrorism, one for white-collar stuff, one for crimes against kids, and then mine, Unit Four, which works crimes against adults."

"Cool," Miki said. "Like, serial killers?"

"Among other things, yes."

"You ever catch one?"

"He caught several," Tom said. "Single-handedly."

The girls looked at him, wondering whether he was joking.

"Never single-handedly," Hugo said. "I worked with a team, which included other agents and local law enforcement."

"And Tom worked for that unit, too?"

"No," Hugo and Tom said together. Hugo glanced at his friend, who was looking down at his plate. *Enough about that*, he knew they were both thinking.

Merlyn seemed to take the hint. "So why did you leave, Hugo?"

"Oh, there was no one reason." He shifted in his seat, uncomfortable with the half-truth. "I got tired of all the death, with dealing with the dark side of humanity."

"And by that he means all the paperwork," Tom chipped in.

"Actually, the bureaucracy had a lot to do with it," Hugo agreed. "That and the fact the bad guys we put away kept getting released."

"Yeah," Tom said, giving Hugo a meaningful look. "Ain't that the truth."

CHAPTER SEVENTEEN

Toward the end of the meal, Merlyn excused herself to the restroom and, when she tottered, Tom leapt up to go with her. Hugo took the opportunity to talk to Miki.

"How's the book research coming along?" he asked.

She laughed, her eyes glassy and shining from the champagne. "Actually, quite well. I hooked into a small group of people with some inside knowledge. Helped me out a bit."

"An online group?" Hugo asked.

"No, some people here in Paris."

"Inside knowledge, sounds intriguing." Hugo smiled but said nothing else. Experience had taught him that silence was a powerful force in getting people to talk; it hovered like a black hole needing to be filled. Especially when someone on the other side of the hole could fill it by talking about their passion. Even more especially when they were properly lubricated.

"Nothing too concrete, not yet," she said. "But there's this one guy who's been chasing the secret Severin papers for the longest time. He had access to some stuff at one point but . . ." She trailed off, as if reminding herself not to say too much.

"So you still think it's true, there's stuff being held back from the collection."

"I'm sure there is."

"Who's in charge of it? Who's holding it back?"

Her eyes dropped to the table. "Well, it's hard to say."

"Michael Harmuth is in charge of all that now, isn't he?"

"He and Michelle Juneau, yes."

"So either one of them could tell you."

She snorted. "Could, maybe."

"What about Isabelle Severin herself? I went out there to talk to her yesterday morning. She's a little forgetful but seems in good health."

Miki's eyes widened. "You did? You were able to talk to her?"

"Well, I went unannounced, which turns out to be a bad idea. But you can call and make an appointment."

"She still sees people?"

"Not everyone, but I think so sometimes. It's worth trying." Hugo smiled. "Imagine that, a cozy visit to the old woman and she spills her guts in person to you over tea."

Miki nodded. "Now that would be something."

"A book, I imagine."

Miki laughed, then hiccupped. "So, what were you doing out there?"

"Same interest as you, to be honest. Trying to figure out if there's anything to the Severin legend."

"Why do you care? I mean, that sounds harsh, but . . . why?"

"Two people are dead, one of whom was curating her collection of papers. If there is a secret hidden away, maybe it's related somehow."

"How?"

"No idea."

"Some detective you are." She winked exaggeratedly and took a gulp of champagne. "So did you find anything out?"

Hugo pictured the letter opener. "Maybe, hard to say at this point."

"Ah, can't reveal anything from an ongoing investigation?" She slurred the last word, and Hugo looked up gratefully as Tom and Merlyn returned. Merlyn nipped ahead of him and took his seat, beside Hugo.

Tom plonked down next to Miki and rubbed his hands together with delight as the waiter wheeled up a three-tiered cheese cart.

"So, are you and Tom looking into the deaths of those two people?" Merlyn asked.

Hugo nodded. "We were just talking about that."

"And?" Merlyn looked back and forth between Hugo and Miki.

"And it's too early to say much. Paul may have committed suicide and it looks likely that Sarah had some help meeting her maker."

"Delightfully put," Tom said.

"He didn't have a heart attack?" Merlyn asked.

"He had a drug in his system. One that would have made it look like he'd had a heart attack." Hugo held up a hand. "And before you ask me which one, I can't say."

"Wow," Merlyn said. "Poison in the library. But you said suicide, and who the hell poisons themselves?"

"Ahem." Tom rattled the remains of his scotch and ice. "I've been trying pretty hard for the past fifteen or so years. Is there anyone on the planet who doesn't put some bad shit in their system?"

Miki Harrison laughed, but added, "Michael Harmuth might qualify. Guy doesn't drink, smoke, and he's into all this alternative medicine."

Hugo glanced across. "He told you about that?"

"He was proud of it. We were taking about Isabelle Severin living so long, and he said it's probably because she's avoided bad food, drugs, that kind of thing."

"Does he know her personally?" Hugo asked.

"Oh, no, it sounded like he was speculating. And when I say drugs, I mean pharmaceutical stuff, the ones doctors prescribe." She popped a square of cheese into her mouth, chewed, and then pointed to her plate. "He doesn't eat animal products, drink caffeine, and he told me he has a little herb garden behind his place where he makes his own medicines."

"Is he some kind of weirdo?" Tom asked.

"No, he's not," Hugo said. "Lots of people agree with him, about the food stuff and medicine. I doubt he's too radical, he'd have his appendix surgically removed if need be. But for headaches, upset stomachs, that kind of thing, a lot of people are turning to more natural remedies. I can see the appeal of it, frankly." *And that explains why he wants the ground-floor apartment, so he'd have access to a garden.*

"Goddam hippy," Tom scoffed.

"No," said Merlyn, leaping to Hugo's defense again, "it's true. When I had sleep problems, my doctor gave me all kinds of drugs. I hated taking them."

"Did they work?" Tom asked.

"Yes, they did. But I felt groggy the next day, and I didn't like the idea of being reliant on . . . whatever they were. Anyway, I stopped taking any pills and took melatonin."

"Those are pills," Tom said.

Merlyn shot him a look full of daggers. "You know what I mean."

"Sure, I do," said Tom, clearly enjoying needling her. "And if he gets cancer, he's gonna make bat-wing soup and drink it with a spoon carved from a virgin's leg bone?"

"Actually," Miki snapped to Merlyn's defense, "he did know someone with cancer. He said they cured it with, oh shit, I don't remember. 'Di-menthol sulfate' or something."

"What the hell's that?" Tom asked.

"No clue. Can't even pronounce it, but he said it was on *60 Minutes*, that American show. That's how they knew to try it."

"I can't imagine there's a natural cure for cancer," Hugo said. "It'd be on more than one episode of *60 Minutes*. I'd bet whoever it was also had chemotherapy." He felt bad undermining Miki and Merlyn, but the words were out before he could stop himself.

Merlyn, on her fourth or fifth glass, wasn't backing down. "Sure, but who knows which one was the main cure? Maybe they helped each other. And how can a natural remedy be bad, even if you're having conventional medicine?"

"Oh, it can't," Hugo said hurriedly, "I'm sure. I was just saying . . . Never mind."

They sat in an awkward silence for a moment, then Miki Harrison spoke up. "So where are we going after dinner?"

"Bed," said Hugo.

She batted her eyelashes. "You think I'm that easy?"

"Oh, please," Merlyn said. "Hugo goes to bed at nine or he turns into a pumpkin. Plus, he has a rich girlfriend."

"Oh, yeah? Why isn't she here tonight?" Miki asked. "Which is to point out, she's not here tonight."

"I was under the impression you'd met someone here," Hugo countered.

"Not that way."

"Weren't you with him all day?" Merlyn asked. "And last night?"

Miki shook her head, a big smile on her face. "No. Not like that, anyway."

"Anyone we know?" Tom asked. Hugo got the distinct impression Tom was both disappointed and hopeful. He clearly had a thing for Miki Harrison.

"I told you, it's not like that. At all." Now Hugo detected a hint of disappointment in her voice, but she rallied. "I was busy working on the Severin story, last night and all today."

Hugo looked down as his phone buzzed. *Camille Lerens* showed on the screen. "Excuse me, guys," he said, "this could be important." He stood and walked to the café's entrance. "Camille, what's up?"

"How's your weekend off?" she asked, humor ringing in her voice.

"Yeah, good one. Something happened?"

"You could say that. Have you been drinking?"

"Like any good French policeman, of course. One Americano and one scotch."

"Well, don't drive. Where are you? I'll send a car."

"If you hurry, I won't have to pay my bill. So where am I going?"

"Paul and Sarah's apartment."

"Oh, no. What now?"

"Don't worry, no one died," she said. "But someone broke in and searched the place."

"Any idea if they took anything?"

"None. That's why I need you here." She barked an order at someone, then spoke to Hugo. "*Bon*, order yourself a coffee. But quickly, a car will be there in ten minutes."

CHAPTER EIGHTEEN

The driver whom Lerens sent was a uniformed *flic* in his midforties, with a bald head and a friendly smile. He drove an unmarked police car, a black Peugeot, and when Hugo slipped into the front seat he was surprised to hear the man introduce himself in English.

"Paul Jameson. Nice to meet you, sir."

Hugo shook his hand. "You're English?"

"God no," Jameson said with a wink. "Scotsman."

Hugo laughed. "Sorry for the offense."

"Just don't let it happen again," Jameson said. He checked his mirrors and looked over his shoulder before pulling away from the curb.

Hugo was curious about his driver, and asked, "How does a Scotsman become a Paris policeman?"

"Always loved the city, used to come here as a kid with my dad and brother. Served ten years in naval intelligence, where I learned French, Italian, and some Mandarin. Once I got out of the forces I thought I'd spend some time over here, work in a bar or something. Then I met a beautiful woman, fell in love, and she wanted me to have a real job. I'd thought about being a cop back home in Toryglen, but she suggested I apply here. They're all about diversity and really welcomed a French-speaking Scot, so here I am."

"You like the job?"

"Aye, love it. Started working for Lieutenant Lerens about two months ago, best officer I've ever met. Tough, smart, and treats her people well."

Jameson had clearly learned to drive as well as speak three foreign languages, and had probably spent years behind the wheel of a car. He weaved expertly through the nighttime traffic, not using lights or sirens but quick signals and even quicker lane changes. In less than ten minutes, Hugo was following the policeman up to the Rogers apartment and shaking hands with Camille Lerens. They got straight down to business.

"Who reported it?" Hugo asked.

"Madame Rogers, actually."

"She was up here?"

"No, she thought she heard footsteps and, of course, knew the place was supposed to be empty. She called the police and we got lucky. It took a little while, but the operator connected this address with the Gregory and Rogers investigation, sent units as soon as she realized."

"Smart operator."

"Right, I wouldn't have put money on her making that connection. You can bet she'll be getting some praise from me in her file."

Hugo recalled Jameson's words: *She treats her people well.* He looked around, but the apartment looked almost exactly the same as the last time he'd been here. If this was a burglary, it was a targeted one, not a ransacking. "When did Madame Rogers call this in, exactly?"

"Not even an hour ago. The first responding officers cleared the place, then staked out the front and back entrances to the building and waited for me."

"Good. Do you know what was taken?"

"No. I don't know whether anything was, actually. It could be the intruder heard sirens and fled."

"No, I don't think so. There would have been several minutes between him getting in here, Madame Rogers calling the police, and the sound of sirens. If it was a random burglar, the place would be at least partially wrecked. But I think he knew what he was looking for, and most likely went straight to it."

"You said *He*."

"Yes." He bounced on his toes. "These floors were redone a couple of years ago, they're not the old, creaky originals. For Madame Rogers to have heard footsteps, they'd either be from a man or from a woman wearing loud shoes."

"And women don't wear heels to a burglary."

"They might, but I've never seen it."

Lerens smiled. "I know I wouldn't. So if this was a targeted burglary, what was he after?"

"It has to be related to either the deaths, or the Severin collection. Or both."

"Evidence of one or access to the other," Lerens said.

"Well put." Hugo walked over to the fireplace. On the floor lay a broken plastic orb. "Is that a camera?"

"It was. Mine, actually."

"Explain," said Hugo.

"I've begun a habit of putting motion-sensing cameras at crimescenes like this, ones that are supposed to be secured. According to a paper written by someone I consider an expert, around ten percent of criminals return to the scene of the crime, either for the thrill of it, or to remove or plant evidence. This seemed like a good candidate for a camera like that, wouldn't you say?"

Hugo was grinning. "You consider that guy an expert, eh?"

"I understand he had a pretty good clearance rate for his cases and, given my broken camera, it'd be hard to argue that he's wrong."

"Well, I'm flattered." And impressed. Hugo had written that paper almost ten years ago for a conference in Milan. It hadn't been particularly revolutionary, more a synthesis of his and his colleagues' experiences, combined with interviews of captured criminals and an application of logic. But the fact that Lerens had read it and then acted on it showed a willingness to learn, to think outside the normal parameters of police work. "So how does it work? Any chance it caught the intruder before he destroyed it?"

"A good chance, yes. I'm waiting to hear from my people. Saturday night isn't the greatest time to get the techies on the phone. But unless he's wearing a mask, the camera should've caught him coming through the front door."

"Great. I assume it was locked?"

"We're not sure. We assume so, too, but I've not figured out who was the last person here to check. It would be pretty bad police work to leave it unlocked, but sometimes, as you know, one cop assumes another cop is taking care of it."

"So either he had a key or he found himself an open door."

"Right. I'm thinking he had a key anyway, though."

Hugo thought the same thing, but he was curious to know if Lerens's reasoning was the same. "Why?" he asked.

"Whether he was here because of the murders or the Severin collection, this is a murder scene, it'd be a huge risk coming here. I doubt someone would take such a risk on the off chance that the door would be left open."

"Agreed." Hugo thought for a moment. "Speaking of keys, have you found any?"

Lerens shook her head. "No, but I've not looked specifically for them. What are you thinking?"

"Let's check, see if we can find a set. Paul's keys would've been given to Sarah, right?"

"That's right."

"And she died here, so hers should be somewhere in the apartment. We need to find two sets of keys, at least."

"*Bon*, let's look." Lerens gestured for Jameson to help them, and the three pulled on latex gloves and began methodically searching the apartment. Hugo stayed in the living room, the Scotsman went into the kitchen, and Lerens tackled the bedroom. They worked quietly, just the thunk of furniture being moved, the scrape of drawers being opened and closed. Hugo started in the most obvious places, the clay pot on the stand beside the front door, followed by the drawer underneath it. Both were empty, except for the thin spider's web in the pot that told Hugo it wasn't a place they kept keys, or anything else.

Hugo looked up as Jameson appeared in the doorway to the kitchen. "*Monsieur. J'ai trouvé des clés.*" He jerked a thumb toward the kitchen. *I found some keys.*

Hugo and Lerens converged on the kitchen, looking into the open drawer separated by compartments. The keys sat in a compartment between an empty one and one filled with rubber bands and coins. Lerens pulled out her phone and took pictures before picking up the keys and inspecting them.

"Given the pink key ring, I'd say these were Sarah's," Lerens said. "And I'm wondering if that empty compartment was for Paul's."

"Let's keep looking. If we don't find them, I'll be inclined to agree with you," Hugo said.

The three went back to their search, more painstaking this time, less urgent. But after thirty minutes they met in the living room, no more keys found.

"*Voyons,*" Lerens said. *Let's see.* "Did either of you find anything else disturbed or obviously missing?"

"Not me," Hugo replied. They looked at Jameson.

"*Rien,*" he said. *Nothing.*

"In that case," Lerens said, "Assuming he had a key to this place already, I think I know why he needed Paul's set."

"His key to the library," Hugo said, and Lerens nodded.

Jameson caught on quickly. "I'll get on the radio and have a unit sit outside, keep an eye on the place."

"Good. And let me just check something." He took out his phone and dialed Michael Harmuth, who answered quickly.

"Hugo, is that you?"

"Yes, sorry to bother you. A couple of quick questions."

"Sure, fire away."

"I'm assuming Paul had keys to the library, yes?"

"Of course."

"Do you know whether the library ever got his keys back after he died?"

"I don't know, to be honest. I can check on Monday, but I'd be surprised if we did now that you mention it. It wouldn't have been a priority for anyone."

"Who else has keys?"

"Well, I have a set. Paul did, of course. Michelle might, I don't know."

"What about Nicole Anisse?"

"I doubt it. But it sounds like I should do an inventory."

"The sooner, the better," Hugo said.

"Did something happen? Why are you asking about his keys?"

"I can't really say at the moment, sorry."

"Do I need to worry about the library being secure?"

"We're taking care of that right now," Hugo said. "Do you have an alarm system?"

"Yes and no. We do for the basement but not for the main level or upstairs lounges."

"Can I ask why not?"

"You saw the sloping glass roof over the teen lounge area?" Harmuth asked.

"I did."

"For some reason, pigeons like to fly into it. Through it. Once a month we're replacing broken glass and responding to the alarm going off. In fact, they told me that two years ago someone from the neighboring apartment threw himself out a window and went through our roof."

"Quite the mess," Hugo said.

"Right. And we've not had permission to get a real wall and roof put in. Partly it's a money thing, but since it's the outside of the building, we need permission from seven different bureaucracies and you know how that goes. So for now we're stuck with cleaning up glass every so often. Paul had the upstairs alarm disconnected because of that and, when we talked about it at the time, he pointed out that anything worth stealing is either in the safe, which no one's moving without a crane, or in the basement."

"That sounds reasonable enough," Hugo said.

"What's going on, Hugo? Will you please level with me?"

"I can't right now, I'm sorry." Hugo thought for a moment. "Do you know Alain Benoît?"

"No, I don't think so. Why, is he suspect number one right now?"

Hugo chuckled. "I'm not at liberty to say. Just, if you run into the guy, and there's no reason why you would, be careful. I'm not accusing him of anything, but . . . enough people have been hurt, I'd prefer folks to be careful."

"Sure," Harmuth said. "Will do."

"Thanks for the help, Michael. I'll come see you on Monday morning; we should have more information to share then. Oh, if we need to go into the library during off-hours, do we have your permission?"

Harmuth hesitated. "Why would you need to do that?"

"I don't know that we would. But if we do, and we don't have permission, it might invalidate any evidence we find."

"I guess so, then. Can't see why not. You need a key?"

"Not right now, but I'll let you know if that changes."

"Okay, sure thing. Let me know how else I can help."

When Hugo hung up, Lerens was on her phone, a serious look on her face. A moment later she disconnected but held the phone in front of her, looking at the screen. "That was my tech guy. They got some footage from the surveillance cam; he's forwarding it to me now."

"Could he tell who it was?"

"No, he doesn't know the players. But you were right, it was a man, and from the description, I think I know which one." She glanced up at Hugo, a mischievous smile on her lips.

"You're gonna make me wait, aren't you?" Hugo said.

"Wouldn't want to make wild accusations and defame someone's good name, now would I?"

"No," Hugo said, resigning himself to wait, "That wouldn't be very nice at all."

CHAPTER NINETEEN

W hen the video came in, Hugo and Camille Lerens hunched
over the screen with Paul Jameson edging in behind to look
over their shoulders. The action began with the opening of the apartment's front door, but for a full minute they could see nothing, just the
vague shapes of furniture in the room. The time stamp in the bottom left
corner told them the break-in happened at around 7:15 that evening, but
even though it was still light outside, the apartment had been shuttered
up after Sarah's death and the August sun was all but blocked out.

Hugo shifted, his eyes glued to the little screen.

"There," Lerens said, and he saw it, too, a figure moving into the
room, nothing more than a silhouette. "Come on, turn on a light," she
muttered.

The figure didn't, just moved carefully between the pieces of furniture, slow and sure.

"If he gets up close, we'll be able to see his face," Hugo said.

And then the figure moved forward, finally coming into view, a tall
and handsome man, eyes darting left and right as if looking for trouble,
finally settling on the camera, a look of surprise on his face turning to
dismay when the penny dropped. He turned his back the moment he
did, but it was too late. The backward walk to mantelpiece and the
shirt pulled over his face were good countermeasures, but they were
too little, too late to save Alain Benoît from being captured by the little
device that cut off a moment after he reached it.

173

Hugo spoke first. "No great shock there."

Jameson cleared his throat gently. "May I ask, who is that?"

"Alain Benoît. Freelance journalist and friend of Paul Rogers and Sarah Gregory. Perhaps especially Sarah Gregory."

"They were having an affair?" Jameson asked. Hugo liked that Lerens didn't shut the uniformed officer down, put him in his place as some senior officers might.

"No direct evidence of that," Hugo admitted.

"We should get over to the library," Lerens said. "He was here almost two hours ago, I doubt he'd wait to let himself in."

"He might if he thinks about the camera," Hugo said. "Better to be busted for one break-in than for two. Maybe none—if he had a key from either Paul or Sarah, he'll be free and clear for letting himself in here."

"I'm not counting on him being that smart."

"One way to find out," Jameson muttered, fishing his car keys from his pocket. "I'll get you right over there."

They rode to the library in silence, Hugo in the back seat behind Jameson. Half a mile away, Lerens had the marked police car withdrawn from the front of the building, an inducement to Benoît if he was lurking nearby. They parked at the western end of Rue de Général Camou, facing east toward the library entrance. The Eiffel Tower glittered behind them, its gray girders sparkling in white lights, a spectacular watchman to keep them company.

Hugo dragged his eyes away from the beautiful structure and looked along the dark street. "I'm worried the police car out front may have scared him off," he said.

"Maybe," Lerens said. "But if he was desperate to take that key, maybe he'll be desperate to get into the library."

"I assume there's an alarm he'll have to turn off or disable?" Jameson said.

"Only in the basement," Hugo said. "Which he might know, as a friend of Paul and Sarah's."

"He may also know about that secret door you told me about, and get in that way," Lerens said.

"Maybe, but then he'd also need a key to access the university building to get down to that door. I think it's a risk, but not much of one."

Lerens shifted in her seat. "The more I think about this . . ."

"What's wrong?" asked Hugo.

"We need to be very careful here. Not to screw up the case, I mean." She turned to look at Hugo. "Say he had a key to Paul's apartment and claims permission to come and go as he pleases. We can't disprove that."

"True. Go on."

"What if he claims, also, he had Paul's permission to go into the library at will? It doesn't need to be true, remember. If he realizes that and we bust down the door after him, take him away in cuffs, then . . ."

"Then he knows we're onto him and will lay low," Hugo finished her thought. "What do you suggest?"

"*Merde*," she muttered. "I think we need to sit tight and see if he goes in. Make it up from there."

Hugo chuckled. "You've been learning investigation techniques from Tom." The thought seemed to hit them at the same time, and a smile spread across both of their faces.

"It might just work," Lerens said.

"I didn't . . ." Jameson began. "I feel like I'm missing something."

"You said you were in naval intelligence, right Paul?"

"Yes, sir."

"You ever come across those guys who did things for you without filling in too many requisition forms, without filing too many after-incident reports?"

"Well, yeah. I mean, not officially, and I couldn't name them, of course, but we all knew they were out there." He grinned. "Somewhere."

"I happen to have one living with me," Hugo said.

"Och, is that right?" Jameson glanced at Lerens, who shook her head.

"I've no idea what he's talking about," she said emphatically. "I've never met anyone like that, don't want to, and wouldn't ever endorse any kind of police activity that didn't result in reams of paperwork and numerous reports."

Hugo pointed to the café two blocks down on their left, its tables spilling out across the sidewalk and lit under an orange canopy. "I bet they have a bathroom in there, if you guys need one."

"I'm fine," said Jameson.

"No, you're not." Lerens opened her car door. "We both need a restroom. Hugo, text me . . . in a while. We may take a break and get coffee while we're there."

"*Bien*," Hugo said, his phone already in hand. "See you guys soon."

"Right," said Jameson, following Lerens out of the car. He handed Hugo the car keys. "Just in case. Sorry for being so dense just now, a piss and some coffee will fix things."

Hugo laughed. "No worries. Enjoy both." When they'd gone, he dialed Tom. "Hey, you sober?"

"As a judge. What's going on?"

Hugo listened hard for slurring in Tom's voice but heard none. "I mean it. Can you help me out with something?"

"Are you with Camille?"

"Kind of."

"Need some black ops, eh?"

"I need you to focus and be serious."

"Seriously, I'm fine. Hanging with Miki and Merlyn, but sober. I promise."

Tom had many issues, Hugo knew, but he was always happy to admit it when he'd been drinking. Or drinking too much. It was like a badge of honor, regardless of what Hugo said.

"OK, then," Hugo said. "Grab an Uber and make your way to the corner of Rue de Monttessuy and Avenue de la Bourdonnais."

"By the Eiffel Tower?"

"It's real pretty tonight, you'll appreciate that. When you get out, walk south along Bourdonnais until you get to me. Black Peugeot."

"Gotcha. What's the job?"

"I'll fill you in when you get here. Oh, if you see Camille and a bald cop in the café as you go by, keep walking. They don't know you and you don't know them."

"Story of my life. See you soon."

Tom opened the passenger door a split-second after Hugo spotted him.

"Impressive," Hugo said.

"Huh? Taking an Uber isn't impressive, there were about fifty of them hovering like flies outside the restaurant."

"No, you sneaking up on me. Didn't know your stealth gene was still operational."

"Oh, I've still got it, you better believe that. By the way, I think I was followed here."

"You *think*? Suddenly I'm less impressed."

"Well, a taxi was behind me from the restaurant, with a driver and someone in the back seat. They slowed when we slowed but drove around the corner when I stopped, so I don't know if whoever it was got out or not."

"Were you follow—"

"Dude, I'm not an idiot," Tom interrupted. "Of course I wasn't followed to this car. Now what are we doing here?"

Hugo filled him in on the new burglary, the identification of Alain Benoît, and Lerens's concern that there may be a technical defense to the man's entry of the apartment and the library.

"We just want to know what he's doing at this point. We have Harmuth's permission to go into the library, so if you can get in without being seen, I'd like for you to just watch."

"Watch?"

"Yeah. I don't know why Benoît took the key, whether it has to do with the Severin papers, the deaths of Paul and Sarah, or something totally different."

"But he's up to something."

"He is. Late-night reshelving perhaps, but we need to know."

"Got it." Tom rolled his eyes. "*If* I can get in unseen. Please."

"Remember, just watch, don't confront. If there's enough light and you can get close, maybe film whatever he's doing. But don't interfere unless he's murdering someone in there."

"The place should be empty, right?"

"Should be. And I'll be out here. Reception inside is a little suspect, nonexistent away from the circulation-desk area, but I'll try to text you if he shows up."

Tom slipped out of the car and made his way along the street to the front door of the library, inset slightly from the street. He knelt and within two minutes was inside, the door swinging gently shut behind him.

His phone buzzed, and Hugo replied to a text from Lerens, saying, "Enjoy your coffee a little longer." Then he put the phone on the armrest beside him and turned his eyes to the quiet street. Night had settled in now, and the few people who used Rue du Général Camou were headed to or from a watering hole, couples or clusters of friends too preoccupied, or tipsy, to pay attention to a man sitting like a statue in his car.

He stayed there for an hour, sending Tom a test message and getting an obscenity in return. Hugo let his eyes wander every time the street was completely empty, knowing that if he stared nonstop at the library entrance, he'd risk nodding off. After an hour of nothing, he gave Lerens and Jameson the go-ahead to come back.

Hugo gave up the driver's seat to Officer Jameson, who handed him a small to-go cup. "Probably cold, but it'll wake you up."

"Thanks," Hugo said. "Never known a Paris café to serve to-go coffee, though."

"They don't to the public—you'll get a nose in the air if you ask. But for cops, they will. They know sometimes we have to take off pretty quickly, or need something to keep us awake and alert while we patrol." Jameson grinned. "Now you know the secret, you're sworn to silence."

"Scout's honor." Hugo returned the smile, then took the lid off the paper cup and tested it with his lip. Still warm, so he knocked it back with one slug. "Just the jolt I needed."

"No action?" Lerens asked, as Hugo let himself into the back seat.

"Not outside or inside," he said, giving her a knowing look.

"*Eh bien.* I suppose that's good." Lerens looked out of the window at a couple who'd stopped to look up at the Eiffel Tower, arms locked together. "You want to take shifts? No point in all three of us spending an uncomfortable night out here."

"I don't think any of us need to," Hugo said. "If he's not here by now, I doubt he's coming."

Lerens looked at her watch. "It's eleven. He may be waiting, wanting to do it later, when there's no one around at all."

"Even if he does," Hugo countered, "unless we catch him in the act or detain him afterward, we likely won't know what he was doing in there."

"Wait, I thought—"

"I said *we* wouldn't know," Hugo went on, hurriedly. "Whether we're sitting out here or not, someone *else* will know exactly what he's up to."

"I see," Lerens said. "Then I suppose we should drive you home. You want to . . . let anyone know that you're leaving? Might be a little rough to just disappear."

"No. A night in a library couldn't possibly do anyone any harm." Hugo smiled. "All those books, all that peace and quiet."

"And maybe a murderer," Lerens cautioned.

"That's the thing about libraries. So full of potential, aren't they? Anything can happen, and does, between those walls."

"Very philosophical, Hugo, but I'm serious," she said. "I don't like leaving someone alone in that situation."

Jameson coughed. "Lieutenant. Why don't you let me stay? I'm working the night shift and I just drank enough coffee to float a battleship."

"You sure?" she asked.

"Aye, absolutely." He looked around and then pointed to a plane tree surrounded by shrubbery. "I even have my own restroom, what more could a man want?"

"Works for me," Lerens nodded.

"How will I know . . . . who to look for? And I don't mean Benoît."

"Ah," Hugo said with a smile. "He'll be the one appearing on the sidewalk at dawn, using some very bad language when he finds out I'm no longer here to hold his hand." Hugo took out his phone. "Give me your cell number." When he had, Hugo flipped through the photo album on his phone, selected a picture, and sent it to the Scotsman. "Do me a favor. When you see him in the morning, be sure to tell him what time I knocked off. Oh, and ask him to be nice and quiet so as not to wake me when he lets himself into the apartment."

"Right," Lerens laughed, "and then call for an ambulance. Hugo's going to need one."

CHAPTER TWENTY

Hugo slept late the next morning, Sunday, later than he meant to. When he rolled out of bed just before nine, he checked his phone and saw a text from Camille Lerens letting him know Benoît hadn't shown up at the library. He also had several texts from Tom saying the same thing, but using different words, and expressing extreme disapproval for being left alone at the library while Hugo went home to a comfortable bed.

He padded through to the living room, surprised Tom hadn't brought the house down to wake him earlier, wondering if his friend had even come home. But Tom's door was closed and Hugo heard the not-so-soft sound of his friend snoring.

Hugo made coffee, as best he was able to, and sat at his desk. He turned on his computer and stared at the home screen. He felt stymied. He didn't know which way to turn and felt like he was letting his friend, Paul Rogers, down.

In the past when he hit a brick wall in an investigation, he'd stepped outside of his immediate suspicions to get perspective, a fresh look. He'd done it many times, to make sure he wasn't missing anything and to keep his mind actively engaged in the case without pressuring himself to come up with the final answer there and then.

So he opened a Google search page, wondering which people, places, or things to start with. He typed *Isabelle Severin* and smiled at the list of a million-plus results. He'd already plowed through many of them in a hunt for the secret Severin collection, but he had found that most just repeated the same stories and rumors. He tried adding keywords like *American Library*, and *dagger*, and *Alain Benoît* but learned nothing new.

He tried Sarah Gregory next and was surprised by how little information there was about her online. Most of it connected her to Paul Rogers, so eventually Hugo found himself reading more about his friend, and his mother, Claire Rogers. Hugo reread the story of Paul's brother and wondered whether he'd been affected during his life by the tragedy of his brother's death. In Hugo's experience, the lack of a body often made it harder for the family to get closure, and there was every chance that Paul had lived his whole life in the shadow of his mother's grief, a sorrow that would never go away as long as there was some slight hope, no matter how ludicrous and far-fetched, that her only biological child would come back home.

She'd be in her new apartment soon enough, and Hugo resolved to visit her, aware that with a second son now lost and living in a strange place, her mind would likely deteriorate even more quickly than before.

Hugo shook off the sadness he felt for the old woman and tried to find out what he could about Michelle Juneau. She'd been secretive about her connection to Isabelle Severin, but Hugo couldn't see any reason why she'd want to hurt Paul or Sarah.

After an hour, Hugo decided to clear his mind completely, stretching out on the couch with a copy of *Stone Cold Dead*, a murder mystery by James Ziskin. It was the third in the series, and Hugo enjoyed the 1960s setting and the tough protagonist, a female reporter called Ellie Stone who reminded him more than a little of Claudia. His mind drifted into the pages, his own mystery disappearing into the distance, and the stress washed out of his lower back and shoulders as he settled deeper into the couch, soaking up Ziskin's persuasive portrayal of upstate New York in an era before cell phones and the Internet.

His peaceful world was interrupted at noon, when Camille Lerens called. "You don't mind me bothering you on a Sunday, do you?"

"Why should I?" Hugo replied. "I let you bother me on a Saturday."

"*C'est vrai,*" she said. *That's true.* "I did a little digging into Alain Benoît, but the guy seems clean. No criminal history, just your average barely known freelance writer."

"Yeah, I didn't find much on him either."

"I did put someone outside his apartment, though. Just to keep track of when he comes and goes, and who with."

"Good idea." A thought struck Hugo. "Does he have a girlfriend?"

"Not that I know of. And I don't want to spook him by asking too many questions of his neighbors."

"That's smart."

"So how's Tom today?"

"Haven't seen him yet. Speaking of odd, he didn't throw things at me when he got in this morning."

"Too tired, maybe. He said he'd stayed awake the whole night."

"I'll give him a pat on the back when he wakes up," Hugo said. "What's your plan today?"

"I'm going to take a few hours off, actually. I'll stay available in case something happens with Benoît, but otherwise I plan to sit in the bath and watch some football."

"You have a television in your bathroom?"

"I have one in every room."

"You sure you're not an American?"

Lerens laughed. "Fairly certain. You guys allow transgender cops over there?"

"I would hope so," Hugo said.

"Come over and watch the game if you like," she said. "I'll even get out of the bath for you."

Hugo looked at his screen as his phone buzzed. Merlyn was trying to call him. "I'll leave you to soak in peace. Call me if something happens."

"Will do."

Hugo clicked over to the incoming call. "Merlyn, what's up?"

"Miki's being a bore. Can we grab lunch?"

"Sure. Just you and me?"

"Yes. Her new boyfriend called her early this morning and she ran out to see him. Wouldn't let me tag along."

"So are you guys an item or not?" Hugo asked.

"I told you, it's complicated. I don't have an issue with her dating him, if that's what you're wondering. She just doesn't need to be weird about it."

"Meet me at Café Laruns in ninety minutes, we can talk about it."

"Deal. Thanks, Hugo."

Café Laruns sat on the crease of the Sixth and Seventh Arrondissments, a place where most of the patrons were French, or at least lived locally. Hugo put the lack of tourists down to the location, the café being between two magnetic fields on either side: the fancy stores and cafés of the Saint-Germain area to the east and, on the west side, the museum of Les Invalides and, a little further along, the Eiffel Tower itself.

As he took a table outside, he heard nothing but French being spoken, which always pleased him. The price of a cup of coffee dropped here, too, a couple of euros lower than at the cafés closer to the tourist sites, and that pleased him more. All around him, conversation swirled as families, couples, and friends settled in to order their coffees and carafes of wine, their omelets and steak-frites, waiters sliding between crowded tables like matadors as they delivered baskets of bread and little plates of olives to whet the appetite.

Hugo looked inside, past the crowd of heads to the more-peaceful interior of the bistro. Two old men, each alone at his own table, ate peacefully by themselves. One picked up fries with delicate fingers as the other spooned an ice cream sundae into his mouth, both protected and seemingly immune from the surge and retreat of customers around them. Hugo wondered how long they'd been coming here, whether it was months or years. Did they know each other, even a little bit? But Parisians, in Hugo's experience, didn't do nodding acquaintances. Either you shook hands and talked for a moment or you passed each other by, familiarity and proximity be damned.

Merlyn arrived late, and flustered. "I'm beginning to wonder why Miki wanted me to come with her," she said.

"What now?"

"Oh, nothing," Merlyn said, taking a deep breath. "I've barely seen her, is all."

"What time did she head out this morning?"

"No clue, she left me a note. Before I woke up, that's for sure."

Hugo grinned. "How romantic, a new love in Paris."

She stared at him for a moment, then couldn't stop herself from smiling. "Whatever. But she's supposed to be here for that book, the Severin stuff, not chasing Parisians around town."

"True, seems like she's not that into the Severin story if she's so quick to be distracted by a guy. Is she actually doing any writing?"

"Not that I can tell. Perhaps that's not fair. She was gone all yesterday, maybe she was writing and maybe not, I don't know. I know she went to a café to do some writing after dinner, too. So yeah, I'm not being entirely charitable."

"But no breakthrough on the secret papers?"

"I don't think so. She seems excited still, so she must have something in mind. She's always been a little secretive, like she is with this new man, so I'm not surprised she hasn't said anything."

"Have you met him?"

"No, and that's a little weird."

"Afraid you'll steal him?"

"No clue. Maybe you can ask her for me. Anyway, enough about her." She picked up a menu and studied it for a minute. "Do all these cafés serve the same thing? This menu looks like all the others."

"Pretty much. The difference is usually in the food itself, not the menu. If you want something specific they don't have, let me know. We can go elsewhere."

"No, it's fine. Do they do veggie burgers?"

"God, I hope not."

She stuck her tongue out at him. "Fine, I'll get the grilled salmon."

"Fish, eh?"

"It's good for the brain. Apparently the oils are absorbed by the brain and . . ." She waved a hand. "And something or other."

"So," Hugo began. "Moving on from Miki Harrison and her mysterious paramour, let's talk about you. Which direction is your life headed?"

"Straight forward, with very little looking back."

"Sounds fun."

"I quit working at the hotel," Merlyn said. "Doing a lot of freelance genealogy work still, which I enjoy."

"So much for not looking back."

"Ha! I meant in my life. I travel as much as I can, see old friends when I can." She gave him a smile. "I'm happy. I don't put great expectations on other people, so I'm rarely disappointed."

"Seems like you're looking at people wrong, then. That's a glass-half-empty approach."

"I'm not looking at it wrong. Life is a beautiful glass, whether it's full or not."

"I like the sound of that." Hugo looked down as his phone rang. It was Lieutenant Lerens, so he answered it and said, "Camille. I need to get my own ringtone for you."

"Where are you?"

"Brunch with a friend."

"Can you get away?" she asked.

"If you give me a good-enough reason."

"I can try. Some Russian tourists just pulled Alain Benoît out of the River Seine," Lerens said. "That good enough?"

CHAPTER TWENTY-ONE

Hugo met Lieutenant Lerens in front of the hospital Hôtel-Dieu on the Ile de la Cité, one of those imposing buildings that millions of tourists walk right by as they take in the more famous, and even more beautiful, cathedral of Notre-Dame alongside it, to its east.

The hospital, like many nineteenth-century hospitals, was essentially a rectangle with a central courtyard, its sides connected by colonnaded walkways. Hugo had been here before and he couldn't quite decide whether the chill the hospital gave him was the nature of the place, or something else.

Whatever it was, he was glad of Lerens's company, and that she already knew the way. He followed her down a long corridor and up two flights of elegant stairs to a nurse's station where a uniformed officer stood talking to a pair of nurses. When the *flic* saw Lerens, he snapped to attention and all but moonwalked back to his station, the closed doorway to a single room.

"No one's come by here," the officer said defensively.

"Thank you," said Lerens, giving the man a less-than-appreciative look.

"I don't understand," Hugo said. "Why his body is up here and not at the morgue?"

Lerens looked at him with a puzzled expression. The she said, "Oh, I'm sorry, Hugo, I just assumed. . . . I'm an idiot. So, he was pulled from the river dead, but he was revived. Well, sort of, he was unconscious and not breathing but one of the Russians was a paramedic and somehow got his heart started."

"Do you know what happened to him?" Hugo asked.

"I don't have any details. As soon as I heard about him being found, though, I sent some officers to try and find witnesses. So far, no luck."

"Did he jump from one of the bridges?"

"We don't know that."

"Nor how long he was in the water?"

"*Non.* We really don't know anything yet, Hugo. He may not even make it."

Hugo drew her down the hallway, out of earshot of the policeman and nurses. "So tell me what you're really thinking."

"I can't decide, to be honest," Lerens replied. "On the one hand, it makes perfect sense that he'd jump. If he killed Paul Rogers and Sarah Gregory, I can see him committing suicide."

"And his motive?"

"He wanted Sarah for himself, but after he killed Paul she rejected him. Either she killed herself out of despair and he followed suit, or he killed her and then himself out of guilt. Either one could be plucked from the police textbook."

"Could be. But you're not convinced."

"I'm not. We have no actual evidence of any affair, or that he was even in love with Sarah. We're just speculating, and I don't close cases based on speculation. Plus, the manner of Paul's death. I mean, poison isn't the first weapon to come to mind when you want to kill off a love rival." She paused, then added, "Unless you're a woman."

"I wouldn't know," Hugo said with a smile.

"That's reassuring." Lerens returned the smile. "I'll let Claudia know. But seriously, if it's him, how did he do it? Rogers was the one running searches on curare. We basically agree it was impossible for anyone to administer the poison to him, thanks to those security cameras."

"There's another possibility, you know. What if Benoît and Sarah were having an affair, and Paul found out. Maybe he confronted Benoît, who refused to back off. Unable to end the affair, and unwilling to leave

Sarah, Paul committed suicide in an unlikely way. Using curare. In other words, he killed himself figuring that we'd look into his death and maybe would blame Alain Benoît. A few days later, Sarah realizes what happened and kills herself out of remorse, or perhaps she rejects Benoît and he loses his mind and kills her, too. Not able to face what he's done, and knowing he's a suspect, Benoît takes a dive into the Seine."

"Paul Rogers getting revenge from beyond the grave, eh?" Lerens said. "I don't know, maybe."

"Seems a little far-fetched, I agree, but it makes some sense."

"But it doesn't explain why Benoît would take Paul's keys, the keys to the library. If, in fact, he did. We still don't know for sure."

"I'm pretty sure he did, but you're right, we still don't know why exactly he would take the keys," Hugo said. "But I think he took them for a reason, and if he knew he was going to commit suicide, seems to me he'd likely execute whatever plan he had in mind before killing himself. He wouldn't care about the consequences at that point."

"Everything takes us back to the library, doesn't it?" Lerens said. "I think it's time to find out once and for all whether there's more to this Severin collection than we know. Figure out if there really is a secret being protected by people there."

"And being ferreted out by someone else. What's your plan?"

"You know the people down there better. Who do you think I should I talk to?"

Hugo thought for a moment. "If it were me, I'd bring in Michelle Juneau in for a few questions. She's pretty tough, but I'm betting she's a lot tougher behind her desk at the library than she is in a police interview room. Start with her."

Hugo stood with Officer Paul Jameson, looking through the one-way glass at an irritated Michelle Juneau, who sat fidgeting with her purse and phone. Hugo didn't know whether she was irritated at being there or at being kept waiting.

"You brought her in?" Hugo asked Jameson. "Weren't you up all night?"

"Had a few hours' kip, I don't need much more than that. And this case fascinates me."

"Me, too," Hugo said.

Jameson gestured to Juneau. "And yes, I brought her here. She wasn't happy at first, but then I told her I'd be happy to come by her place of work tomorrow and be a little more persuasive. She preferred the idea of a Sunday-afternoon chat over a Monday-morning embarrassment."

"Nice work. She say anything on the way over?"

"Just asked what it was all about, so I played dumb. Not hard, under the circumstances."

"Yeah," Hugo said. "It's not much more than a fishing expedition at this stage." He fell silent as Camille Lerens let herself into the interrogation room. She glanced at the one-way glass, as if checking Hugo was in place. She spoke to Juneau in French, and her voice came through to the observation room as tinny and metallic, but loud enough and clear enough.

"Madame Juneau, I am Lieutenant Camille Lerens." She didn't shake hands, just sat down opposite Juneau and put a file folder between them. "This is probably obvious, but I wanted to point out the cameras that will record everything, sound and sight, that goes on in this room. We do this to preserve our conversation and to ensure there are no questions about what was said today. Is that all right with you?"

"*Oui*, I understand."

"Good." She flipped open the folder and picked up a photo. Hugo leaned to one side, then saw that it was a picture of Alain Benoît. "Do you recognize this man?"

"No, I don't think so."

"Look closely, please, it's important."

Juneau reached out and took the photo, studying it. "Maybe I have seen him. At the library, I think. I don't remember names, though." She passed the photograph back. "Who is he?"

"A friend of Paul Rogers and Sarah Gregory. You knew Sarah, yes?"

"A little. She'd come by the library sometimes, informally to see Paul and also when we had events. I didn't know her socially, though, if that's what you were wondering."

"You told Hugo Marston about an incident at the library when you heard someone in the basement with Monsieur Rogers."

"Yes."

"Can you repeat that story for me, please?"

Juneau nodded. "Of course." She seemed to gather herself, then started on the account of that night, repeating the story she'd told Hugo. He listened carefully for variations, omissions, or additions, but other than the occasional word choice, the story remained the same. When she'd finished, Lerens sat quietly for a moment.

"You know about the secret door, right?" she asked.

"In the basement?" Juneau smiled. "It's not so much secret as, well, we're not supposed to use it. It's totally off-limits."

"The person you think you heard. Could he or she have used that door to get away?"

"I suppose so, yes. If they had a key."

"Rogers could have given them one, right?"

"Yes, true."

"If you go through the door and into the university library, where can you exit? Which street or streets?"

"I don't know. Honestly, I've never used the door and I don't know anything about the building it leads into."

"*Bon.*" Lerens shifted gears seamlessly. "Tell me how you got your job."

"I applied." She shrugged. "How else do people get jobs?"

"I see." Lerens kept her tone light.

"You think I was gifted the job because of the Severin collection?"

"I don't know, that's why I'm asking."

"Look," Juneau said. She leaned forward. "I applied for the job. When I interviewed, I told them it was possible I could talk to Isabelle about getting her papers housed there. I made no promises, nor did anyone else. So if you're asking whether there was a quid pro quo, there wasn't from my end, so you'd have to ask . . ." Her voice trailed off.

"Paul Rogers? Except we can't very well do that, can we?"

"No, I'm sorry. I'm just trying to tell you that I got that job the same way anyone gets a job."

"I've no doubt you're very qualified." Lerens gave her a warm smile. "So the next thing I'm wondering about is the same thing everyone has asked you."

"Ah, of course," Juneau said. She leaned back in her chair, as if suddenly relaxed and in control. "The secret papers of Isabelle Severin."

"And the dagger," Lerens said playfully.

A smile spread over Juneau's face. "You're right, several people have asked me about her so-called secret papers and the dagger. Well, I can tell you one thing about that dagger. And one thing about the story that goes with it."

"Please do."

"First, the story, the legend. All I can say is that somewhere in the depths of her mind there is a true story, but it's one that has grown in the public, on the Internet, and I couldn't tell you what's true and what's not. No, I don't know what the truth of that is anymore. But the dagger itself, that's very real indeed."

CHAPTER TWENTY-TWO

The moment he heard those words, Hugo felt a need to be in the interview room, if not asking questions then able to look Michelle Juneau in the eyes as she answered those posed by Lieutenant Lerens. He pulled out his phone and texted her, willing his friend to notice the message. She did, and she seemed to study the words longer than necessary.

Say yes, Hugo thought.

Lerens put the phone slowly back in her pocket, turned to the one-way window, and nodded. Hugo didn't hesitate, leaving being a startled Officer Jameson as he strode out and pushed his way into the interview room.

"*Bonjour* Michelle," he said. Lerens announced his arrival for the record, and he jumped right in. "Two Americans are dead and the police aren't entirely sure what happened, so I'm just helping out where I can."

"*Dites-donc.* I thought our talk at the library was . . . informal, if not private."

"It was," Hugo said. "But at this point we need a few things on the record. Like, for example, the dagger. Does Isabelle Severin use it as a letter opener, by any chance?"

"*Oui, mon dieu*, she does." Juneau smiled. "How did you know that?"

"I paid her a visit," Hugo said. "It was right there in plain sight. A little smaller than I'd imagined, but it sure looked like a dagger."

"And what better place to hide it?" Juneau said. "When I first realized, I told her she was crazy. That she'd lose it or someone would recognize it and steal it. She wouldn't confirm any of the rumors about its meaning, but she did ask me how many times I'd seen it and not known, how many times I'd been in the same room and had no idea. So, like you said, hidden in plain sight."

"Except someone else realized, and took it."

The smile fell from her face. "What?"

"Someone went to her house and stole it," Lerens chimed in. "Do you know who might have done that?"

Good cop, bad cop? Hugo wondered.

"No," Juneau protested. "I haven't seen her in weeks. Check the sign-in log, the appointments register where she lives, that'll tell you."

Lerens threw Hugo a look. "Yeah, well, it seems that not everyone signs in when they pay her a visit."

"They're supposed to, I always do. Check and see."

"We will," Lerens said. Her phone buzzed again and she took it out and looked at the display. "I need to step out for a moment. So as not to waste more of Mademoiselle Juneau's time, Hugo, feel free to ask her any questions you may have."

Hugo nodded and watched as Lerens let herself out of the interview room. Then he turned to Juneau and spoke in English. "So the dagger is real—what about the secret stash of papers?"

Juneau looked at the recorder. "Should we speak in French?"

"Your English is better than my French, and I'm sure they can translate it if they need to. It's not like you're a suspect, as far as I know."

She gave a tight smile. "That's a relief."

"It's true. You were saying, about the secret papers not part of the main collection."

"Ah. That's less straightforward," Juneau said.

"Try."

"In a word, yes."

"What are they?"

"I don't know. Not exactly."

"Explain what you mean by that."

"When we were packing up her papers to send to the library," Juneau began. "After I got hired, this is. Isabelle and I went through most of her stuff and I created kind of a list. A manifest, whatever you want to call it. That way, the library would know what they were getting and could plan for where they put it all."

"Where's that manifest now?"

"I don't know. Paul had it, I suppose Michael does now. Maybe in the big safe?"

"OK, go on."

"So we had all this stuff piled up in Isabelle's living room and the spare bedroom, trying to keep it in order. I used her desk to create the manifest, on my computer. But right when we were done she came out of her bedroom with a metal box. Say, twice the size of a shoe box. It was heavy, too. She put it with the other things but asked me to keep it locked away, preferably somewhere at the library or at my apartment. I didn't know the library had such a large safe, but that was perfect, and Paul let me put it in there behind some other stuff, books and papers that I didn't really look at."

"What was in the box?"

"That's what I'm trying to tell you, I don't know. It was locked and she didn't give me the key."

"Did you have any instructions? I mean, it doesn't make sense to give you a box and no key, and just say nothing."

"I was getting to that. She told me to keep the box until she was gone, passed away. Then I could open it and add it to the rest of the collection. She made me promise not to sell it, to profit from it in any way, which I'd never do. She was so good to me, there's no way I'd betray her trust and do something like that. Just no way."

"And the key?"

"She must have kept it."

"So how are you supposed to open it when she dies?"

"I assumed she'd leave it to me in her will."

Hugo shook his head. "I don't know. It just seems like, if she trusts you with this Pandora's box, she'd trust you with the key."

"I won't lie, I did wonder about that, but I never asked. I mean, how could I?"

"Do you have a theory?"

"Actually, I do. She could have kept the box with her, taken it to her new home and left that to me in her will. So I think that it's not so much her trusting *me* with the box, as her *not* trusting other people. In other words, because she was moving to a new place and would be surrounded by strangers, she felt like she didn't have much of a choice. And she knew she was getting dementia, or at least going a little senile. I'm sure she'd have preferred to keep that hidden from me and everyone else, but she didn't trust herself, or the place she was moving to. I mean, think about it. A famous person moves in with a mini treasure chest, you can see how she'd worry about someone taking it, taking advantage of her situation."

"That makes sense, I guess."

"Also, she doesn't have family here but she does in America, distant family. What if they contested the will and the box ended up in the hands of some far-off cousin only interested in making money from her past? Much safer to let me have the box and only risk losing the key."

"Very true. But that doesn't explain why she wouldn't just give you the key," Hugo said.

Her face softened and she smiled. "You've not dealt with many old people, have you?"

"No, but I think I'm beginning to see what you mean. She wanted to hang on to her most precious possessions as best she could, keep just a little bit of her past in her control."

"Exactly. These possessions, whatever's in there, must be some of the most private and meaningful things she's owned. It makes sense to me that she'd want to at least seem like she has some control over them."

Hugo nodded. "Do you have any sense of what's in the box?" he asked. "Not specifically, but whether they confirm the old stories about her."

"Are you asking for the investigation, or out of curiosity?"

"Both, I guess."

"Then no, I don't know. I won't until I open that box and give its contents to the library."

Hugo smiled. "Somehow I don't believe you. But that's OK."

They both looked up as Camille Lerens reentered the interview room. "All done?" she asked.

"Yes," Hugo said. "Do you have any more questions?"

"Probably, but we have someone else to focus on right now."

"Who's that?" Hugo asked.

"Come with me." She led Hugo out of the room and closed the door so Juneau couldn't hear. "I'm talking about Alain Benoît. More specifically, whoever murdered him."

The morgue smelled like every other one Hugo had been to, from Barcelona to London to Wichita, Kansas. That hollow smell of disinfectant and bleach overlaid by something cloying. In this case, pine scent, as if a man-made odor would let the people who worked there imagine they were somewhere a little less grim.

Hugo and Lerens were shown into Doctor Sprengelmeyer's office at nine the next morning, and the doctor got straight to business.

"Please, sit down," Sprengelmeyer said. "So, your friend Monsieur Benoît is dead, and while it's not my job to say, I would not rule out murder."

"Why do you say that?" Lerens asked.

"Because he spent some time upstairs before coming to see me, and we know he wasn't in the water that long." He held up a hand to silence Lerens's next question. "He did have water in his lungs, and that's what killed him, he drowned. But he also had a bruise on the back of his head that was not caused by the water."

"He could have bumped into something, a boat or the concrete banks of the river," Hugo suggested.

"Possibly, but two things make me think not. First, I drove alongside the river where he likely would have floated, and the water is moving very slowly right now. I don't think it would have propelled him with the force necessary. And, as I said, he wasn't in there that long." He opened a folder in front of him and turned a photograph so Hugo and Lerens could see for themselves the bruise he was talking about. "But more importantly, you'll see that the bruise is over the occipital bone, a little above the superior nuchal line."

He paused, and Lerens prodded him. "And that means?"

"It means," Hugo interjected, "that most people float facedown or face-up, not in a way that he'd get a bruise right there, even if he did bang into something."

"Correct," said Sprengelmeyer. "If he was facedown, how did he get a bruise there? Same question if he was face-up."

"Someone hit him and dropped him in the river," Lerens said. "Anything else suggest to you that this was murder?"

"That's your job," Sprengelmeyer said. "But I did check for curare, just in case. His system was clean, of everything."

"Can we see his belongings?" Hugo asked.

"Of course, come with me." Sprengelmeyer got up from his desk and led them into the autopsy room, pushing through double-swinging doors that whooshed shut behind them. Hugo looked around as Sprengelmeyer went to some metal lockers to their right and worked on a padlock, twisting the combination and muttering as he got it wrong. This room smelled even more of disinfectant, and Hugo's eye was drawn to the three autopsy tables that took up the center of the large, white space.

He'd watched a hundred autopsies in his time at the FBI, maybe more, but somehow the three empty metal tables, shallow and clean, were as portentous and disturbing as the ones he'd seen bearing bodies. It was as if they were lying in wait for their next victims, as ominous and patient as three open graves. He suppressed a shiver and was glad of something to do when Dr. Sprengelmeyer handed him a large paper bag.

"That's everything," he said.

"Hang on." Lerens took a pen from her breast pocket, and Hugo held the bag still as she signed the custody sheet taped to it. She looked around, and Hugo felt like she was avoiding the autopsy tables, but they were the best place to do their work, and she eventually gestured for him to put the bag on the closest one. Hugo did so, but not before making sure the table was as clean and dry as it looked.

The bag was stapled shut, and Lerens pried the large staples open with the tip of a pocket knife. She fished inside and pulled out individual plastic evidence bags. The morgue staff had packaged each item of clothing separately, and Hugo inspected each one in its bag, looking for one thing in particular, but not finding it.

"You see what's missing?" he asked Lerens.

"Tell me."

"Paul's keys, the keys to the library," he said. "If we're still assuming he took them."

"I think we are. They could have fallen out of his pocket when he was in the water," she said.

"True." Hugo picked up a small bag that contained what he thought at first was Benoît's wallet.

"For his phone," said Sprengelmeyer. The case was rectangular and made of soft leather, now heavy with water, and a zipper ran along the top of it.

"The phone wasn't inside?" Hugo asked.

"No. We didn't find it, anyway."

"Interesting," Hugo said, as much to himself as his companions.

"I'll have someone check with the hospital staff upstairs, see if anyone messed with it," Lerens said. "It was attached to his belt?"

"Yes," said Sprengelmeyer, "I took it off myself and bagged it after they sent his things down."

"I'm taking it as an indicator that you're right about murder, for now anyway," Hugo said. He looked at Lerens. "And if we're right about that, it seems like we may need to find a brand-new suspect in the deaths of Paul Rogers and Sarah Gregory."

CHAPTER TWENTY-THREE

"Revenge?" Tom wondered aloud.

He and Hugo were in their apartment, Hugo had come home to shower the smell of the morgue from his skin. He stood by the window and looked down at Rue Jacob as an early-afternoon rainstorm pounded the street and soaked the few pedestrians brave enough to venture outside.

"You mean, he killed Paul and Sarah, and someone killed him in revenge?" Hugo said, absentmindedly. "I guess it's possible. Maybe."

"Fine, a stupid idea. So what's your solution?"

"I don't have one." Beneath him, a mother and daughter scurried hand in hand along the sidewalk, both trying to stay under an umbrella that was just a fraction too small. *No one tests umbrellas for size*, he thought. *But if you're sharing one . . .*

"Stop moping, will you?" Tom snapped.

"I'm not. I'm letting my mind wander, it's not the same thing."

"It puts me on edge. An unfocused Hugo is . . . weird. You wanna go out and drink, get even more unfocused?"

"It's raining."

"Yeah, see, I was thinking we'd go somewhere with a roof. Wacky new invention the French have nowadays. Chez Maman? Not been there in an age."

"No, thanks." The last thing Hugo felt like was the cramped confines of the hole-in-the-wall bar, sitting on a hard wooden chair under the curious eyes of its owner and customers. Sometimes the ancient tavern had its own charm, but sometimes it just seemed downright depressing.

"Come on, man. It's Monday and it's raining, two things I fucking hate, so can we get some action going?"

"The Severin collection," Hugo began. "I wonder—"

"Dude, if that's the key, just get a damn search warrant, open up the box, and see if it contains the secret to all this crap."

"Lerens and I already talked about it, and we called a magistrate about two hours ago. No go, we simply don't have any factual basis for one. Isabelle Severin isn't talking, and so no warrant." He shook his head in frustration.

"How do you know the old lady isn't talking? I mean, I know she's been all secretive so far, but if you tell her that her little box has something to do with a murder case, maybe she will."

"You're still a step behind our good friend Camille. She sent the local police to talk to her after our chat with Michelle Juneau drew a blank yesterday. Apparently the sweet old lady gave them an enigmatic smile and little else."

"Why isn't there enough for a warrant?"

"The magistrate said so. As she explained it, to get a search warrant you have to be looking for something specific, and have a good reason to be doing so. The best we can say right now is, 'We're looking for clues from the past to help us out with what we're pretty sure are murders, but we don't really know what we might find or how it might help us.' Not really good enough."

Tom snorted. "Well, no shit, when you put it like that."

"The magistrate did. That box is the old lady's property and we have no evidence it's connected to a crime, so unless we get the old lady's permission it stays closed."

"Well, that's just great."

Their musings were interrupted when Tom's phone went off. He dug it out of his pocket. "Hello? Oh, hey. Really, why?" He listened for a moment, then spoke to Hugo. "Our new girlfriends are leaving town."

"Today?"

"First thing tomorrow." He pointed at the phone. "This is yours. Merlyn."

"Is something wrong? Why didn't she call me?"

"She says she did, but you didn't answer."

Hugo patted his pockets. "Oh, my phone's charging in my room. Tell her to come by."

Tom relayed the message, listened, and then disconnected. "Miki is stopping by the library to drop something off before it closes for the day, then they'll be here. She said to order pizza."

"Pizza? We're in Paris."

"So the pizza should be good," Tom said. "Fuck it, I'll order one myself. Extra garlic for you. Oh, but I don't have any cash and I don't want to run out to the ATM in this weather."

"Like you would anyway. Pizza joints accept credit cards, you know."

"For the tip," Tom said. "I'll let you get that, and maybe I *will* pay for the pizzas, just to show you."

"First time for everything, they say." Hugo turned back to the window. The rain had lightened a little, encouraging a few more people out into the open. "Why would . . . ?"

"'Why would' what?"

"Nothing. ATM, you said."

"Hugo, you're being weird, please stop it."

"I wonder . . ." Hugo strode into his room and picked up his phone. He opened the map application and typed in the address of the library, zooming in when it came up. Using the library as a focal point, he searched the neighboring streets until he found what he was looking for. He dialed Camille Lerens. "There's a bank on the street behind the library. Facing the American University."

"OK, go on."

"Can you send someone over there to see if it has an ATM out front, and if so to pull the security footage from it the night we staked out the library?"

"Sure. What are you expecting to see?"

"I think Benoît was headed there that night, but someone called him off. Not just called him off, but came and picked him up. That's why we never saw him."

"And you think whoever picked him up might be on that footage."

"Yes, I do."

"It's worth a shot, although that kind of tape can be pretty grainy if it's at any distance. We may be able to see the person but not be able to tell who it is."

"That's OK," said Hugo. "I just need the tape to confirm my suspicions."

"What do you mean?"

Hugo paused for effect and flashed a smile at Tom, who stood in the doorway, watching intently. "I mean, Camille, that I already know who it is."

The pizza was good, and probably because Tom had requested extra garlic on it. On them. He'd ordered three, a vegetarian one for Merlyn and Miki, a meat-laden one to share with Hugo, and an extra one for his breakfast the next day.

"Indian food still big in England?" Hugo asked as they gathered around the coffee table. He'd put Band of Horses on his iPod, their *Mirage Rock* album playing gently in the background.

"Always," Merlyn said. "Like pizza, it'll never disappear." She took a bite. "Napkin please," she said to Tom, who handed her one.

"Don't wipe your fingers on my couch," Hugo said.

"You're safe." Merlyn studied her fingertips, then the crust of her pizza on its plate. "How is it that pizza crust looks totally dry, but it's impossible to eat it without getting grease on your fingers?"

"Great philosophical question," Tom said, pouring red wine for everyone. "I imagine it's the same reason that a mosquito always flies past your ear before biting your ankle."

"What the heck are you people talking about?" Hugo asked. But his eyes were on Miki Harrison, who'd said virtually nothing since coming in. She picked at her pizza, took tiny bites, and chewing seemed like a conscious effort.

"The great questions of our time," Merlyn said.

"I have one," Hugo said. Something in his tone of voice had all three looking at him. "Why are you heading back so suddenly?"

"It's not sudden," Miki said, with a sharpness to her voice that she noticed herself. She looked down and softened her tone. "At least, not really. And we're just across the Channel, we can be back in a couple of hours if we need to be."

"Well, I'm sorry, but you can't leave," Hugo said. "Not just yet."

"Aww, that's sweet, Hugo, you'll miss us?" Merlyn batted her eyelashes at him playfully.

"Actually, I'm serious."

Tom rubbed his hands together with glee. "Here it comes."

"Here what comes?" Merlyn looked back and forth between them all, her eyes lingering on Miki, who stared down at her barely touched food. "Hugo, what's going on?"

"That was my question for Miki," Hugo said.

She looked up slowly. "What are you talking about?"

"I'm talking about the reason you're leaving Paris in such a hurry."

"I told you, I'm not, we're just—"

"You're scared," Hugo said. She said nothing, just looked at him, so he went on. "And I don't blame you for that, but you can't leave. For one thing, running away never solved anything, and for another you're now a witness."

"A witness to what?" Merlyn said. "Hugo, stop messing with us."

"I'm not. Something you said to Tom on the phone today made me wonder, set me to thinking. You said Miki had to drop something off at the library."

"So what?" Merlyn said.

"I'll let you tell her," Hugo said to Miki, but she got up and went to the window. "Fine, I'll do it myself. Miki's writing about Isabelle

Severin, using her collection as source material. Which made me wonder what exactly was Miki dropping off." Hugo silenced Merlyn with a gesture. "Would I be right if I said you have no idea?"

"I mean, a book," Merlyn said. "I assume a book."

"Except all the books about Isabelle Severin are now part of the collection, none of which can be checked out."

"Oh, I didn't know that," Merlyn said.

"So what was she dropping off?" Tom asked. "Or wasn't she?"

"She was. Right Miki?" Hugo said. Miki flashed them a look over her shoulder, then went back to staring out of the window. "She was dropping off some keys. A set of keys that belonged to Paul Rogers, to be more precise. I'm guessing she dropped them somewhere in the stacks, or maybe the conference room. Somewhere they'd be found pretty easily."

"Why would she have Paul Rogers's keys?" Merlyn asked.

"And how?" Tom chipped in. "You thought Alain Benoît stole them."

"So he did," Hugo said. "And I'm an idiot for not putting this together sooner."

"For fuck's sake, man, spit it out," Tom said.

"Yeah, what the hell's going on, Hugo?" Merlyn asked.

"Miki's scared because her partner, Alain Benoît, was killed. He and Miki had started collaborating on the Severin stuff. I don't know if they were planning on writing a book together or what, but they were working together to figure out whether the legends about her were true. Right, Miki?"

At the window, she gave an almost-imperceptible nod and her voice was a whisper. "How did you know?"

CHAPTER TWENTY-FOUR

Hugo stood and went to Miki Harrison, guiding her to a chair beside the couch. When she sat, she had tears in her eyes.

"Holy cow," Merlyn said quietly, "that guy Benoît was your boyfriend."

Miki laughed quietly. "Not my boyfriend, but I was interested." She looked at Merlyn, Tom, and then Hugo. "He's gay, you know. So yeah, that was going nowhere."

"You're sure he's gay?" Hugo asked.

"Yes, I heard him talking on the phone with his boyfriend."

So, Hugo thought, *he wasn't having an affair with Sarah Gregory.* "How did you meet him?" Hugo asked.

"Online, while I was in England doing initial research into Severin. Then we connected here." She looked at Hugo. "How did you know?" she asked.

"I didn't, to be honest. But it was the only thing that made any sense."

"How so?" Miki pressed.

"Once we assumed it was Benoît who took Paul's keys, the only reason I could think of was an interest in the Severin collection. He was obviously planning to sneak into the library and get into the safe to see what he could see. We couldn't figure out why he didn't show up at the library, but it dawned on me that someone had called him off, and probably gone over there to pick him up."

"But how did you know that person was Miki?" Merlyn asked.

"The first connection was the interest in the Severin collection, of course," he said. He turned to Miki. "And you mentioned something that didn't click with me initially, while we were at Deux Magots," Hugo said. "You told us you knew someone who once had access to the Severin collection, but no longer does. That describes Benoît. He was a friend to Paul and, of course, is also a journalist."

"That's right," Miki nodded.

"Tom said he was followed that night. But he came straight from the restaurant after talking to me. Whoever followed him had to have done so from there."

"Yes," she said sheepishly. "There were several taxis right outside."

"I'm sure, at a tourist spot like that." Hugo held up a finger to stop Merlyn from interrupting. "Last of all, since you'd not said anything about being in competition with Benoît, which I think you would have if you were up against each other, I could only conclude that you were working together."

Miki nodded. "You're right, but that's not all."

"What do you mean?" Hugo sat back on the couch as a light came on in his head. "Wait, I've been assuming you sought out his help, as a local, as a journalist, and as a friend of the man in charge of the collection. But that's not right is it?"

"No," Miki said. "It's not."

"He was the one in the basement. The one Michelle Juneau heard that night."

"I don't know what you mean."

"The point is," Hugo continued, "he was working with Paul, wasn't he?"

"I don't get it," Merlyn said. "Paul Rogers and Benoît were working on what?"

"I think," Hugo said slowly, the cogs starting to spin in his mind, "that Paul was taking advantage of his position. Using his access to the Severin papers to provide information to Alain Benoît."

"He was," Miki said. "It's not as bad as it sounds, though. I mean not as sneaky."

"Looks pretty fucking sneaky from where I'm sitting," Tom said.

"No," Miki insisted. "They were going to honor Isabelle Severin's wishes to keep it all secret until after her death. But Paul said that they needed to have a book ready to go when she died. I mean, when that happens there's going to be a ton of interest and just imagine, imagine a tell-all book revealing new and amazing secrets from her days in the war."

"Instant bestseller," Hugo said.

"Totally. Compare that to having to wait to begin everything, how long it would all take. Writing the book, getting a publisher, the editing and marketing, and all the time interest in her waning."

"It makes perfect business sense," Hugo said. "Is that what Paul was working on in his *atelier*?"

"No," Miki laughed. "That really was his novel. That's why he wanted Alain to help, to actually do the writing. It sounds mean to say now, but he wasn't a confident writer, really. I saw some of his novel and it was fine, some of it pretty good but he didn't think so. Anyway, he said he'd never written in a journalistic way so that's why he secretly brought Alain on board."

"But when Paul died, Benoît was left on his own," Hugo said. "And he couldn't suddenly start working in the open because people knew he was friends with Paul and Sarah, it would look strange. That's why he needed you."

"Yes," Miki agreed. "And he thought I'd have more access since I was friends with you, since you knew Paul and were at the library a lot."

"Back up a minute," Tom said. "How did you know to call off Benoît from breaking into the library on Saturday night?"

"Luck, I guess," she said. "I happened to call Michael Harmuth after Hugo did. He said Hugo warned him to stay away from Alain, and that the police were making sure the library was secure. Something like that. Anyway, something in my voice gave away to Michael that I knew Alain, and he accused me of being involved."

"Were you?" asked Merlyn. "You bloody better not have been."

"No. I didn't know he was going to those extremes, I promise." She frowned. "I may be wrong, but I think he was trying to cut me out of the loop."

"Why do you say that?" Hugo asked.

"Well, he didn't tell me about this. And he'd started being secretive, calling and texting someone and not telling me who. I mean, maybe he was cheating on his boyfriend, but he could've told me about that, I don't care. He seemed to be actively hiding stuff from me."

"Wait, back to Saturday night," Hugo interrupted. "Where did you go when you picked him up?"

"Back to his place. He gave me the keys to the library and said I should return them, drop them anywhere in the building. He even wiped his prints off them."

"So the question becomes," Tom said, his eyes firmly on Miki, "who killed Alain Benoît?"

"Don't you dare accuse me!" she said, indignant.

"You have a suspect in mind?" Hugo asked Tom.

"Maybe and maybe not." Tom said. "But we probably shouldn't ignore the fact that the last person to see him alive was also about to be cut out of a very lucrative book deal."

Miki Harrison paled as Tom's words sank in. "Me? No!"

"Tom's right," Hugo said gently. "You definitely can't leave the city, and I need to let Lieutenant Lerens know all this. It's your choice what to do, Miki, but running away doesn't look good."

"But I didn't do anything!" she insisted. "I could never hurt someone, no way. And for a book? It's important, but I wouldn't commit a crime for it."

Hugo shook his head. "Well, that's not entirely true, is it? Something else I noticed about our discussion the other day. I told you I'd been out to Isabelle Severin's home and you didn't ask me any questions about where it is. That suggested to me that you already knew."

"What do you mean?" Miki asked, her eyes wide, fearful.

"Let's just say that it might speak well of you if you give it back."

Miki swallowed. "Give what back?"

"The thing you and Alain Benoît stole on Saturday morning," Hugo said. "The Severin dagger."

CHAPTER TWENTY-FIVE

On Tuesday morning the sun was shining again, but the rain had worked its magic on the temperature and the Paris air was ten degrees cooler than it had been for weeks. Hugo opened his windows wide to air out the apartment as the coffee pot gurgled in the kitchen.

When it was ready, he poured himself a cup and went into his bedroom, opening that window, too, and sitting at his desk as the morning breeze drifted through the room. He started his computer and e-mailed his secretary and the ambassador to let them know he was working from home still. He then wrote a second e-mail to the ambassador, giving him a short update on the death of Alain Benoît over the weekend, and the possibility that an English woman, Miki Harrison, may have been involved.

The update was short because, in truth, Hugo was uneasy.

At that very moment Miki Harrison was being questioned by Camille Lerens at police headquarters. He'd called Lerens the previous evening to let her know immediately what Miki Harrison had admitted. When she showed up to Hugo's apartment, they spoke alone in the downstairs lobby and the police lieutenant had not been pleased.

"You interrogated her here?"

"No, we were talking generally and a few things fell into place," he said.

"Hugo, if you knew something, you should have told me."

"About what?"

"About Harrison and Benoît being the ones who stole the dagger. *Merde*, about the fact they even knew each other."

"I'm telling you, Camille, I basically figured most of this stuff out just now."

"Most of it," she said, suspicion in her voice.

"Look, I told her to cooperate, that she couldn't leave. And then I called you, straightaway."

"*Bon*, I'll take it from here. She has a lot to answer for."

"You think she killed Benoît?" Hugo asked.

"I don't know, I've not questioned her yet."

"OK, calm down, Camille, I told you I wasn't playing cop here today, I was hosting pizza."

"And in doing so, made yourself a witness." She gave him a meaningful look.

"Wait, no," he began. "Don't tell me that. I want to be there when you interview her."

"You know that's not possible now. She made admissions to you, and that puts you in the witness box."

"No," Hugo said emphatically. "If she makes admissions to you, you get to stay in the investigation so the same applies to me."

"If she makes admissions to me, Hugo, they will be in an interview room, under full caution, and they will be digitally recorded on film and audio. They will not be made over pizza in my apartment. See the difference?"

Hugo did, and he knew she was right. But he was less than happy at being kept out of Harrison's interview, mostly because he had more questions, but also because Merlyn had begged him to protect her. The most he'd been able to do, though, was call his counterpart at the British embassy and let him know what was going on.

Hugo jumped when his phone rang at ten o'clock, and he was pleased to see Lieutenant Lerens's name on the display.

"*Bonjour* Camille. Are you done already?"

"She came in at eight, just like she said she would."

"And?"

"And it seems like she's my best suspect."

"What did she tell you?"

"Pretty much what she told you, I think. But she said it was Benoît who stole the dagger, not her."

"She did?"

"According to her, it was his idea to go out there and talk to Isabelle Severin, she just went along with it, and while they were there he spotted the dagger and took it. She claims she didn't even know until they were in the car on the way home."

"Do you believe her?"

"Not really. When I told her we didn't find anything like that at his apartment, she said he'd given it to her for safekeeping."

"What's wrong with that?"

"Come on, Hugo, seriously?"

"Yes, seriously. We know he was prepared to steal for this book, he broke into Paul's apartment and helped himself to a dead man's keys, so he could then break in somewhere else, the library at the dead of night. That enough criminal activity for you?"

"Maybe someone was pulling his strings."

"She's a criminal mastermind now?"

"She may not look like one, but I do find it odd that Harrison claims not to have known about the theft of the keys and the library break-in, yet she's the one who winds up in possession of the keys. Then she claims she didn't know about Benoît stealing the dagger, yet she has that, too. And it's not her who shows up floating in the Seine, is it? No, it's Alain Benoît, and not only was she the last person to see him alive, but she has a pretty good motive to kill him."

"I can't argue with any of that," Hugo conceded. "But do you really think she did it? Why at that moment?"

"Maybe he snagged some other piece of prize information and wouldn't share it. She said she thought he was holding out on her over the book."

"Yeah, she told me that, too."

"There you go. She saw him about to disappear into the wind and take all the glory himself and decided not to let that happen."

"If that was his plan, why would he leave the dagger with her? That makes no sense."

"Maybe she took it in the first place. Or after she killed him."

"Possibly. What did she say about the last time she saw him?"

"That she stayed with him after picking him up from the library, but left after midnight and got a call very early that morning to meet him at a café. He'd received a text from someone, he didn't say who because he wanted to talk to her in person about it. Anyway, he didn't show up, so she waited an hour and then went home."

"She have any guesses as to who texted?"

"She says she doesn't know."

"It might explain why his phone was missing," Hugo said.

"What do you mean?"

"If someone sent him a message, and maybe insisted on meeting him early on a Sunday morning before he saw Miki Harrison, that person might want to destroy that message, which likely would mean also destroying Benoît's phone."

"And someone would lure Benoît that way because a phone call would be traceable, but a text isn't."

"Right."

"My head's spinning, Hugo. Are all these deaths related or is Benoît's nothing to do with the other two? I mean, we can't even be a hundred percent sure that Gregory and Rogers didn't both commit suicide. Maybe there's just one murder, and even that one might have an alternate explanation." She spread her hands wide. "Maybe there are three suicides here, or two suicides and an accident."

"Perhaps, but I don't think so," Hugo said grimly.

They disconnected and Hugo sat quietly for a moment, thinking. His head was also swimming with the possibilities, although there were several things that especially bugged him, things that suggested he swim in a particular direction. Nothing concrete, but a few coincidences and inconsistencies had started to pile up along the way and, sitting there, Hugo decided that the pile was now large enough to warrant closer inspection.

He opened the folder containing Paul Rogers's book-checkout history, then picked up the phone and called the main number at the library.

"Nicole Anisse, please," he said.

A moment later, she came on the line. "This is Nicole, can I help you?"

"Hey, it's Hugo Marston. Quick question for you."

"Oh, hi. Sure, whatever you need."

"I'm looking at Paul's book history that you gave me. Is there any way to tell exactly who physically checked out a book, as opposed to whose card was used?"

"I'm not sure what you're asking. You have to have a library card."

"But people can borrow other people's cards, right? Or you could sign out a book under another library employee's name?"

"I suppose so, yes. Sure."

"Good to know, thanks," Hugo said. "Hey, would you put me through to Michelle Juneau?"

"She just left the building, sorry. Anything else I can help with?"

"I was just wondering about the funeral arrangements."

"Oh, then I can help you. Well, kind of. I think she got Michael to help with that. I heard them talking about it. Want me to see if he's here?"

"No, that's OK. But I just thought of something else."

"Fire away."

"I need a peek at someone else's checkout history, would that be OK?"

"I don't know," Anisse said, her voice hesitant. "I could get in trouble for that, if it's someone who works here or is a current patron. Paul's was different because . . . well, obviously."

"I know, but it'd be our secret," Hugo said, coaxing her. "No one would ever know, I promise."

She relented with a gentle laugh. "I suppose it's OK to be naughty once in a while. For a good cause."

"It certainly is that." Hugo gave her the name and Anisse promised to e-mail the information right away. She ended the call playfully, saying, "You owe me big time, Hugo. Big time."

Two minutes later, her e-mail arrived and Hugo opened the attachment. He scanned the list of books, and when he saw one in particular a shot of adrenaline made him sit up straight.

"So why would *you* need that book?" he muttered to himself, and sat back in his chair as the pieces started to edge toward each other, not slotting into place as yet, but aligning themselves enough that he thought he could finally see a face.

But he needed more. More evidence, more proof, and if there was one thing guaranteed to help him get a new, and hopefully clarifying, perspective, it was a trip out of town. But before he could make any arrangements, his phone rang.

"Hugo, it's Merlyn." She sounded breathless, panicked. "What the hell is going on?"

"What do you mean?"

"There's a frigging police car outside our apartment. Miki's been told not to leave Paris. Jesus, Hugo, she was interrogated by your cop buddy this morning."

"Interviewed, not interrogated," Hugo said calmly.

"She's a suspect?" Merlyn said, incredulity in her voice.

"Not for me, no. But right now I'm not the one who matters."

"The police. Hugo, they're staking us out. What the hell is that?"

"Merlyn, calm down. Remember when we were charging around England looking for a murderer? We weren't quite sure who or what or why, remember?"

"Yes, I do. And you ended up in the trunk of his bloody car at one point."

Hugo laughed. "Yeah, I'm gonna try and avoid that situation again. But listen, I'm just saying you need to stay calm. I'm a few hours away from being sure what this is all about. Just be cool in the meantime, ignore the cops, and stay where you are. Watch some movies or something."

"They're all in French."

"That happens when you go to Paris. So read a book."

"You have to clear her, Hugo," Merlyn insisted. "Miki may be head-strong but, my God, she's not a cold-blooded killer. That's ridiculous."

"I know, but right now she's the best suspect the police have. They've got motive and opportunity for Alain's death, at least."

Merlyn was quiet for a moment, then asked, "What are you going to do?"

"The less you know, the better." That wasn't true, not really, Hugo just didn't want to explain, answer questions. And he didn't even know if he was right. Not yet. When they disconnected, he called Lerens back. "Quick favor."

"What is it?" she asked suspiciously. "Related to this case?"

"No," Hugo said. "At least, I can't say it is right now. I need you to get me access to a very old file in another jurisdiction."

"Only if you promise to tell me what you're up to."

"As soon as I know, I will. Call it a hunch for now, and I know how you hate acting on those instead of firm evidence."

"*C'est vrai.*" Lerens laughed gently. *That's true.* "But I'm more than happy to let you act on one of yours. Tell me what you need."

She listened quietly as he explained, and she agreed to make some calls for him.

"Are you still convinced Miki Harrison is responsible?" Hugo asked.

"It doesn't look good for her. I know she's got an excuse and an explanation for everything, but she's neck-deep in all of this. I forgot to tell you, during the interview I asked her where she was around the time Sarah Gregory was killed. She said she was with Alain Benoît."

"Not much of an alibi," Hugo agreed.

"That's the thing. I can't verify any of the stories she's telling me. Of course, as yet I can't disprove any of them, either."

"You have people watching her, I gather."

"How did you know?"

"My friend Merlyn called, less than happy."

"We don't have enough to arrest her, not yet. I'm getting a warrant for her computer to see if she has anything on there, but the magistrate kicked it back first time, said she wanted more."

"Well, you do your thing and I'll do mine, maybe we'll meet in the middle."

When he hung up, Hugo logged in to the SNCF website to book two tickets, first-class, on an afternoon train out of the Saint-Lazare train station. He then sent a short text, hoping for a quick response. Tom wandered into the room just as Hugo was starting to pack.

"In the old days, you had a go bag ready in the closet. Where are we off to?"

"Don't you knock anymore?"

"I never did," Tom said. "I asked where we're going."

"That depends." Hugo checked his phone and smiled. "You're going nowhere. I'm going up north with Claudia for a day or so."

"Odd time to take a vacation."

"You think so? Half of Paris is on vacation now."

"Half of Paris isn't involved in a hunting a serial killer."

"Neither am I."

"Three bodies in a week, seems like it'd qualify. I mean, you're the expert but I've read enough fiction to get the gist."

"Funny."

"Where up north?"

"So you can tag along?"

"No, I wouldn't do that. I'm just curious." Tom smiled broadly, his attempt at looking innocent.

"I thought some fresh sea air would be good. A quick trip to Dieppe."

"Dieppe?" Tom's eyes narrowed. "Wait a minute. I told you that story, you should be taking me."

"Love your company, Tom, but you still come in second for over-night trips."

Tom grunted. "Guess I can't blame you there."

CHAPTER TWENTY-SIX

The train left just before three that afternoon, giving Hugo and Claudia a chance to eat at the station's renowned *brasserie*, the aptly named Lazare. Hugo had expected to buy a sandwich for the train, but Claudia insisted they'd be able to get a table without a reservation. She had her hair in a ponytail and was wearing jeans and a loose, white shirt. Her skin seemed to glow, and every time he looked at her, she was smiling.

"It's a Tuesday, and it'll be later than most people eat." She hadn't mentioned until they were seated that she knew the chef and his wife.

"Always full of surprises," Hugo said. He felt good in her company, he always did. She was one of a handful of people he'd ever met who made him feel utterly comfortable and himself. His first wife, Ellie, had been like that. And with Claudia, too, he had no desire to guess what she was thinking, analyze and parse her words, second-guess her intentions. It was, he knew, because she and Ellie were without guile or artifice; they said what they were feeling and meant it. He may not always like or agree with what Claudia had to say, but she would always tell him the truth.

"Try the roast chicken," she said.

"Is that an order?"

She winked. "If you want it to be."

They ate slowly, Hugo checking his watch every now and again to make sure the train's departure time didn't sneak up on them.

They both had the roast chicken and followed up with cappuccinos, resisting the dessert list and cheese cart. At the end of the meal, Hugo let Claudia pay when she insisted it was only fair, since he'd booked the train tickets and the hotel room.

"Thank you," he said as they walked toward the train. "That chicken really was good."

"So was the company." She put an arm around his waist and he put his around her shoulder, a closeness that felt natural, almost inevitable.

As the train pulled out of the station, Hugo felt a surge of excitement. Traveling always made him feel this way, but this time he had Claudia with him, and he felt a growing certainty that the vague, almost spectral theory that was taking shape in his mind, might actually be real, even provable.

The train gathered speed and he watched the city slip away, the grubby industrial yards and gray factories that always seemed to sit alongside city rail lines replaced by ever-larger patches of green and gold, the pastures and fields of wheat and barley unfurling across the train's large windows. As they sped north, the land stayed flat and Hugo stared out at the stone villages that dotted the open farmland. Sometimes he and Claudia talked, but mostly they sat quietly next to each other, holding hands and looking at the world speeding by.

The sun was low in the sky when they got to Dieppe, bright and warm still, and the air smelled fresh and just a little salty. When they walked out of the front of the station, an unmarked police car was waiting.

"Camille really did pull out all the stops," Claudia said. "Although an afternoon at the police station doesn't sound like a huge amount of fun. Mind if I head to the hotel?"

Hugo kissed her forehead. "Of course not. Maybe find somewhere for us to eat tonight, a restaurant with a view of the sea."

"Consider it done."

He waited as she climbed into a taxi, then walked over to the police car and shook hands with the uniformed driver, who introduced herself as Genevieve Hillier. She was pretty and probably in her early thirties, and, Hugo guessed, of Filipino descent.

MARK PRYOR   221

"Sorry to keep you waiting," Hugo said in French.

"It's not a problem," she said. "But do you mind if I practice my English?"

"Not at all."

She chattered on the way to the Dieppe police station, talking about the movies she watched and learned from, the books she was trying to read, and how she was determined her son would speak English like a native. Hugo appreciated her enthusiasm and her company; most police officers were more hesitant and taciturn when an investigation bled into their jurisdiction. But when they got to the station, he discovered that she was only his driver when she handed him over to an older detective. He was a burly man with a thick, silver mustache and curiosity in his eyes. His handshake was firm and his smile welcoming.

"Georges Bazin," he said. "I'm two weeks away from retiring and am dying to know why you're interested in this old case."

"Hugo Marston, pleased to meet you," Hugo replied. "I just wanted to check on a few things I'd been told about it, see whether they were all true."

"Of course. You know, it was my first month on the job and I was the first officer on scene, and this case always bugged me, something about it." He led Hugo past the reception desk, down a long hallway to a small conference room. A small, round table dominated the windowless room, and four plastic chairs were tucked neatly under it. On the table was a cardboard box. "Everything related to the case is in there," Bazin said.

"You said case, not accident."

"I did. Help yourself and take as long as you like. If you need to make copies of anything, just let me know." He pointed down the hallway. "That's my office at the end."

"Thanks, I may take some pictures with my phone if that's OK," Hugo said.

"Whatever you want, that's fine. This case has been closed for decades, so you can't do any harm." He hesitated. "If you find anything odd, let me know. Like I said, I never quite swallowed the official story, never quite believed it happened the way the final report concludes, but," he shrugged, "I was a young officer and didn't have the guts or the rank to do anything about it. Nor any evidence, I suppose. Just one of those things, you know?"

Left alone, Hugo sat at the table and took the lid off the box. Inside, half a dozen bulging folders had been stacked on top of each other. He piled them on the table and sorted through them. The top one contained the initial report filed by young Officer Bazin, and some subsequent crime-scene reports from other officers. The next had photos of the accident site, and Hugo was eager to see the precise location for himself. The third folder had been labeled "Witness Statements," but it contained only one, and Hugo read it carefully, then read it again. He took out his camera and photographed the single page, and then a few of the pictures from the scene.

For the next hour, Hugo sifted through the reports one by one. As the pages passed under his fingertips, his conviction grew that the Severin collection was little more than a blinding flare, a clever distraction being exploited by a cunning and imaginative killer so that the Paris police would keep chasing their tails, and maybe run right into a brick wall. Not that people weren't trying to uncover the true story behind Isabelle Severin's role in the war, they were. But they weren't the ones who'd committed murder.

As he closed the last file, a deep sadness fell over him, a sorrow not just for the people who'd lost their lives, but for the person he had to unmask. He knew that people killed for many reasons, and very rarely for pleasure. Paul Rogers, Sarah Gregory, and Alain Benoît had all died not to amuse their murderer, not to assuage some sick fantasy that couldn't be controlled. No, this was about survival, and about keeping a secret buried that if quite literally unearthed, would mean the end of the road for a person who'd spent far too long looking over both shoulders and living as a fraud.

Hugo called Claudia. "Did you find us a place to eat?"

"I did. Table for two at eight."

"Would you hate me if we canceled?"

"Hugo, what's wrong? You sound...depressed or something. What did you find out?"

"Honestly, I thought this would be a wild goose chase, that my theory couldn't possibly be right. Or maybe I just hoped that."

"You wouldn't tell me what it was," she said, "so I couldn't really say one way or the other."

"Let's just say we should head back to Paris. I need to tell Camille what I found, show her some of this stuff."

"So they were murdered, all three of them?"

"Yes, they were," Hugo said.

"Who? Who did it?"

"Can you get us a rental car? I'll explain on the drive down." He thought for a moment. "But there's someone here who needs to know the truth about a case he worked on. Text me the address and I'll meet you at the restaurant, we'll get something from there and eat on the road."

Hugo knocked on Georges Bazin's door.

"*Entrez*," Bazin called.

Hugo went in and sat across from the French policeman. "Well, it looks like you were right." He'd brought a few of the crucial documents, photographs mostly, and placed them on the desk. "Look at these and I'll explain."

Georges Bazin sat quietly and listened, and when Hugo was done, his eyes locked on a photo of a stretch of coastal road, a broken barrier, and a steep but not precipitous drop to the sea. After a moment, Bazin looked up.

"Makes more sense now." A wry smile played on his lips. "I feel like I should've seen this before. I mean, really seen it."

"Hindsight," Hugo said. "Makes fools of us all."

"But three more people died because I didn't."

"You weren't the only one. You weren't even the one responsible for figuring this out."

"No," Bazin sighed, "I suppose not. You'll be needing to get back, be there for the arrest."

"I'll drive down this evening."

"You need a ride anywhere?"

"Just to a restaurant, thank you."

Bazin picked up his desk phone and called Officer Hillier, who appeared in the doorway two minutes later. Hugo stood and shook hands with Bazin.

"Thanks again for your cooperation," Hugo said.

"Of course. You know, I feel like I should be happier you solved this. Instead, I just feel . . ." The policeman shook his head sadly.

"I know what you mean," Hugo said. "Anytime an accident turns out to be murder, well, you wonder if you've discovered a moment of evil. An accident causes enough grief and sorrow, but to use a tragedy to disguise something like this, when you figure it out there's not much to celebrate."

CHAPTER TWENTY-SEVEN

Officer Hillier knew the restaurant, Chez Nous, and dropped him at the entrance to the busy parking lot, away from the line for the valet parking. Cars nudged forward and young men and women dressed in black zipped back and forth, swapping keys for tickets, trying to keep their hungry customers moving into the restaurant. Those unwilling to pay the extra five euros crawled through the parking lot proper, looking for empty spaces, stalking those leaving, and in some cases forcing their vehicles into manufactured spaces that meant an exit through the sunroof.

"Summer up here still," Hillier explained. "Most Parisians have gone home, but this week people come from everywhere else before school starts. Hope you booked a table."

Hugo said nothing. He was impatient to get on the road. It was already eight o'clock and the light was beginning to weaken. Clouds had started to fill a sky that had been blue all day, threatening to bring rain or, at the very least, an early sunset.

On the drive over he'd exchanged texts with Lerens, convincing her to keep a team on the only person Hugo suspected, despite the fact that she was still inclined to hold Miki Harrison accountable. He'd detected a note of uncertainty in Lerens's tone when she was talking about Harrison as a suspect, which Hugo appreciated. Neither of them could dispute which way the evidence pointed, but in Hugo's experience a good cop had good instincts, and learned to trust them. That

225

didn't mean ignoring the facts, it just meant keeping an open mind and making sure your eyes were open to other possibilities.

Hugo hurried across the parking lot, sliding between the crowd of cars and, at one point, almost stepping out in front of a tiny Renault. He wondered whether it'd do much more than bruise his shins, and the car's weak horn, more like a squeak, didn't convince him otherwise. He was eager to get back to Paris and find out whether his instincts had pointed him in the right direction, whether he'd uncovered the real truth. The confirmation lay in Paris, quite literally, and he wanted to be there when Lerens and her team revealed it.

He stopped to let another car pass, a dark-blue Peugeot. He was on the driver's side and frowned with impatience as the car slowed and the window came down. He was preparing to tell the driver that he didn't live here, couldn't give him directions to an alternate parking lot, or anywhere else, when he saw the gun pointing at him.

Michael Harmuth had turned his body so that his left arm also hung out of the window, blocking any side view of the weapon, like they were just two friends, chatting.

Hugo's breathing slowed and he forced his eyes away from the steady black barrel, forced himself to look at the person behind the gun.

"I'm surprised to see you up here," Hugo said.

"I could say the same, although given your reputation, perhaps I shouldn't be."

"Am I next on the list?" Hugo asked. He thought about running, but the gun was just too close, he'd never make it three steps. *Talk first, run if I have to.*

"There was never a list, you know that, right? I never wanted it to play out this way."

"You'd be amazed how many times I've looked into the eyes of a murderer and heard those same words," Hugo said.

"I'm not a murderer!" The gun wavered, but only for a fraction of a second. "Well, I suppose I am technically, but not in my heart of hearts."

"Four deaths, Michael. You're directly responsible for four people being killed."

"Ah, I see," Michael Harmuth said. "Then you really do know."

"I wasn't positive, but yeah, I was pretty sure."

"You want to make it five?" The words were intended to be menacing, but Harmuth looked suddenly tired.

"No, and you don't either."

"Want, need," the steel was back in Harmuth's voice. "Not always the same thing. Get in the back seat."

"And if I don't, you'll shoot me right here?"

"Why not? What do I have to lose at this point? Get in."

"If I run, you'll miss."

"I have your pretty lady friend in the trunk, Hugo. I won't miss her."

Hugo's eyes flickered to the trunk, but there was no way to tell if Harmuth was lying or not. His fingers itched to grab his cell, call Claudia and make sure she was all right. But if he did have her, if she was in the trunk, he couldn't run. He reached out for the handle, opened the rear door, and slid into the back seat. He pulled the door shut and called out, "Claudia! Can you hear me?"

Harmuth shook his head. "Ever the gentleman. I imagine she's waiting for you in the restaurant." In a quick move that surprised Hugo, Harmuth had his door open and was letting himself into the rear seat, beside Hugo. "You'll be driving. Climb through."

It was a squeeze and at one point Hugo thought he might be able to land a kick into Harmuth's crotch, but Harmuth sensed it, too, and locked eyes with Hugo. "I swear to god, Hugo, two things are true. If you cooperate with me, I will not kill you. But if you fuck with me, like you just thought about doing, I will shoot you and then lure your pretty girlfriend out here and shoot her, too."

"And you're not a murderer." Hugo dropped into the driver's seat.

"No. And you probably think I'm being insincere, but the fact you didn't take a chance with her life, that was admirable."

"Excuse me if I'm not flattered by any compliment from you," Hugo snapped. "Where are we going?"

"My mother still has that house outside of Dieppe. I'm assuming you know who my mother is."

228 THE PARIS LIBRARIAN

"Claire Rogers."

"I'm curious to know how you figured this out, but we don't have time. Your phone and gun, please." Harmuth was sitting right behind Hugo, his gun pointed at the back of Hugo's head between the seat and the headrest. Hugo was angry, not just at Harmuth, but at letting the man put him in such a vulnerable and indefensible position.

"I didn't bring my gun."

"Bullshit. We had that chat already, you take it everywhere. Fingertips, please."

Hugo reached slowly beneath his jacket and took out his gun, holding it between his fingertips as ordered. Harmuth snatched it, then took away Hugo's phone, and tucked them both under his leg.

"Did you follow us up here?" Hugo asked.

"No, actually. I called Miki Harrison; she said you were on your way up here, to Dieppe."

"How would she know that?"

"Beats me. I'm guessing your friend Tom told her, but it doesn't matter. When I heard that you were coming here, I was sure you'd figured it out. Not positive but as good as. I called a few hotels and asked for you, and when I located the hotel I went there. I saw Claudia and not you, and stuck to her until she got here. I just waited, and then when I saw you get out of a police car, well, that was that." He gave a short, hard laugh. "Imagine if I'd been wrong, if you didn't know anything?"

"Pretty embarrassing for us both," Hugo said.

"Yeah," Harmuth said. "Let's go to the house. Behave and I'll leave you there, send someone to get you in a day or two."

"Why would I believe that?"

"Because you don't have many options right now. Believe and behave, don't and die."

Hugo turned and looked through the front window. Harmuth was right, his options were as narrow as they could be, for now. He put the car in drive, and drove slowly through the parking lot to the main road. "Which way?" he asked, through gritted teeth. *If nothing else, I can put a few miles between this lunatic and Claudia before that gun goes off.*

On any other evening, under any other circumstances, Hugo would have appreciated the drive out of the city of Dieppe, the lessening of traffic as the car took them off the main road, angling upward, parallel with the English Channel, toward the angry red ball of the sun that sunk lower and lower and spilled its light like blood across the horizon.

"Here, turn left," Harmuth said.

Hugo steered the car into a narrow road that snaked between high hedgerows that cut off the view, the quick twists of the deep-cut lane throwing Hugo's sense of direction out of whack. He tried to focus on the direction, but with few visual markers, it was difficult.

"Coming up," Harmuth said. "Left again, this driveway."

The track was rutted and the car bounced left and right before hitting a smooth patch that led them up a steep slope to a stone house that looked like it had been built into the hill, the roof at the back seeming to touch the rocky slope behind. Several of the windows were broken, and the ground was littered with tiles that had slid from the roof. To their left a ramshackle shed tilted toward them, its roof half gone.

"This your vacation home?" Hugo asked. He looked at Harmuth in the mirror and considered driving the car straight into the stone wall of the house, but Harmuth reached forward and unclipped Hugo's seatbelt, so he stopped the car.

"Get out," Harmuth said. "I told you, do as I say and I won't hurt you."

"You'll forgive me if I'm skeptical," Hugo said. But he opened the door and got out, Harmuth doing the same behind him.

"I only need a couple of days," Harmuth said. "Maybe even just one."

"To do what?"

"Walk toward the house. Move." He gestured with the gun and Hugo started walking. "To disappear," Harmuth continued. "What do you think? I managed it once, didn't I?"

"With your mother's help, yes."

"I was a kid then. I've been preparing for this eventuality, I'm ready."

Hugo thought of his own go bag, the one he had packed and ready when he was with the FBI, the one he no longer needed. *What did Harmuth have in his? Money and a new passport?* They made their way to the house, and Harmuth produced a key from his pocket. The heavy front door unlocked easily enough, and Hugo wondered if Harmuth had been here recently. If he really did have a backup plan, an escape plan, it would make sense to use this place as a staging point.

Harmuth stood aside and indicated with his head for Hugo to enter. Inside it was dark, and the air was damp and cold. Hugo felt sure that even if Harmuth had been here recently, he'd not spent much time in the house.

Harmuth flicked a switch and a weak light fell over the main room, the kitchen to their left, and some heavy chairs and sofas making up the living area, arranged around an open fireplace in the wall to their right.

"To the kitchen," Harmuth said, flicking the gun barrel in that direction.

"Good, I'm hungry," Hugo said.

"Hugo, you wouldn't believe me if I told you I was sorry, would you?"

"If you're sorry, put down the gun. I believe actions, not words."

"I meant it when I said I'm not going to kill you, that's about the best I can do." Hugo paused and looked over his shoulder. "Unless you try to stop me," Harmuth added, his jaw set.

"Where do you want me?"

"That door, open it." It looked like a pantry door, with thick panels and an iron handle and hinges, but Hugo realized that it must be more than that. When he opened it, the air was even colder and he stared into a storeroom that seemed to have been chiseled out of the rock itself. The room was roughly ten feet wide and twenty deep, with a stone floor worn smooth from use over the years. To his left, plastic crates had been stacked on top of each other and looked to be full of bottles of water and wine. To his right, wooden shelves had been affixed somehow to the rock wall and bore dozens of cans of food, beans and soup, and other dry goods.

"Go inside," Harmuth said.

A sense of dread washed over Hugo and he stopped in the doorway to the little room. He tensed himself to fly at his captor, make one final attempt to save himself from being entombed in this place and prevent his killer from getting away. But Harmuth seemed to sense Hugo's aggression and put another two feet of space between them, raising the gun an inch or two to show Hugo he was ready.

"You said you weren't going to kill me," Hugo growled. "I'll die of exposure in there before someone finds me."

"I think there's a blanket somewhere. And you have wine and food, so you'll be fine for two days. That's all I need, just two days."

"Whether I live or die, there's nowhere you can go we won't find you."

"Get in," Harmuth repeated. "Don't make me shoot you." He lowered the gun toward Hugo's leg, and Hugo instinctively backed into the storeroom. "That's better. Now go to the back."

Hugo complied, resisting the urge to grab a can and hurl it at Harmuth's head. When Hugo got to the back of the storeroom, he said, "You don't want to know how I figured it out?"

"Not playing that game with you, Hugo. It's time I need, not a story about how clever you are. Oh, and I apologize for the lack of light."

Without another word, Harmuth swung the door closed and Hugo heard the bolt slide into place as darkness enveloped him. Hugo started forward but in the blackness lost his sense of balance and clattered into a stack of crates on his right. He swore and tried to right them, hoping that none of the bottles would topple out and smash on the rock floor. The last thing he needed was to be locked in the pitch black with broken glass all around. But by feeling carefully, Hugo managed to set everything properly upright, and he steadied himself before moving slowly forward, using his fingertips to guide him. His nostrils stung with the dust and cold, and he made a conscious effort to slow his breathing, to calm himself.

He reached the door and felt for the handle, trying it even though he knew it was useless. He pushed and pulled against the door, but it didn't budge. *As sturdy as it looked*, he thought. He traced his fingers around the edges and realized that Harmuth must have turned off the light in the house and left already.

He turned his back to the door and felt to his right, hoping for a light switch, wracking his brain for what he'd seen on the shelves, but he couldn't picture anything that'd be much use. Hugo continued his search for a light source on the left side of the cell but felt no switch, no wires, nothing that would contradict Harmuth's parting words, *I apologize for the lack of light*. He waved a hand in front of his face and thought maybe he saw movement, but he wasn't sure.

One thing, and one thing only, was for sure—Hugo was a prisoner, locked tight in this stone room, and shackled further by complete blackness and a silence that was absolute.

He tried cheering himself with humor, cursing at Harmuth for not leaving him a cork screw, but the darkness wouldn't let up, pressing in on his body and soul, making movement difficult and stifling his thoughts, blurring the sharpness of his mind and disrupting his attempts to think his way out of his prison.

He waited what felt like five minutes, but perhaps it was just two, for his eyes to adjust and he thought maybe it was working, that the blackness was less absolute. Even so, he couldn't see objects either side or ahead of him. He started to feel around for the blanket Harmuth had mentioned, but a moment later he thought he heard a noise from inside the storeroom and he froze, listening intently. He moved into the middle of the small room, still listening, but either it was his imagination or one of the crates he'd knocked into earlier had just settled back in place.

There must be something useful in here, he thought, and started to run his hands over all of the shelving he could reach, careful not to dislodge objects that might land on his head, and careful, also, to avoid getting splinters from the shelves themselves. He was halfway along the room when he felt something, a wash of relief flooding through his veins as his fingers closed around a large box of matches. He gave it a reassuring rattle, opened the box, and struck a match. The flash of light and sharp smell of burnt chemicals in the cold air were as welcome as anything had ever been, literally a tiny beacon of hope. Hugo sheltered the flame and used its light, and the light from two more matches, to finish his inspection of the shelving, finding more matches and a box of tea-light candles.

Finally, some luck, he thought.

He lit four of the candles and placed them around the storeroom, making its walls glow and giving him enough light to complete his search. He hoped to find a set of tools, something he could use to break down or through the door, but his luck extended only to the newfound light source.

He went to the back of the room to put out the candle there, to preserve it, and his gaze rested on a knee-high wooden barrel. *Too flimsy to break the door down, but . . .* he lifted its lid and on top of a mound of dried beans sat a metal scoop. Hugo picked it up. It was heavy in his hand, solid and well-made. Not the axe or crowbar he'd have preferred, but better than nothing. He took it to the door and pressed the leading edge of the scoop against the miniscule gap between two of the thick boards that made up the door. He squared his stance and applied as much pressure as he could, trying to force the boards apart. His hand felt like it might slip on the metal handle, but he kept going until the little shovel snapped out of the gap, sending a large sliver of wood flying into the dark.

Not much, Hugo thought, *and this is gonna take a while. But it's a start.*

He worked for five minutes, then took a break to rest. As he leaned with his back to the door, he thought he heard another noise, this time from the other side, a soft thump from the kitchen, like someone was moving in there and trying to be quiet.

Hugo's mind raced. *Did Harmuth forget something? More likely he changed his mind about killing me . . .*

His blood ran cold when the noise came from the door itself, a gentle scrape, once, and then a second time. Hugo shuffled to his left, pressing himself against the shelves, preparing himself to rush at Harmuth as soon as the door opened.

He heard one more clank, the bolt being slid across, and a moment later saw a line of gray where the top of the door should be. He waited for the gray line to broaden and as soon as it did, Hugo launched himself at the door, charging it with his shoulder, his fists balled and ready to fight.

The door thumped into a body on the other side, and Hugo slammed himself into it again. It gave under his weight, faster than he planned, and he sprawled out of the storeroom and landed facedown on the floor. He struggled to catch his breath, his hands scrabbling at the form lying next to him, trying to use his weight, his strength, to immobilize his captor.

A white hot pain slashed across his left forearm, and he cried out, but the cut made him angry, angrier than he'd been in years, and he swiveled on the ground and lashed out with his foot, aiming the toe of his boot at the dark figure trying to rise. His foot connected and for a moment Hugo froze in place, a disconnect trying to right itself in his brain, the high squeal of pain from his adversary not registering, not making sense. And then, through the fog of anger and pain, and in the dark of that cold, stone house, his mind made the connection, recognized the voice.

"Claudia, it's me. It's Hugo, stop fighting!"

The dark figure froze and the voice, when it came, was hesitant. "Hugo?"

"Yes, it's me." But they'd already recognized each other, the low light allowed them to see that much, and as their panic ebbed away they came together in relief, both on their knees with their arms wrapped tight around each other.

"My God, Hugo, I was so scared. Are you all right?"

"Yes, I'm fine." She squeezed him and he winced. "I was until you rescued me, anyway."

"I'm sorry." She moved away, sitting back on her heels. "I cut you."

"Let's find a light." Hugo stood and moved between the black outlines of furniture to the front door, when he fumbled for the light switch. Claudia hurried to him, as Hugo rolled up his sleeve. "It's fine, looks worse than it is."

"I'm sorry, maybe there are bandages here."

"We need to get going, find Harmuth. How did you get here?"

"Taxi," she said, "but I sent him away. The police should be coming, I called when we were driving here."

"How did you . . . ?" He wasn't even sure what question to ask.

"Two guys having dinner in the restaurant, they kept staring at me, and I could tell they were preparing some sort of move. I wasn't in the mood, Hugo, so I told the waitress I was going outside for a cigarette. I was going to wait for you there. I saw you walking across the parking lot, I waved but you didn't see me." She reached out and put a hand on his arm. "Then I saw the car pull up, I saw you get in. I couldn't see who it was, I didn't even know why you got in with him. But I knew something was wrong so I got in a taxi and followed."

"And called the police?"

"Not until we were out of the city." She looked down as if she'd done something wrong. "I didn't know what was going on, and I didn't want to call them over nothing. But I figured you wouldn't stand me up without calling, and you wouldn't answer your phone."

"He took it. He had me at gunpoint."

Claudia looked at her watch. "I called about ten minutes ago. I figured he'd done something . . . God, Hugo, I assumed it was you in there but then you attacked me!"

"I'm sorry, I thought he was coming back, I had no idea you were here."

"That's OK, I'm just a little . . ." She shivered. "Are you OK?"

"I'm fine, he didn't hurt me."

"No," she laughed through tears, "I did that for him."

"You said the taxi left?"

"Yes, just in case. I didn't want to put anyone else in danger."

"Brave woman."

"More than you know," she said, looking up at him with a soft smile.

"Meaning?"

"Meaning Harmuth's not getting very far," Claudia said.

"Why not?"

"My knife. I used it on his tires."

Hugo grinned. "Are you serious?"

"Yes. When I got here I didn't know what was going on, but I figured he'd use that car to get away from here. I only got two of the tires before I heard the front door opening, then I ducked behind that little shed. Like I said, I didn't know exactly what he was doing, but I was pretty sure it wasn't good." She shrugged. "If I was wrong, I'd be more than happy to buy him two new tires."

Hugo shook his head. "You weren't wrong, not by a long shot."

CHAPTER TWENTY-EIGHT

The distant wail of sirens grew louder, and Hugo turned on every light he could find to help the arriving officers see inside and outside the stone house. Before they arrived, Hugo used Claudia's phone to connect with an emergency operator and update them on their exact whereabouts and the situation. He emphasized the importance of finding Harmuth's dark-blue Peugeot, hopefully stopped by the side of the road. The city lights way below them twinkled orange and white, but Hugo knew it was dark on these country roads, and unless the police were actively looking for Harmuth's car, they could easily drive right past it.

"You need to call for an ambulance," Claudia said when he'd hung up.

"I'm fine."

"No, it's either that or a trip to the hospital when you faint."

Hugo smiled and did as he was told, asking for an ambulance to be sent along with the police. In the meantime, Claudia rummaged through the house and found a clean packet of gauze, which she pressed onto his wound.

"Thanks," he said, wincing as she tied it off.

"Try to keep it up and not move too much, I don't think it's all that bad."

They stood in the doorway, waiting for the police, watching as the headlights flashed into the driveway. Two police cars arrived at once, their sirens extinguished but blue lights raking across the front of the building. Hugo and Claudia stood with their hands up as two officers, one man, one woman, approached cautiously, their hands resting on their holsters. Once they'd confirmed the couple's identities, the officers relaxed and went back to their cars to switch off the overhead lights and update the dispatcher.

The policewoman approached and introduced herself as Audrey Chapuis. "We have every unit available looking for your man, he won't get far."

"He's pretty slick," Hugo said, "and he's been ready to disappear again for a while, if what he said is true."

"Maybe," Chapuis said. "Hang on." She pressed her fingertips to her left ear, making sure she could hear the radio chatter. They waited for a moment, then she looked up and smiled. "They have him. He drove into a field, may have burst a tire."

"May have," Hugo repeated, and gave Claudia a nudge with his elbow.

"Told you," she said.

"*Bon*," Chapuis said, "they want me to run you down to where he's being held to do a field identification. A formality, but we need to do it after the ambulance has seen to you."

"Of course," Hugo said. "Was he hurt in the crash?"

"I don't think so," Chapuis replied. She gave him a conspiratorial smile. "Unless you want him to be, I'm sure we could arrange something."

They laughed at her joke but Hugo wondered, just for a second, if they'd give him the time and space to plant his fist into Harmuth's face if he asked them to. Victims and their assailants rarely encountered each other once the police were involved, at least in his experience, and he wouldn't have allowed that kind of revenge, but he was beginning to see the appeal of it. His arm was beginning to ache, and he was relieved when the flashing lights of an ambulance appeared at the foot of the driveway.

A pair of paramedics hopped out of the vehicle and waved a greeting at the *flics*. Chapuis pointed to Hugo, who held out his arm.

One of the paramedics pulled on blue latex gloves, while the other opened the back of the truck.

"They said you're American," the taller paramedic said in broken English.

"*Oui, mais je parle français,*" Hugo replied. *Yes, but I speak French.*

"*Bien.*" He took Hugo's arm and gently unwound the bandage, then looked at the cut. "Not as bad as it looks. I'll put a couple of stitches in, bandage you up, and you'll be fine."

"Glad to hear it," Hugo said. Once it was cleaned, stitched, and bandaged, he flexed his arm and thanked the paramedic.

"Don't thank us," he said, "we don't usually get to leave the city. Made for an interesting drive." He snapped off his gloves and made his way to the front of the ambulance. The other paramedic slammed the doors shut and gave Hugo and Claudia a friendly wave.

As they drove off, Hugo and Claudia walked toward the police cars.

"You doing OK after all that excitement?" Hugo asked her.

"Yes, but I think I'll leave the action to you and Tom in the future. I'm not so used to it."

"You did great. Better than great."

"Thanks." She smiled up at him. "And speaking of Tom, I need a strong drink."

"As soon as we get this field ID done, I'm right there with you."

When they got to the cars, Chapuis held the passenger door open for Hugo. "*Monsieur*, you can ride with me. *Madame*, perhaps you can go with my colleague."

"*Bon, d'accord,*" Claudia said. *Yes, OK.*

Hugo felt a pang of disappointment at being separated from her, and that surprised him. He gave her a strong hug and resisted the temptation to pat her behind, but watched as she climbed into the front seat of the other car.

Chapuis turned to her colleague. "Guillaume, wait here until the crime-scene unit arrives, keep the place secure. Then take her wherever she wants to go."

"*D'accord*," Guillaume said, then nodded at Hugo as Chapuis slid behind the wheel and they pulled away. Hugo waved at Claudia, but she was saying something to her new companion. *That's my Claudia*, he thought. *Friends with everyone.*

They drove in silence along the coastal road, and Hugo lowered his window to enjoy the fresh, salty air. It'd been a while since he'd visited the coast, and he made up his mind that he'd have a proper vacation up here, soon and preferably with Claudia.

Ten minutes later, they came to the crash scene, and Hugo quickly saw what had happened. Harmuth had tried to drive on his flat tires, shredding them completely, the wheels themselves digging into the roadway and then, as he failed to steer around a corner, he'd run into an iron gate. The bottom half of the gate had broken from its post, tipping upward, and the hood of the car had lodged underneath. The top of the gate had shattered the windshield, breaking it inward over Harmuth. Another ambulance was here, and Harmuth sat as Hugo had done, in the back of it on a gurney, as he received treatment for his cuts. Four policemen hovered close by, making sure the patient didn't try any more escapes.

Officer Chapuis arranged the car so that her side faced the back of the ambulance. A nearby *flic* motioned for the paramedics to stop what they were doing and step aside for a moment. When they were clear of the ambulance, Chapuis turned on the spotlight by her window, and trained it on the rear of the vehicle, smothering Harmuth in light. He shielded his eyes but lowered his hands when an officer barked orders at him. He blinked into the brightness and Hugo was startled by how pale he was. Perhaps from the crash, surely to some degree, but it was more than that. He looked ten years older, his expression blank and his shoulders slumped. The red scratches and cuts on his face seemed all the brighter for the contrast with his blanched face, and as they watched a cut on his forehead trickled blood into his right eye. Harmuth reached up and wiped it away, then turned his face from the light.

"That's him," Hugo said. "No doubt at all."

"*Merci.*" She turned the spotlight off, then reached for the gear shift but stopped when her phone rang, answering it instead. She gave her name, then listened for a moment before handing the phone to Hugo. "It's Detective Georges Bazin."

Hugo smiled as he took the phone. "Georges, I'm glad someone contacted you."

"Is it him? Is it really Michel Rogers?"

"Yes, it is. And this time he's not getting away."

A long sigh came down the phone. "I knew it. I always knew it. Are you headed to the station? We'll have to charge him with your kidnapping before we can dig up his past, just to make sure we hold him."

"Can I do it in the morning?" Hugo asked. "I'm pretty beat and have a beautiful young lady waiting to buy me a drink."

Bazin chuckled. "Of course. How could I get in the way of that?"

"*Merci bien.* You know, I'm not sure I'd have been afforded the same accommodation back home."

"This is France; we know where our priorities lie. I'll see you tomorrow morning at the station." He paused and Hugo heard the smile in his voice. "If you're a little late, I'll know why."

They sat on the bed and ate pizza. Neither Hugo nor Claudia wanted the formality of a restaurant, and what they both needed most was comfort food, washed down with good wine that they drank out of the hotel's glass tumblers.

The television played in the background, a mix of news, weather, and commercials, but the sound was low and neither one paid any attention to it, focused more on reducing the size of their pizza, slice by slice.

"Did you call Camille?" Claudia asked, after a while.

"I did. They're going to hold off on the digging until tomorrow, no need to do it tonight after so long."

"Digging? Hugo, you still haven't told me what this is all about."

"No?" He smiled. "I guess I didn't yet, did I?"

"No." She threw him a sharp look. "But if you've finished stuffing your face, I'm ready."

"I'm not done stuffing my face, actually," he said. "But I'll tell you anyway, if you promise not to make fun of me."

"For figuring it out?"

"For being so slow."

"You always say that," she laughed. "But since you're always the first one to solve these crimes, I don't think anyone else is in a position to complain about you being slow."

"Yeah, I know." Hugo grimaced. "It always seems so obvious to me after the fact."

"Tell me anyway. When did you first suspect him?"

"It's hard to say, honestly. I didn't have a moment of clarity when suddenly I knew it was him. It was more a case of seeing little clues pile up in my mind, hints and suggestions, and things that I couldn't quite make sense of. And, looking at the other players, I just couldn't see any reason for anyone else to be guilty of these crimes."

"Especially when your main suspect was killed."

"Benoît? Yeah, that was a gamble on Harmuth's part. I mean, if it'd worked and we'd fallen for the suicide angle, he was in the clear. Game over and he wins. If not, then it was obvious someone else was doing this."

"Why do you think he took that gamble?" Claudia asked.

"The same reason most people make a bet. It looked like a good idea at the time, and he thought he'd win. I mean, he was right in some respects. Benoît was looming large to the police as the killer, and everyone knows cops love to close their cases. I can see how a dead Benoît works out perfectly for Harmuth."

"And he didn't have much time to make that decision."

"Right, I'm sure it occurred to him and he had only a little while, minutes, maybe an hour or two, to weigh the pros and cons. He probably thought that we'd eventually eliminate Benoît for some reason or another so, yeah, I can see why he did it."

"But it narrowed the list of suspects."

"Definitely."

"So then, how did Harmuth even end up on it?"

"Like I said." Hugo wiped his hands on a napkin. "A whole bunch of little things. Imagine a kaleidoscope of shapes and colors, and at some point they start to come together."

"For example?"

"Well, some things struck me as odd or interesting at the time, but they didn't mean much until I thought about them later. Like his pronunciation of the French word *atelier*."

"I don't understand."

"He told me he didn't speak much French at all. And that's a simple-enough word when you see it written down, but it's actually quite hard to pronounce perfectly. Yet he was able to. It didn't click at the time, I was just impressed. But later, when I started to wonder if he was who he said he was, it seemed like maybe it meant something."

"What else?"

"Well, he claimed to be big into security at the library. Remember, he was the one who had the security cameras installed. And yet, when Paul's keys were stolen not only was he unsure whether his library key had been returned, but he also didn't know who else had keys. Whether Michelle Juneau or even Nicole Anisse did. Again, a small thing that didn't resonate much at the time."

"Wait, I'm not getting that. Why did he care about security?"

"He didn't. He cared about the cameras. He planned the murder carefully, laid the groundwork for his alibi by putting them exactly where he needed them."

"OK, two big questions," Claudia said. "How and why?"

"Short answer, because Paul and Michael, or Michel, were brothers."

Claudia's eyes widened. "What? Are you serious?"

"Paul never knew, of course."

"That story wasn't true? He survived the crash?"

"There was no crash. Well," Hugo corrected himself, "there was a crash with an empty car."

"But a part of her was found in it!"

"Yes, and one of the things I did up here was look at the original crime-scene photos. The leg had been severed cleanly at the knee. Not only that, but they had good pictures of where the car went into the ocean. It wasn't a cliff, nothing steep enough to cause that kind of injury. No, he staged the whole thing to look like an accident."

"Why didn't the police figure that out back then?"

"It looked cut and dried, you can't blame them. The press was reporting it as this Romeo and Juliet story, as if it was some sort of romantic tragedy."

"That's ridiculous."

"Yes, but that's how it was reported, and that's what the police believed." Hugo thought of Georges Bazin. *Most of them.*

"So what do you think happened?"

"I'm pretty sure that Michael Harmuth, or Michel Rogers, killed his girlfriend at his mother's apartment. Together they buried her body in the backyard and engineered his escape."

"Oh my God, that's awful."

"Hence the digging tomorrow," Hugo said. "They'll get a warrant and do it by daylight. It's a small space, it won't take long."

"So, Harmuth killed Paul Rogers because he knew something?"

"No. He did it to protect his secret. Paul and Sarah were planning to build onto the apartment, and to do that they would have taken up part of the garden. The chances were better than good that they'd uncover the body, and that would be that. A few years ago, Harmuth might have gotten away with it, but with DNA they'd almost certainly figure out who she was, which would mean his story about an accident would crumble."

"The police wouldn't just be looking for him, they'd have to arrest Claire Rogers." Claudia shook her head sadly. "How did she live with a secret like that for so many years?"

"Because she had to. Michael, or Michel as he was, was her son, and most mothers will do pretty much anything to protect their children. She's most mothers."

"But how did you know?"

Hugo smiled. "As a matter of fact, she actually said it at one point, I didn't even pay attention. When we were at her apartment, she almost called him her son, or so it seemed to me. I put it down to the dementia, and he played it very cool, I must say."

"You told me she was protective of her garden. It wasn't the flowers at all, was it?"

"No, she was in on it, no question."

"All those years, and they didn't try to move the body."

"I can see why," Hugo said. "Harmuth had to stay away as long as possible in case someone recognized him, and it's so much easier for Claire Rogers to just leave the body there. Why take the risk if you don't have to?"

"And then she started to get ill."

"Which sped up the clock for Harmuth. He had to come back and figure a way to keep their secret buried. He probably thought he'd done it with his plan to move in to his mother's apartment, but at some point he realized that Claire and Paul had agreed to switch, move Paul and Sarah into the ground-floor apartment and give Harmuth the floor above."

"And with the extension they were going to build . . ."

"Yeah, that sealed the deal, I'm sure."

"So that's the why," Claudia said. "What I don't understand is, how? Paul was in that room alone; he was fine when he went in, and he had no contact with anyone before he died. So how in the world did Harmuth manage to poison him? And how the hell did you figure it out?"

"As to how I figured it out." Hugo smiled and pointed at their food. "This."

"Pizza?"

"Yes," Hugo said. "More specifically, the crust."

CHAPTER TWENTY-NINE

The following morning, Hugo went to the station early to give his statement. He didn't enjoy climbing out of bed, but he was eager to get back to Paris and wanted to get the formality over with. Georges Bazin was one of the detectives there in the interview room, and he shared Hugo's eagerness to complete the statement and see what would be found in Claire Rogers's flower garden.

They shook hands on the steps of the police station as Claudia pulled up in a rental car. She stayed in the driver's seat; Hugo had a phone call to return to Camille Lerens, who had many of the same questions that Claudia had the night before.

"I want to know why you suspected Harmuth," Lerens said, echoing Claudia.

"A couple of days ago, Alain Benoît said something that I thought about a few times afterward. It was a throw-away remark, about how Michelle Juneau looked a little like Madame Rogers."

"Wait, Juneau has something to do with this?" Lerens asked.

"No, no, nothing like that. It just got me thinking about people not being who they appear to be, and so I started thinking about people who'd come into this little circle recently. And whether people were presenting themselves accurately. As I said to Claudia, there was no one moment that it all came together, just a few things that made me look more closely at Harmuth."

"His recent arrival at the library. What else?"

247

"A couple of obvious things that we all saw or heard, but paid no attention to."

"Except you."

"Better late than never," he said. "First, his name. Michel and Michael. As you probably know, people like to hang onto their names, even when they change them they often keep the same initials."

"True," Lerens said. "He didn't do that, he kept his first name and changed his last name."

"Right. Obvious clue number two was when Claire Rogers almost called him her son, of course. And that same day, when we asked him to come to Sarah and Paul's apartment, he suddenly appeared, knocked on the door, remember? That meant he didn't need to be buzzed in, he had a key. I assume now that he got it from his mother. I eventually put all these things together and figured that I should look into him, and that accident."

"So what prompted the flight to Dieppe, exactly?"

"Yeah, I decided that was necessary after seeing Harmuth's checkout history."

"His what?"

"The books he checked out of the library."

"Sounds exciting, but I'm not following you," Lerens said.

"The book that Paul was using, the guide to firearms. Before he checked it out, Michael Harmuth had it."

Lerens was quiet for a moment, and Hugo could almost hear her putting it together. Finally she said, "He had to make sure it was there when Paul wanted it. But I'm not clear on why."

"Ah. That comes down to the way he killed Paul."

"Yeah, I was getting to that," she said, humor in her voice. "The curare. Do you know how he administered it?"

"I think you'll find that he used dimethyl sulfoxide."

"Means nothing to me."

"It's a chemical compound; it was in the news a while back. A lot of people were selling it as a cure for cancer, a homeopathic remedy. Miki referred to it, but she just called it the wrong thing."

"*D'accord*," Lerens said. "But I thought we established that curare was the poison, and that you were safe if you just ingested or touched it."

"Right, it has to go straight into the blood stream. And it did. Dimethyl sulfoxide was the delivery mechanism, which I realized when we were having pizza the other night."

"Pizza," Lerens said. "Are you serious?"

"I am. Merlyn asked something like, *How is it that a pizza's crust looks dry, but you can't eat it without getting grease on your fingers?*"

"And the answer?"

Hugo smiled as Claudia looked over at him. She'd heard this story the previous evening. "He mixed the curare with dimethyl sulfoxide, which is able to penetrate the skin and basically carry another substance with it. That's one of its primary qualities. All Harmuth had to do was put the mixture on a nonporous substance and wait for Paul to touch it. Curare is so deadly, it didn't take much."

"And he had access to Paul's computer to make it look like it was Paul searching for and ordering it."

"Right, except none of his Internet history showed anything being ordered. Plus, Paul did all his research at home in the evening so he'd be ready to write the next day."

"How would Harmuth know about the other substance?" Lerens asked. "The dimethyl whatever it is."

"Dimethyl sulfoxide. Because he was big into homeopathic remedies. Even if he'd never had cause to use it, he'd have known about the controversy surrounding it as a cancer cure, which means he'd have read about the substance's real uses."

"Makes perfect sense. Do you know how he got it onto Rogers's skin?"

"It had to be a nonporous surface, so I'd guess the door handle, on the inside. That's why he knocked on the door an hour or so into Paul's writing time, to get him to come to the door, touch the inside handle. And you remember on the video, Harmuth leaned back into the room? Supposedly because he was having trouble believing Paul was dead, but I bet that handkerchief we found on the floor was what he used to wipe off any residue. He'd need to do that to make sure no one else got poisoned." A thought struck Hugo and his stomach dropped. "Wait, Camille, get everyone out of the library. Do it now!"

"Why?"

"Get off the phone, get the library cleared, and call me right back when it's done. No one is to touch any of the books, please hurry."

The phone clicked and Claudia shot him a look as they slowed behind a truck in the outside lane. "What's going on?" she asked.

"I think Harmuth had a backup way to make sure Rogers touched the poison. He used that book, the one he dropped off outside the *atelier*. It had a plastic cover and I'd bet that he smeared some of the mixture on it. I'm almost certain that Laurent Tilly, the janitor, touched it when he was helping to reshelve books."

"If so, and if curare is so lethal, why didn't he die?"

"Because the poison doesn't kill, it just paralyzes you so that you suffocate. Tilly didn't die because he was given mouth-to-mouth, and when the poison wore off—which it does quite quickly—he was able to breathe on his own."

"Didn't Harmuth help save him?"

"Yes. I think he realized what was happening and didn't need another death on his conscience."

Claudia snorted. "As if that man has a conscience."

"Yeah, I know, it's easy to think of all murderers as monsters," Hugo said. "But he could've killed me, and he didn't."

She took a hand off the steering wheel and squeezed his leg. "Thank heavens for that."

"I really think he killed those people because he felt he had too. I'm sure he's telling himself that right now, it allows him to see himself as a decent human being still."

"He really planned this out, didn't he?"

"Very carefully, yes. Hard to keep all those lies straight, though."

"You caught him in one?"

"I called the library right before getting tickets," Hugo said. "I got Harmuth's checkout history but also found out that he was the one who'd arranged the funeral. Specifically, cremation. He'd told me Michelle Juneau was doing it, which was a lie."

"Cremation. Charming."

"I know." Hugo's phone rang and he answered. "Camille, is the library empty?"

"Yes, you want to tell me why?"

Hugo explained his theory about the curare on the book, and the potential risk of someone touching it.

"How long is that stuff dangerous?" Lerens asked.

"I don't know. Contact your hazard-materials experts; I'm sure you have them. They'll know, and be able to tell you how to make sure the place is safe."

"I'll do that right now. When will you be in Paris?"

"A couple of hours, depending on traffic."

"All right. I'm going to let Miki Harrison know she's free to leave town, and get the library safe," Lerens said. "Go straight to Claire Rogers's apartment. We'll probably have started the dig."

"I texted you about Paul Rogers's keys likely being dropped in the library somewhere," Hugo began.

"We have them. Left on a shelf in the stacks, as you predicted," Lerens said. "But I have about fifty more questions rolling around in my head, so hurry back."

Hugo laughed. "Be there as quick as we can."

The body lay ten feet from the house, an intact but incomplete skeleton sewn into to the earth by the roots of a still-blooming rose bush, right where the extension would have ended.

They'd hoped Harmuth would save them some time and give up his girlfriend's final resting place, but he wasn't talking, not to anyone. Claire Rogers had also been taken into custody, based on her estranged son's admissions to Hugo, and after her small garden was excavated foot by foot until the shallow grave was found. A tent was quickly erected, and the pace of work slowed to glacial as every piece of evidence was found and preserved.

Doctor Sprengelmeyer had set up in the old woman's living room, the furniture moved out and a large table erected to make an initial study of, and to catalogue, the bones. When the poor girl's skull was brought in, Sprengelmeyer paid it special attention, using a magnifying glass to inspect every part of its surface.

Hugo and Camille Lerens watched from the doorway, both silent and captivated by the slow but precise dance playing out before them. They straightened as Sprengelmeyer gently put the skull down and walked over to them.

"Well, she's definitely dead," he said. When neither Hugo nor Lerens smiled at his dark humor, he shrugged. "Has a crack in her skull. Big one. I'm guessing that's what killed her, and if experience is any guide, at this point you're just wanting guesses."

"I prefer to call them opinions," Lerens said.

"*Bon*, so far no lower left leg, as Monsieur Marston here surmised. I'll bring in a colleague to help me look over the entire skeleton at the hospital, she's an expert in forensic anthropology." He looked at Hugo. "From your part of the world, as it happens."

"Jen Winkler?" Hugo asked.

"That's the one. You've worked with her?"

"The best," Hugo nodded. "I'm glad she'll be helping out."

Lerens looked around the apartment, her brow creasing. "Being here reminds me: What was the deal with the missing wills?"

"A question for Harmuth, I'm afraid," Hugo said. "If I had to guess, I'd say he didn't know about the central registry and stole the copies thinking they were originals. I expect he just wanted to remove any and all obstacles to him getting this apartment, and the chances were high that the wills addressed that issue, Paul's and his mother's. Having spent most of his adult life in America, he'd have no reason to know about the registry."

"If he decides to talk, I'll ask him," Lerens said.

Hugo ran a hand over his face, suddenly exhausted. "If you don't need me, Camille, I may take off. Grab some sleep and then touch base with you later."

"*Bien sûr*, that's fine. I'll have Jameson drive you."

"You should let that guy get some sleep, too."

"He's a Scotsman. They don't need sleep, they take walking naps. Or in his case, driving naps."

"Very encouraging," Hugo said.

Lerens took out her phone and made the call. "He's outside, waiting. Talk to you later."

"No doubt about it."

He turned to go, but her voice stopped him. "Hugo, one quick question."

"Fire away."

"Well, you solved this business here. But I'm still wondering about the Severin collection. Is there anything to the stories about her and the Resistance? Or did that little mystery have you stumped?"

Hugo gave her a tired smile. "We may have to wait until the old lady dies to figure that one out. There's a dagger and a box of her stuff that'll stay under wraps until she passes, but I don't know whether those are love letters or secret Resistance papers."

"You should help that girl pay Severin another visit. On the record this time."

"Feel bad for arresting her?"

"I didn't, I just questioned her," Lerens responded. "But yes, a little. I think she knows how it goes, this song and dance that we do. Sometimes we hit the right notes, sometimes we don't. I'm sure she understands." When Hugo didn't respond, her tone was quizzical. "Hugo, you're thinking about something. What did we miss?"

Hugo looked up. "Nothing. Keep going here, I'll catch up with you later. And if it makes you feel any better, you may have just given Miki Harrison a proper apology. One she can actually use in her book."

That night they celebrated with, appropriately, pizza.

Hugo ordered the same three again, and paid the delivery man at the door as Merlyn, Miki, and Tom sat around the coffee table, downing some of the cheap wine Merlyn had sprung for. Hugo's eyes lit up as Claudia appeared behind the departing delivery man, clutching three bottles of Chateau Pichon Longueville.

"That's nice wine for this crowd," Hugo said, putting the bottles in the kitchen and wrapping both arms around her.

"I'm sure they'll appreciate it," Claudia said.

"Pichon Longueville?" Hugo laughed. "I hope so."

"You know, they have a very nice hotel there," she said, nudging him gently.

"You don't have to ask me twice," he said.

"Get a room, you two," Tom called from the living room.

"We're working on it," Claudia said.

Hugo uncorked a bottle, and he and Claudia watched Tom slide two large pieces of pizza onto his plate. She looked up at Hugo. "What's wrong?"

"Tom's a little subdued," he said quietly.

"With two pretty girls at his disposal? That's not good."

"Precisely."

"Any idea why?"

"No. Well," he frowned. "No, I don't."

"What are you not telling me?"

He put his hands on her shoulders and looked at her. He leaned in and whispered in her ear. "I know I can trust you with anything, tell you anything. And I will. I think maybe something from our past has popped up, and I promise that I'll tell you all about it. Just not tonight."

She nodded and kissed him gently on the lips. "*D'accord.* I can wait."

"Go see if you can cheer Tom up. Some of that good wine should do it."

Hugo leaned against the kitchen counter and watched as Claudia walked over to the gathering in the living room. Merlyn shifted over to give her space at the coffee table, and Claudia sat next to her, cross-legged.

Miki stretched her arms over her head and looked over at Hugo. He inclined his head. *Come here.*

She hadn't wanted to come tonight, had even called him that afternoon to say she was giving up on the Severin project and going home. There was something in her voice, anger or resentment, as if Hugo had been the one interrogating her. He'd reminded her, in his gentle way, that he'd been the one to ensure she was no longer a suspect, that he'd solved a riddle that threatened to ensnare her. She'd acceded finally, but not out of gratitude.

Now, she got up and walked over to him. "I'm glad you made me come tonight," she said.

"Good," Hugo replied. "Did you bring the Josephine Baker letters? The sheet music?"

"In my bag." She indicated a large purse on the floor by the front door.

"Bring them into my office. Which also happens to be my bedroom, now that Tom's here taking up space in my spare room. If you don't mind."

"Not at all." She winked exaggeratedly, and somehow it came across as less salacious than before, just funny. She grabbed her bag from the floor and followed him into his room, ignoring the quizzical looks from the others and the low whistle from Tom. Hugo didn't.

"We're gonna make sweet music in here, please excuse us," he said with a grin. In his room, Hugo closed the door.

"What's this about?" Miki said. "Like I said, I've looked at the letters, there's nothing there. Just talk of her schedule and those sheets of music."

"Are you musical? Have you tried playing them?"

"Yes, and yes." She dug in her bag and handed over three thick envelopes.

"And I'm guessing it sounded pretty bad, right?"

"I wasn't sure if it was me or the music—I'm pretty rusty."

"I'd bet it was the music." Carefully, he took the pages out of the envelopes and spread them on his desk. "I'm not very musical myself. Learned as a kid, dabbled as a young adult, and tried more recently to get back into the piano."

"Maybe you can play this better than me, then," Miki said.

"It wasn't meant for playing," Hugo said. "You notice how each letter has just three pages of sheet music?"

"Yes, I did."

"I think you'll find that the notes were code," Hugo said. "And it'll be decipherable in one of two ways."

"Code?" Miki's eyes widened. "Are you serious?"

"It's going to be a nice little puzzle for you to solve. The dates and places of the letters, who sent what to whom, and then what they said."

"Wow!" She turned to look down at the music. "Wait, you said there were two ways to solve this?"

"If I'm right, it's called a musical cryptogram. The musical notes translate into letters to relay a message."

"But musical notes are only A through G," she said.

"Right. So she used either the French or the German method. The French . . ." He held up a hand. "Anyway, now isn't the time or place to go into how each one worked, it can get a little complicated. You'll have to research it and take the time to decode any message, but you could have quite an interesting little twist to this tale."

"If you're right," she said with a wry smile.

"Indeed. But that's the fun of history, isn't it? All the digging around and finding stuff. A few dead ends never hurt."

"Easy for you to say."

Hugo smiled. "I know." They looked up as someone tapped on the door. "Come in," he said.

The door opened. "Only me," Tom said.

"Holy crap, you actually knocked. What's wrong?" But the look on Tom's face told Hugo that something really was up. "Tom?"

"You lovebirds done? I need a word with the gentleman of the house." The flatness of his tone didn't match the levity of his words, and Hugo's stomach sank.

"Yeah, we're done," Hugo said.

They watched as Miki gathered up the letters and sheet music. "Thanks, Hugo. If this turns out to be something, well, it'll be amazing. Just amazing."

"You can put me in the acknowledgments," he said.

"Most definitely."

Tom stood aside as she left the room, then he closed the door. "You're pretty smart for figuring this mess out," he said. "Nice job."

"Thanks. But you're welcome to say that out there, in front of everyone."

"Not a chance."

Hugo perched on the edge of his desk. "So what's up?"

"What's up is that while you're busy getting things right, I got one thing wrong. Very wrong."

"What are you talking about?"

"Our little chat the other day. I just got a call from a friend in Houston. Our buddy Rick Cofer just got paroled."

"Are you serious?"

"For once in my life, I am."

Hugo stared at his friend for a moment and couldn't help but ponder the parallels. Two cases, one recently solved and one much older, not closed exactly but out of sight, buried. In the new one, Michael Harmuth's past came back to haunt him, pushing him to commit further atrocities just to keep his ill-gotten freedom. And in the old one, starring Rick Cofer and his brother Steve, small-time hoodlums with big ambitions, itchy trigger fingers, and a startling lack of conscience.

"What are you going to do?" Hugo asked eventually.

"Nothing. Don't worry."

"Then it's no big deal. He'll be out on parole, screw it up, and get sent back to prison." Hugo shrugged. "Or he'll be a good boy and leave everything well alone."

Tom snorted. "He ain't gonna do that, my friend. The Cofer brothers never flew straight a day in their lives."

"Then he'll end up behind bars again."

"He's smarter than that. If he does go back to what he was doing, he won't get caught this time."

"How's that your logic?" Hugo asked. "He got caught before."

Tom held Hugo's eye. "We know why and how, don't we? Can't see that happening again."

"Look, what happened, happened. If he's not coming here and you're not going there, we have nothing to worry about. It's not like he's writing his memoirs; and even if he did, he's a murderer and a thief. So let's just go back to the wine and pizza. Especially the wine."

"I'm just saying, some secrets are best left buried."

"That was Michael Harmuth's view of the world," Hugo said. "And look where that got him."

Tom grunted. "He was hardly a pro."

"Drop it, Tom."

"Fine. Wine and pizza it is." Tom turned and, without another word, opened the door and walked back into the living room. Hugo pushed himself up from the desk and followed him.

"There you are," Claudia said. She was seated on the floor, her back to the couch. She smiled up at him, but worry sat in her eyes. "Join us?"

Hugo slid in behind her and put his hands on her shoulders, squeezing gently. She kissed his hand, and Merlyn nudged Miki. "If it's massage time, you do me first."

"Some chance," Miki laughed. "I'll need more wine first."

Hugo looked over at Tom. *On any other day, he'd be the first to offer a massage to Merlyn. And Miki.* Tom caught Hugo looking, and rallied himself. He reached for the wine and topped everyone up. "Get a room, you two," he said. "Or did I say that already?"

Claudia smiled at him. "We have several to choose from. Maybe later."

"You foreigners," Merlyn laughed. "One-track minds."

"From the kinkiest woman in the room," Miki said, smiling and raising a glass. "Anyway, here's to Hugo."

"What's that for?" Tom asked.

"Being a brilliant detective, and helping me with my little project," she said. "May the secret life of Isabelle Severin be as exciting as her public life."

They all raised their glasses and clinked them together over the coffee table and the remnants of their pizzas. Hugo gave Claudia's shoulder another squeeze and leaned down to whisper in her ear. "I was going to invite you to the Normandy coast for a few days," he said. "But thanks to this wine I'm wondering whether a trip to the Loire would be even better."

She tilted her head back and kissed him. "You treat me to one, I'll treat you to the other."

Tom smiled finally. "I need to find me a girlfriend like that. Rich and beautiful."

"Yeah, don't we all?" Merlyn laughed. She picked up another slice and spoke through a delicate bite. "Still, sharing pizza and wine in Paris with friends will do for now. Very nicely indeed."

ACKNOWLEDGMENTS

I'd first like to thank the people who made my visit to the real American Library in Paris such a treat: Charles Trueheart, Abigail Altman, and Audrey Chapuis. I'm sorry I had to reveal your secret door and coopt the *atelier* for my murderous purposes, but they were too good to ignore!

I should also thank my wonderful friends and readers who play the name game with me, letting me use their names as characters in the books. I hope it's as much fun for you as it is for me.

Many thanks to the two people who helped me with my medical and chemical concerns, Doctor Kenneth Youens and Dr. Lee Ann Grossberg.

Also much gratitude to my wonderful cadre of readers: Patricia De Méo, JoAnne Bagwell, Nancy Matuszak, Nan Martin, and (as ever) Jennifer Schubert.

I am ever grateful to so many people in the book world, especially my agent, Ann Collette, and the wonderful folks at Seventh Street Books: Dan Mayer, Jill Maxick, Jon Kurtz, Jade Zora Scibilia, and Jake Bonar. Also the amazing booksellers at BookPeople, Murder by the Book, Poisoned Pen, and MacIntyres, to name just a few.

I'd also like to thank a family of new friends whom I've never met, but hope to. The Harmuth family, who were led into my life by the late and very great Michael, for whom a major character in this book is named and dedicated. Your family's strength in the face of adversity and your love for each other has been an inspiration.

I also want to thank you, the reader, and I truly hope that you enjoyed *The Paris Librarian*. There is no greater reward for a writer than to know that his or her work is enjoyed by the reader. If you did enjoy it, or any other Hugo story, please tell others and like it on Facebook, or perhaps review it online—for the greatest support you can give any author is your word-of-mouth-recommendation. Thank you!

Finally, my love and thanks to the four people who continue to encourage and inspire me every single day: Nicola, Henry, Natalie, and Sarah.

ABOUT THE AUTHOR

Mark Pryor is the author of *The Bookseller, The Crypt Thief, The Blood Promise, The Button Man,* and *The Reluctant Matador*—the first five Hugo Marston novels—as well as the stand-alone *Hollow Man*. He has also published the true-crime book *As She Lay Sleeping*. A native of Hertfordshire, England, he is an assistant district attorney in Austin, Texas, where he lives with his wife and three children.